Matthew

Dudley Price

authorHOUSE®

AuthorHouse™ UK Ltd.
500 Avebury Boulevard
Central Milton Keynes, MK9 2BE
www.authorhouse.co.uk
Phone: 08001974150

This book is a work of fiction. People, places, events, and situations are the product of the author's imagination. Any resemblance to actual persons, living or dead, or historical events, is purely coincidental.

© 2009 Dudley Price. All rights reserved.

No part of this book may be reproduced, stored in a retrieval system, or transmitted by any means without the written permission of the author.

First published by AuthorHouse 2/10/2009

ISBN: 978-1-4389-3988-9 (sc)

Printed in the United States of America
Bloomington, Indiana

This book is printed on acid-free paper.

All events and characters in this book are fictitious, and any resemblance to actual persons, living or dead, is purely co-incidental

The belief is real

For my darling Marion

**My life's journey is magical
Thank you for travelling with me**

*To our friend Mary
Dudley
04-03-2009*

The absence of evidence
is not evidence of absence
Dr. Carl Sagan. American Astronomer 1934 - 1996

Science without religion is lame,
Religion without science is blind.
Albert Einstein 1879 - 1955

Reproduced with kind permission of Neil Smart, Vicar, The Parish Church of St. Nicholas, Brockenhurst, New Forest, Hampshire, England

CHAPTER ONE

I needed something, I don't know what. A project maybe, or a challenge in which my very life could be jeopardised. Something to pull me out of a two year descent into suicidal depression, a period during which there were moments I had just wished to die.

Two years ago I had been happily married. Until then and for ten glorious, happy years Jenny had been my wife. She was attractive, intelligent and I loved her to bits.

Then with devastating cruelty she had died. A tsunami of grief swept over me as my world ended. For two years I had mourned, unable to come to terms with her death.

For two years I had ceased to work, ceased to function. Friends had slowly drifted away and I sank into a limbo of despair. I railed at God, railed at the medical profession. I cursed myself, trying in my mind to relive those wonderful years. Could I, - should I, have done more to love Jenny, to make more of what we had - but I didn't know then the cruel events that lay ahead, and now it was too late. But her death was the catalyst for my central role in the most awesome story ever told.

My whole being ached with the loss.

After the first year friends gently suggested that 'perhaps it was time to move on', but I did not want to 'move on' and I pushed them away until I was alone with my memories and the place where Jenny lay.

Then along came Mandy!

Thanks forever to Mandy, a nine year old girl I saw in the park. She was the image of my Jenny and took my breath away. As I watched her walk and skip beside her mother, engaged in animated conversation I couldn't believe her, it could have been Jenny!

I was twenty nine when I met Jenny. Until then I had led a fairly humdrum life.

My early teen years were pretty uneventful. I became friends with Tony Hurd, son of the local MP; he was nearly two years older than me, but we seemed to hit it off and probably his seniority influenced my earlier teenage behaviour, anyway we knocked around together and I was often at his home.

Tony's father Harold, (Known as HH to most), seemed to accept my frequent presence in his home without demur, although he himself was often away in London.

Tony's mother, Jessica, was different.

'Hello. You must be Matthew,' she said, opening the door on my first visit to their house.

I was immediately envious of Tony. Jessica was strikingly attractive, a far cry from my dear maiden Aunt Joan, who had struggled alone to bring me up from babyhood and sacrificed her own chances of love in the process.

Jessica was fairly tall with auburn hair, stylishly cut, falling to her shoulders. She wore soft denim trousers, an ivory blouse under a light blue sleeveless jacket. The top three buttons of her blouse were undone revealing glimpses of breast snuggling into a lacy bra. She had the poise and directness of a typical county woman. She observed me with some curiosity.

I felt gangly, ill equipped in my adolescence to engage in repartee.

'I've come to see…' I started,

'Come in,' she smiled, standing back. 'Anthony is in the kitchen. Come on through.'

As I passed her I caught a whisper of expensive perfume. We walked along a dog legged passage, well carpeted, to the last door. This opened into a large farmhouse style kitchen.

'Matthew's here,' Mrs Hurd announced, as we entered.

Tony was sitting in a high wheel backed chair, reading. He stood, casting the magazine onto the table.

'Hi. Matt. You ready?'

'Would you like a coffee, before you go out?' Jessica asked.

Tony must have told his mother early on that I lived alone with my maiden Aunt, and from the first moment Jessica opened the door, she took to me, first as a surrogate mother, but which later was to grow into something more complex.

Tony answered for me. 'No thanks Mum, we're meeting up in town. We'll get something later.'

Jessica's hand rested briefly on my arm as we filed past to take our leave.

In those days, on Sundays, I invariably accompanied Aunt Joan to church. She had insisted that I joined a Sunday school at age six, and from then onwards Sunday mornings were fully occupied. At twelve I swapped the Sunday school for attending morning service. Aunt Joan was well liked by a large section of the neighbourhood and her personal sacrifice to bring me up as her own was well known. Over the years she had formed an attachment to one or two potential suitors, but the reality of taking on a ready made family, - me, seemed destined to drive them away. She settled for a comfortable, if frugal life, derived from my parent's assets. Aunt Joan was a leading light at the local bridge club, held twice weekly in the church hall. This and the Church provided the main social interaction for her.

Sunday services were generally a matter of rote. I took in the bible doctrine, and learned the gospel stories, Matthew, Mark, Luke and John, but it all seemed distant. The continual exhortation to repent, and the usually dull hymns left me unmoved.

Until the Reverend James visited.

Well built and jolly, he climbed to the pulpit, a broad grin on his face. He thanked the resident vicar, Reverend Parsons, and with a deep chuckle launched into a forty minute sermon that transformed my adolescent view of religion.

'We're all God's children,' he said with an expansive wave of both arms. 'Whether you like it or not we are all related through God's creation. He made heaven and earth and he made you and me,' he grinned delightedly.

'So, He-ll-oo brothers and sisters, I'm going to tell you about God and his works and why we are so important to him.'

The congregation sort of gawped. His odd ball manner was more reminiscent of gospel and evangelical meetings; but murmured disapproval from some quarters was soon replaced with grudging interest. The Reverend James swept all before him, his enthusiastic body language and bold words rolled over the congregation in a wave of fresh ideas. After thirty minutes the congregation were sitting up, attentive and loving every word. The Reverend James's ideas stayed with me for a long time afterwards; it was a year later that another event brought two things together which I later saw was to be the changing point in my life.

I was then fifteen. Living with Aunt Joan was comfortable enough and my Aunt always made sure I was properly cared for, but life was an uneventful routine. Time spent in after school activity was often a more engaging use of an evening, so I belonged to a couple of school clubs.

It was an autumn evening, and at eight o'clock there was a chill in the air; it was dark. I was waiting around near the school entrance; several kids were coming or going to various after school activities. I was waiting for Harry, we played badminton together; I had been hanging around for nearly an hour and it looked as if he was not going to show up. A figure I recognised as the physics teacher, Mark Reynolds walked towards me from the car park.

'Hello Patterson, what are you waiting for then?' he paused, hitching a heavy satchel on his shoulder.

'Harry Meldrew, Sir. – Badminton,' I added, holding up my racquet as proof.

'Ah. He's late, isn't he? The club starts at seven.'

'I don't think he's going to turn up. I've been waiting since seven.'

'Good lord, Patterson you've been hanging about here in the cold for an hour?'

'Yes, Sir.'

'And what have you been doing?'

'Sir?'

Reynolds unhitched his satchel and walked across the entrance road to the boundary wall. He indicated that I should join him. 'Look!' he said gazing into the sky. 'What do you see?'

I stared into the clear night sky, into the vault of heaven; stars twinkled back at me, and as I stared, I slowly made out more and more points of light until the whole blackness was speckled with a myriad of tiny lights.

'Stars?' I said hopefully.

'Not just stars, Patterson. You are staring into the past, billions of years into the past. You are seeing vast distances and millions of worlds, worlds we can only dream of, stretching away forever.'

As he spoke, I kept staring and I felt hypnotically drawn into the darkness. I could feel the dimension of distance and as I looked I felt I could see further and further, almost as if I were being drawn up into the void.

'Heaven stretches before you,' said Reynolds. 'Immeasurable, exciting, - and very busy.'

As we gazed, he and I, another voice entered my consciousness, that of the Reverend James. His voice even after a year still remained with me.

'We're all God's children,' the voice said. 'Whether you like it or not we are all related through God's creation. He made heaven and earth and he made you and me.'

The thought of a God, omnipresent, all powerful, capable of moving through space and time intrigued the adolescent in me.

Reynolds placed a friendly arm round my shoulder. He knew my circumstances and was that rare breed of teacher able to reach out to a young parentless boy.

'Tell you what, Patterson, why don't you come

and join us in the Lab, - get a hot coffee, eh? The astronomy club is there, you can come out onto the playing field with us later and see some of this through a telescope. To-night we're looking at Saturn. – You know Saturn, -with all the rings?'

The evening turned out to be a great success. After half an hour in the school Laboratory seven boys trouped out after Mark Reynolds onto the dark playing field where he had set up a 3 inch refracting telescope. As I took my turn to stare through the eyepiece at the majestic Saturn I was truly fascinated, its moon Titan clearly visible. Reynolds hovered around, commenting generally to the budding astronomers, encouraging us all, by light of dim torches, to sketch what we saw.

'Next week then,' Reynolds said as we broke up, including me now as part of his group.

So it was that by the time I frequented the Hurd household I had developed an interest in both religion and astronomy, I had formed a quiet attachment to both subjects.

One evening I called for Tony. Jessica let me in.

'Hi, Matthew,' she said, ushering me into the kitchen. 'I'm afraid Tony has had to stay back, discussing his placement or something. But do stay and have a drink.'

'I, uh.'

'Look,' Jessica interrupted before I could frame a decision. 'Just help yourself. I've got to go and change.'

She turned at the door.

'Matthew, - tell you what. I'm going to the stables to settle 'Jimjam', you can come with me.'

Jessica left, assuming everything was settled. I mooched around in the large kitchen, taking a cola from the fridge. This had become a habit, though Tony was normally there with me.

From the start Jessica had accepted me into the family and I generally felt relaxed, although sometimes - one to one with her, I experienced both attraction and self consciousness. I didn't really know what to talk about. Her nearness would unsettle me, other times, when Tony was around, we would all indulge in inconsequential chatter.

She re-appeared, dressed in a pair of old jeans and boots, a roll necked sweater and a jacket, hair held back in a short pony tail. She looked absolutely gorgeous and I immediately felt tongue tied. She looked at me with some amusement.

'Are you going to be warm enough?'

Without waiting for an answer she picked an anorak from a miscellaneous range of coats hanging in an alcove and handed it to me. 'Put this on, - it's Anthony's.'

As I shrugged into the voluminous garment, Jessica pulled the collars together, the back of her hand brushing my cheek.

We set off in the Hurd Range Rover just as it was growing dark; the stables being a thirty minute drive. I struggled to think of things to say, in the end we drove mostly in silence although Jessica occasionally softened the silence with amiable comments about her horse riding.

I was introduced to 'Jimjam' an eight year old mare, who stared out of the stable door as we approached.

'Give her these,' said Jessica, 'She will be your friend for life.'

She pulled a handful of biscuity things from her pocket and handed them to me. 'Hand flat out,' she added catching hold of my hand and turning it palm up.

I carefully tendered the offering; it was my first ever encounter with a horse and I was surprised by the softness of Jimjam's lips. The biscuits were soon gone and the horse nudged me for more, head nodding up and down, lips pouting.

Jessica had moved away and was talking to another woman, clearly on the same errand. Another 4X4 pulled into the yard and Jessica became engrossed in talking to the other owners, so I wandered about the yard a bit, poking my nose into several large sheds. Eventually I strolled to the road leading into the yard and leaned on a fence.

My mind drifted as I stared into the darkening clear sky. The night sky had become very familiar to me following my membership of the school astronomy club; I searched out well known stars and constellations but as always my eyes were drawn into the depths beyond the cloudy haze of the milky way. I tried to see the Andromeda galaxy and imagined I could make out its distant smudgy glow with my naked eye. What was really out there? I envisioned new worlds, maybe primeval, maybe even with life. My adolescent mind pondered an intelligence unencumbered outside the physical body. Lost in reverie I jumped at the voice beside me.

'Matthew, what are you doing over here?' it was Jessica seeking me out. She stood close by my side and saw that she had startled me.

'I was, - well I was just looking at the stars.'

'What were you thinking Matt?' she said softly.

Jessica never called me Matt, always Matthew. Her closeness, casual clothes, hair tied back in a girlish bunch and now use of the diminutive swept away the barrier of being Tony's Mum, of being the wife of an MP. Suddenly I felt excited, equal; this attractive woman took the effort to care, to engage me.

'I was thinking about the wonder of it all, the spiritual power at work,' I said, a bit self consciously, my voice husky with the thrill of Jessica's interest and my adolescent fear of being ridiculed. 'I just feel that there is something out there, beyond the moon, beyond the milky way.'

'The milky way? - Can you see the milky way?

'Oh yes, look, - see that cloudy haze stretching right across the sky. That's the milky way, the haze is the starlight from millions of stars, all part of our galaxy,' I directed Jessica gaze. 'All the stars you see are part of the galaxy. Those bright stars you can see are relatively close, look that's Pegasus, the four forming a square.'

Jessica looked at me, her face inches from mine, she could see my features in the starlight, animated; and I saw hers; she knew she had found my quintessence.

'Yes, I see it Matt. You're a very young man to be thinking about the meaning of life?' she put her arm round my shoulder, 'Come on, I've finished here. Let's go home.'

The journey back was different. I relaxed, and in response to Jessica's smiling prompts chattered incessantly about the mysteries of the universe. The journey was over in a flash. I tumbled out of the car and we entered the kitchen. Tony had returned; we were starving, so Jessica made bacon sandwiches all round.

Tony talked about his placement meeting. He had always been interested in biology and decided to study micro biology at the University of Leicester.

'Microbes?' I had exclaimed.

Tony's eyes lit up with missionary zeal as he got onto his pet topic.

'Micro-organisms (viruses, bacteria, fungi, protozoa) are fascinating creatures, Matt, they help purify our waste water and clean up pollution. Mankind has used them for thousands of years in the production of foods and drinks but, - some types can cause devastating diseases.'

'The bad guys!'

'Well, yeah. Microbes are the oldest inhabitants on the planet, yet we have still only discovered a small fraction of those that currently exist, and know what? They're cunning buggers, they can change to evade anything we throw at them.'

'Superbugs? Like MSRA, C Difficile and the like?'

'Right. If they learn to totally resist, we're history, - like dinosaurs.'

'They weren't knocked out by viruses, were they?'

'Well, no. I mean gone. In any case we aren't really certain how they went.'

I didn't reply, a small unease at the back of my mind.

Tony went on. 'Once I qualify I can get a job in any industry. Microbiology is at the forefront of a technical revolution, Matt, there are incredibly sensitive molecular tools, sophisticated computer analytical software; we are unlocking the secrets of life and I want to be part of it.'

After Tony went to Leicester, I continued to make regular visits to his parents. HH seemed to have time for me and we would chat about all manner of things. Jessica continued to take an interest in my progress to adulthood and mentored me more effectively than dear Aunt Joan could ever hope to. I loved them both.

Eventually, my turn came for university, I went into the LSE with two 'A's and two 'B's, well over the standard offer grade. One of the 'A' grades was maths. I studied micro and macro economics then concentrated on political science. I was going to be big in the political/economic field.

What actually happened was that, after graduation, I got a junior job in a government research department; it was utterly boring. Eventually I was 'promoted' to senior researcher and began to get a wider remit, often tasked to produce 'biopics' or 'assessment papers'; it was a bit more interesting and I did get to find my way around a wide range of Whitehall departments, libraries and newspaper offices. A lot of time was spent on the internet.

I became friends with a columnist of a national paper, David Henchal. It became convenient for us to meet for a (mainly) liquid lunch at the 'Wig & Pen'.

David was going around with Liz Hardy, we formed a trio and spent a lot of time drinking at favourite watering holes in Covent Garden. I met a few of Liz's girlfriends and for a time took to a zany girl called Tina. We became 'an item' for six months, enjoying theatre and night spots, but I must have been too staid for her extrovert nature because we began to row about silly things and eventually we broke it up. I was 'pathetic' I overheard her say one day, and so we parted company.

My friendship with David remained strong and we continued to meet up, - the three of us, David, Liz and me; we met other friends, and occasionally an unattached girl would make up a foursome, but none I took a shine to.

I was visiting David and Liz one evening. They had invited me to supper at their apartment; it was during one of my bouts of trying to figure out what a career move might be. Over drinks he suggested I take up journalism.

'You're made for it Matt,' David said earnestly. 'Look, you've been sniffing out facts and figures for your political boss people, you write up reports, you're good at deadlines, you'd do well.'

I was doubtful but sufficiently interested to listen more. 'I've always imagined your life was more exciting than mine I must say,' I said.

'Exciting? - I dunno, the pay's better I guess.'

We talked it over some more. 'Look,' he said. 'Start writing some pieces, I'll look them through and give you an opinion. There's always a market for topical stuff.'

As it happened I did have a bee in my bonnet about a topic that I felt I could write about. I had recently gathered data about the demographics of the European Union for a member of a committee sitting in Brussels. The more I thought about 'The European Project' the more I believed it would end in tears. I couldn't say so, of course, I was paid just to provide the data; it was up to ministers to make assessments. But here was my opportunity to write an article setting out the dangers of eventual break up of the Union.

I believed that the welding together of some twenty seven countries, with different cultures, different languages, and, if the long term aim of getting Turkey on board came about, even different major religions, was a recipe for trouble. I had plenty of case studies, - Czechoslovakia, Yugoslavia, Russia, even before referring back into real history.

Why the major European countries didn't

settle for autonomous Heads of State, but bound by co-operative agreements in Trade, Defence, and okay, even finance was incomprehensible to me.

So far as UK went I always thought that much more could have been made of the Commonwealth. Here was a disparate group of countries spread over the globe, bound only by a common thread of empire, long gone. The Commonwealth in total could be a powerful trade block, strong in unified defence, and a force for stability in the world. Strangely, I found my thoughts flowed easily onto paper and I soon had a reasonable thesis mapped out.

So, about a week later, sitting at our customary place at the 'Wig & Pen', I slid my article self consciously over to David.

'You said you would give an opinion,' I ventured.

David, about to take a swig, paused mid way.

'You young bugger!' he said, 'You were serious then.'

'Don't read it now,' I said hastily, 'Look at it when you've got time, eh?'

It was the next day that David rang me at work.

'Matt, your piece,' he said without preamble. 'Explosive, perceptive, - we all rated it!'

'All?' I said in alarm.

'Well, yeah. You want it read don't you?' his voice was amused. 'Look, our sub editor likes it, he asked if you want to run it?'

'I -I don't know. I 'spose so. I mean can I?'

'What do you mean, can you?'

'Well, I mean, I am working for the Civil Service, I'm not sure if they allow moonlighting. Look, I'll check it out and let you know.'

'Ok. Be sharp eh?'

So began my career move into journalism. A few articles here and there began to turn into a full time occupation. It was with some excitement and trepidation that I gave in my notice to the cabinet office, (Agencies and Public Bodies). Now I was a freelance journalist! Suddenly what had been the luxury of writing for fun became a task master to earn money. It took nearly a year, and most of my savings, before I eventually became self sufficient. I looked back with satisfaction at that learning curve. My first repeat commission was a cause for celebration.

It was a good year and in the September David announced that he and Liz were getting married. I was invited to the wedding and of course, to a stag party. It was a respectable affair, some twenty friends invited to a country pub for a few drinks, and without the wild juvenile antics that was becoming the fashion.

I knew most of the 'Staggers', who were mainly David's contacts I had met during my transition to 'journalist,' he introduced me to Paul Kneale, who was later to become my agent. Paul had been in the business for a long time and after a few trial meetings Paul and I began to meet more frequently as our friendship developed. He would subtlety

'Wonder' about a subject, and 'What did I think,' then, 'Would I like to write about it.'

The system worked well, Paul had an antennae on world affairs and I could be relied on to have strong opinions.

I found that my submissions were well received and over the next five years began to get acceptance as a writer of some substance. During this time Paul seemed to develop a respect for my work.

'There's something about your work that gets to people,' he said soon after we started working together. 'I don't know how you do it, mate, but you seem to connect strands of information and write pretty powerful conclusions. Certainly stirs things up.'

Two things happened which turned my life upside down and, I believe, began the next step in an ordained path to the most life changing episodes ever dreamed of. One: Paul fixed up an approach for me to write the biography of a Reverend Charmin. Two: In order to have constant access to the Reverend I decided to move to the New Forest where the Reverend Charmin now lived.

I had visited Paul in his London office to discuss an article I was writing about: *'Contributions to social breakdown'*. I knew the topic was subjective, and that there were diverse causes, but somehow, from within my soul, I believed there was a common thread and I was trying to enunciate it in a fairly long article he had asked me to produce.

'Ah! Matt,' he said as I was shown into his office by Sheryl, - secretary and good natured dog's body. 'I'm glad you came in, I've got something for you. You're going to love it, babe, - its big,' he grinned amiably.

Paul and I got on really well. He had mentored me in the early days and now it paid off for him as commissions for my work began to arrive on his desk unbidden.

'You'll like this,' he said again as Sheryl fussed around with coffee.

'Okay,' I said, intrigued and putting aside the reason for my visit. 'What have you got.'

'These people want me to sound you out about producing a biography. They specifically asked for you, Matt.'

'A biography. Cripes! I've never produced anything more than about 20,000 words before, - max. I'm not sure I know even what goes into a biography. Well, I mean I know what a biography is, of course, - but writing one?'

'Matt, these people travelled from Nigeria to meet you for God's sake. They know more about you than I do!'

'From Nigeria? What do you mean, 'They know about me'? So what's the deal? Who is the subject?'

Paul grinned widely again and got down to business, he knew he had hooked me and opened a file that lay in front of him.

The subject was a Reverend Richard Charmin, Englishman, who now lived in retirement in Hampshire, - 'Somewhere in the New Forest,' he had spent a lot of his working life in Africa, particularly West Africa, - Nigeria and the Congo. He did a lot of hands on work with charitable foundations; taught clerics and lay people alike the true Christian ethos. He created programmes for AIDs victims and worked tirelessly to educate young Africans in the way of careful sexual encounters. He visited all the churches of the 76 Dioceses, and hundreds of villages yet to be reached by the gospel of salvation.

The Reverend Charmin was looked upon as a saint in areas where he was known, and the desire to have his biography published was made by a number of Nigerian church leaders, almost as a text book for the people. It was to be commissioned by no less than the Anglican Communion of the Church of Nigeria and had attracted a government grant towards the cost. A Reverend Samuel Johnson was in London, 'as we speak' from the first Province to negotiate a deal.

Paul was enthusiastic and, as I scoped the task in my mind, I too, became excited by the challenge.

Paul wasted no time in fixing up a meeting with the Reverend Johnson in London for later in the week. Now Paul was relaxed.

'So, what did you come in for,' he said, still grinning.

I met the Reverend Doctor Samuel Johnson at the Institute of Directors, we sat in the common room, he having booked a table. He was Nigerian, with genial features and ready smile showing perfect teeth. As I was to discover, over time, his shining face and ever dazzling smile cloaked a mind that was sharp as a razor. He was fairly stocky in build, and wore a light blue suit that seemed a size too small.

We talked for over an hour. He spoke on behalf of a grateful and active Christian community in Nigeria and now had received the Anglican Communion approval to commission a biography of a much loved and respected man. As Samuel Johnson talked, I became intrigued and enthused with the idea.

'Why me?' I asked.

Samuel looked at me carefully. 'Let's just say that you have been noticed, Matthew.'

I grimaced, uncomprehending, but left it.

We parted on friendly expectations. He would contact Paul to sort out the contractual aspects and a meeting would be set up with the Reverend Charmin so that I could develop a rapport and plan of action.

As we parted, the Reverend Samuel shook my hand. 'I'm pleased we met,' he said. 'When you have sorted things out you will need to come to Nigeria to visit the scene of Dickie's work. I will act as your guide,' he paused, uncertain. 'Matthew, time is of the essence here. We need to put a deadline on the contract,' he sounded anxious.

'What sort of time are you talking about?'

'We need it published within two years.'

I relaxed. 'I am sure that can be achieved,' I said, and we parted on genial terms.

I was elated and on the way back to my apartment thought of little else. I realised that if I was going to achieve a meaningful work I would need constant access to the Reverend Charmin, and at least one visit to Nigeria. I wondered about Reverend Samuel's anxious need to have the work completed within two years and felt an uneasy twinge; but by the time I got home I had worked everything out of my system and I came to the decision to go ahead and that I would need to move house and live closer to my 'new' subject.

CHAPTER TWO

I felt some unease about leaving London and worried whether I would lose the buzz and contact for source material. In the end I decided that internet access to people and information could be achieved just as well from anywhere. (A few years before I had completed work for my then bosses in the Civil Service while on holiday in Cyprus. My laptop and wifi connected me to all the people and data I needed).

So it was that two months later, with a contract to produce the biography, I acquired an apartment on the outskirts of Lymington, in the New Forest. This necessitated visits to solicitors, estate agents and the local branch of my bank where I arranged to move my account. This I discovered, needed a 'personal interview' and the issue of a 'Relationship Manager'.

I attended the bank as arranged. A receptionist smiled, and taking my name, disappeared behind the scenes, shortly returning to usher me into an empty interview room.

'Your relationship manager will be with you.'

So I sat and waited.

The young woman that entered the room with a welcoming smile on her face was a dream. Elegant in corporate skirt and blouse, a chiffon scarf under her collar, the ends draped down her front. Black tights and high heeled shoes completed her business attire.

'Hi,' she grinned, as I stood up. 'I'm Jenny Richards.'

Indeed, she had a name card pinned to her blouse stating that she was, in fact, 'Jenny'. We shook hands, hers firm yet soft. She moved round the desk and sat, placing the file on the desk in front of her.

'Mr Patterson,' she began. 'I see you've recently moved into the area and want to change your branch. We can sort that out for you now.'

Her eyes looked quizzically at me as she spoke, head slightly tilted, her left hand rested on the desk, her thumb tucked under her fingers. She glanced down at the file, and on returning her gaze to me tossed her head slightly to push back rebellious strands of blonde hair.

She took my account number and brought up details on the screen of her computer terminal, tapping in the change of address. We discussed my requirements for a few minutes, checking on some direct debits that I had on the account. Miss Richards - I saw she was not married, tried a soft sell for a loan, 'for any purposes' bearing in mind moving costs etcetera. I didn't need a loan, and she did not pursue it, however she did get me to upgrade my account from gold to platinum, which increased my overdraft limit to some outrageous figure and included travel insurance and vehicle breakdown. I signed a couple of forms, we shook hands again.

'I shall be your Relationship Manager,' she said as we parted. 'Please feel free to contact me if you need anything.'

I assumed she referred only to banking matters, but said nothing. I must admit I was impressed with what I saw. I think she must have guessed as much because she seemed amused. I left with as much dignity as I could muster.

Over the next couple of weeks I seemed to find a need to call at the bank frequently and started to draw my expense cash out at the bank counter rather than the cash machine in the foyer. I contrived to get to the counter when Jenny was 'on' counters.

'You could use the ATM for this, you know,' she said, smiling after the second withdrawal in a week. 'Save you queuing,' she passed the cash over with the card.

'I, - well, yes, but I wanted two fives,' I said hastily, fumbling, and returning one of the tens. It was all a bit farcical, anyway we settled down to friendly recognition whenever I came to the bank.

It was Saturday. I had gone into Bournemouth to buy yet more stuff for my new apartment. Where in London I had rented, here I had decided to buy and now owned, a three bedroomed apartment. One bedroom was kitted out as my 'office'. I had filled the car boot with various kitchen and bathroom purchases and returned to the top floor restaurant of a department store for a light lunch before finishing off. While eating, I mulled over an article I was preparing about a spat between government and educationalists. I was trying to link this with the ever increasing anti social behaviour of school children.

'Hello, Mr P, - Saturday shopping?'

I looked up, startled to be addressed. There she was! A million dollars would have been in the shade. Jenny Richards! I was used to seeing her in bank uniform, now, blonde hair more tousled, she was dressed in a cowl necked sweater of pink cashmere, black slacks. A trio twist of gold necklace completed the vision.

'Miss Richards, Hi!' I scrambled to my feet. She was passing, holding a loaded tray. 'I didn't know you lived in Bournemouth,' I said, trying quickly to keep her close by.

'I don't,' she laughed, her generous mouth showing perfect teeth. 'I'm like you, shopping. – enjoy,' she grimaced to show that shopping was not really an occupation she liked either. She made to move on.

'Er, would you like to share the table?' I said hurriedly, 'Oh, - I mean if you're with someone. I'm sorry, - I didn't mean to….'

'No, I'm not, - with anyone,' she grinned.

'Thank you,' she parked her tray on the table as I shuffled my notes out of the way. 'Big list,' she said nodding at the sheaves of paper I held.

'Not shopping, just some notes for something I'm doing.'

'What do you do, Mr P.'

I explained that I was a writer, it sounded better than journalist. We got onto Jenny and Matt terms. I told her a bit more about my biography contract, hence the move from London. Jenny told me a bit herself; she had lived all her life in the New Forest; and lived in her parent's house and owned a horse and a retriever. A whole hour drifted by as we chatted. I got seconds in coffee, and more time went by. The rest of the shopping was forgotten.

I was so pleased that this could not be construed as a contrived meeting and that Jenny had paused by my table, not the other way around.

'Do you come here often?' I said, then we both giggled as we realized how daft it sounded.

'Yeah, I spend a lot of time in the department store restaurant,' Jenny said, continuing the absurdity.

'What I meant was, well, could I see you again?' There! I'd said it. 'I mean are you seeing anyone else?'

Jenny said seriously. 'Well, there is someone else, - at the bank….'

My face must have fallen because she laughed. 'This bloke keeps coming into the bank on a pretext to do banking, but we all know he's stalking me!'

My concern for her changed to confusion as I realised that she meant me, then I laughed with her.

'I'm glad we met today,' Jenny said quietly.

'Me too!' I said. We parted soon after. I had given up any interest in further shopping, but drove home, a date with Jenny next week firmly locked in my mental diary.

Back at my apartment I walked on air. The days until our 'date' went by exquisitely slowly. I went into town a couple of times, I cashed funds using the ATM and steered well clear of the bank.

I was to pick Jenny up at her home, which turned out to be a substantial cottage, with a small stable block, and a paddock which backed directly onto the new forest. Jenny met me at the front of the house as I drove up. She was wearing a tan blouse, brown body warmer, brown slacks; and was accompanied by 'Daisy' a beautiful, creamy golden retriever; the dog was quite laid back at my arrival.

Jenny accepted a chaste peck on the cheek in greeting, we stood a little self consciously making small talk about the weather.

'Come and meet Putin,' Jenny suggested.

We walked round the back of the house to a small stable block backing onto the forest. There, the top half of a stable door was open and a horse looked out at us. We strolled across and Jenny reached up to pat the horse's neck.

'This is Putin,' she said.

I approached gently. I think it was first time

I had touched a horse since my teens, when I used to go to stables with Jessica Hurd. Rubbing the horse's nose I remembered the softness, the straggly whiskers. We stood around chatting, then Jenny suggested we went for a walk through the forest into Brockenhurst. There was a good coffee shop there, she informed me. A stile separated her grounds from the open forest, I helped her over and as she jumped down I forgot to let go of her hand, she didn't mind and we strolled through the green enclosures and paths of the forest towards the village. Daisy mooched along with us.

It was one of the few grey and dull days that summer. As we walked we chatted comfortably, and as inhibition fell away we relaxed as if we had known each other for years. We spoke of our parents, hers had been killed in a car crash some years ago.

I wanted to say 'I'm sorry'. But wondered if it was appropriate.

'It was a long time ago,' she said sensing my hesitation. 'Come on, lets walk some more.'

We strolled over the level crossing and up a long narrow road to the parish church. There, built on higher ground, was a small church, surrounded by trees and hedging. The south facing porch and chancel was of stone and clearly very ancient. A small graveyard crowded to a gravel clearing for car parking and I had noticed very extensive burial grounds at the rear facing the village and covered in head stones as far as the eye could see, back down the hill.

'The church is over 1200 years old,' Jenny said as we mounted the few steps to the porch. She walked round the church and we strolled on down through the burial ground which gave way to more open ground but still dotted around with a multitude of trees; oak, beech, larch, birch, hazel and more; the ground was covered in headstones; here and there were benches, all facing the view down the hill to the village. We stopped about half way down. Jenny motioned to a headstone.

'That's where Mum and Dad are,' she said flatly. I gently put my arm round her shoulders, and we gazed at the headstone for some minutes. Then we moved to a nearby bench and sat close together looking down the hill to the village.

We spoke more of her parents; her brother who now lived in America; and about several of her Aunts and uncles. I told her I didn't know anything about my parents.

'My mother was a single mum. I never knew who my father was. Then Mum died when I was still a baby, - there was a lot of mystery about it; her younger sister,- Aunt Joan brought me up and cared for me until I left home,' I paused.

'No brothers or sisters?'

'No, there is no one else in my family except Aunt Joan. I owe so much to her. She is quite old now and in a retirement home, I make sure she has everything she needs. Now the shoe is on the other foot.'

I was telling Jenny more about my personal background than I had ever disclosed to anyone except Jessica. I wanted to change the subject.

'Is this your church?' I asked.

'Yes, I am here most Sundays, - unless there is a horse event of some sort on. I help out a bit as well.'

She hesitated. 'Do you have a church, Matt?'

'No, - well I did, in London - but now I'm down here I'll have to sort something out.'

'Come with me on Sunday, here,' she said. 'You'll like it, its very small, but you will begin to meet some of the locals.'

I told her it was a date and my whole being filled with elation.

'I've read some of your work,' she said suddenly, colouring a little.

I was ridiculously pleased that she said that. I didn't know she even knew of my work.

'Wow!' I said, joshing, 'I didn't realize I was so well known.'

'I, - well I looked you up on the internet after we met in the restaurant.'

'Do you check out all your new customers on the web, Miss Richards? I said in mock severity.

'Only the one's I fancy,' she said mischievously. We fell silent for a moment, gazing across the tombstones in a companionable reverie.

She went on. 'You have strong views of religion?'

'Not really, - well, yes I 'Spose so. I'm not studiously religious, if you know what I mean, but I really do believe in creation. I can spend ages staring into the night sky, imagining the vast distances and the worlds out there, and I feel that God must be out there somewhere.'

'Do you, really? - Do you really spend ages looking into the sky?' she laughed, looking at me with some incredulity.

I suddenly felt foolish, telling a young lady whom I've recently met that I was a stargazer, but before my confusion showed, she went on breathlessly, 'So do I Matt. I love looking into the sky too. It's awesome! I even did some evening classes on the 'Sky at Night'.'

Incredibly we were on the same astral wavelength; my joy was unbounded.

I told her of my university days, my job as a researcher for the government offices, and then my move into journalism and writing. I talked about my work on the biography of the Reverend Charmin.

After a while our animated discussion abated to a peaceful togetherness.

The solitude of the grounds seemed to crowd round us and in the greyness of the day we existed alone, save that is, for a thousand souls that sighed in the air, I could almost feel their presence biding time behind trees and headstones.

'Matt,' Jenny said, a bit self consciously, 'Some of your articles, the way you write, it has a ring of authority, as if you write it the way it is because, well, - somehow you know.'

'Wow, Jen! Steady on. I've really been looking on myself as a bit of an upstart in the literary world. Just stuff for press fodder.'

'I just get the feeling that one day You'll write

something really important, something that will influence the world,'

Jenny paused, as if she had said something she hadn't meant to; we were both silent. I was a bit stunned by her observation; I felt both exhilarated and uneasy.

We steered the conversation back to mundane matters and the crowding souls retreated. We arranged to meet again at the weekend.

Over the next few weeks I threw myself into my work. I arranged a round of weekly interviews with the Reverend Charmin, and built a structure for the work. I could see that it would mean a fair amount of travel (covered in the contract) in order to visit the scenes of much of his charitable work. The initial notes and planning had reached the third month during which time I continued to produce paying articles for the press. I had by now reached an international outlet for my work. The growing workload and Jenny occupied all my time.

I had established a routine with the Reverend Charmin, visiting him weekly, usually on a Friday, by which time I had compiled more questions from the previous weeks work. He had passed me boxes of letters, articles and diaries that would form the basis of the biography and I began to understand the man and his motivation.

On the day we were due to meet again we sat out on the patio at his house near Salisbury. His home was a delightful cottage with a garden that led to the banks of the river Avon. It was a warm summer day; we sipped iced water and chatted companionably on various topical matters of church interest. We were by now on 'Matt' and 'Dickie' terms. He was lamenting on the falling off of church attendances.

'The world is changing,' he said sadly. 'We live in an unstable society, Matt, it's not just this country, there is turmoil everywhere, graft, poverty, war and fewer people are turning to the church for salvation. There is now no more than about two million people in this country who would say they are churchgoers.'

His face was tired. He had spent a lifetime in the service to others, working unselfishly on humanitarian projects in Africa and poorer parts of our own country. Now, in retirement, the years of toil showed through. He went on, 'I think the problem is that the church has not moved with the times. Services, in general, don't put the average person into contact with God. And the church itself has unity problems of its own.'

I thought I knew where he was coming from. I too, had a pessimistic view of mankind's morality and the degeneration of society.

'I suppose the church itself is in trouble,' I said, 'What with the homosexuality schism, for example. Its relations with Islam. Even the ordination of women causes turmoil.'

Dickie snorted. 'Like politicians, the church does not grapple with the real problems. Take the ordination of women. It cannot be wrong to have women priests, - women can proclaim the gospel as well as men, and indeed can be said to provide a more natural pastoral care,' he topped up his water glass, carefully retaining lemon slices in the jug. He went on.

'Is homosexuality wrong? -Yes. Not only is it against the ordinance of God, it is biologically unsound, I believe a major backlash will ensue…'

I interrupted. 'Oh. You think society will turn on the issue?'

'No I don't. Society will continue its blind acceptance in the guise of 'human rights'. The backlash would have come from evolution, but the signs are that God will lose patience before that. You will note that civilisations come to an end soon after sodomy becomes an accepted practice.'

'Really, Dickie? Do you really believe that we are close to a reckoning?'

Dickie Charmin waved his hand impatiently. 'Look around you, the signs are everywhere. This planet is insignificant in the scheme of things, but it is a jewel. Look this way and you see beauty and natural abundance. Look that way and you see terrible destruction and waste. In every country, where there is man, there is killing and maiming, pollution and poison.'

'Crikey! You paint a dismal picture Dickie.'

'I feel the forces of evil closing around us, Matt. The maddening thing is that most people are oblivious to the signs.'

We were silent for a while, each lost in our own thoughts; the afternoon wore on, we chatted amiably, putting the world to rights. The evening chill drove us indoors. Dickie put light to a prepared log fire, which soon crackled merrily dispensing warmth and light to the room, we sat in overstuffed chairs angled to the fire. As I sipped a brandy, the germ of my next article was forming in my mind.

Later, as I was leaving, Dickie took my elbow.

'Matt,' he said, 'Next week, - come on Wednesday, eh? Say ten o'clock.'

'No problem,' I said, assuming our normal Friday conflicted with something else he was doing. 'Anything special?'

'A mystery tour,' he said with a conspiratorial smile.

That weekend I scoured the internet, badgered the information office of the Church of England web site and several dioceses information offices, then completed a lengthy paper which I then attached on an email to Paul.

'What do you think?' was my only message .

The next day he called. 'Bloody hell Matt,' he said, 'this is going to cause ructions. You really know how to wield the knife don't you?'

'I write as I find, Paul, the facts and quotes are correct, I've checked everything.'

'I know you will have, Matt. The conclusions are a nightmare.'

'The point is, will it publish?'

'Too right, it'll publish. There's plenty who would jump at the chance to trumpet on about the 'Broken society'.'

'Broken society, - I didn't say that.'

Paul laughed. 'You wait and see.'

The following Wednesday I arrived at the Reverend Charmin's house at ten o'clock as arranged; he was ready for me.

'We'll go in my car,' he said, and we set off towards Basingstoke turning off the M3 to take minor roads. A few miles short of Basingstoke we stopped in a large village at the school gates. There were a number of cars drawn up on the worn grass verge opposite the gates.

'This is the Parish Primary school,' Dickie said, importing no further clue as to the purpose of our visit. The front door of the school was locked, and was opened in response to a bell by a pleasant woman in a jumper and blue skirt.

'Dickie!' she said effusively 'You're on time as usual.'

They exchanged air kisses. Dickie introduced me. 'This is Matthew Patterson,' he said. 'Matthew, please meet Dorothy, - Head Teacher of the little monsters of this Parish.'

'Ah, ah!' exclaimed Dorothy, all smiles. 'I am pleased to meet you at last. Dickie has told me a lot about you.'

I smiled in return. 'Only good things, I hope.'

It was standard banter, but we all felt comfortable.

We could hear lively raised voices emanating from behind one of a number of doors leading off the hall. We all three proceeded into a large room full of excited children. As we entered the noise stopped and the children stood with a chorus of 'Hello Dada Charmin.'

There were a lot of giggles as they greeted Dickie with a warm show of familiarity.

'*Thank* you, children,' Dorothy said with mock severity. 'The Reverend Charmin has brought a visitor today, Mr Matthew Patterson.'

'Hello, Mr Patterson,' the children chorused.

As the children reverted to their activities, I looked around the room. There were full length benches down two sides of the room. That on the left was covered in books and pamphlets. On the wall above were 'Blue tacked' posters of the 'times tables' and various basic formulae, all written out in different coloured felt tipped pens On the right side were four computer terminals, and again on the wall above were numerous colourful posters, this time concerning IT topics. Overall the room was interesting and busy. I was impressed at the level of learning data displayed on almost every inch of wall space. On the end wall were two clocks one read 10.50 the other 11.50.

The teacher, a youngish man with a mop of black hair, detached himself from the bank of computer screens; they were displaying the same web page.

Dickie shook hands with him.

'Matt, this is Ben, - teacher and Project Manager.

Ben, - Matt,' Dickie said. We shook hands. He went on.

'Matt, this is a little project I have set up between this school and one I used to visit in Nigeria. I thought it would instructive for you to see first hand, and then when you go to Nigeria you can close the loop so to speak. Ben here has been an inspiration, I could not have done it without his expertise.

Ben made disparaging sounds. 'You're just in time,' he said. 'Come on over to this computer, Matt, You'll get a good view over the children's heads. Oh! By the way You'll be on camera,' he grinned.

I followed Ben and Dickie to the bank of computers where Ben had been setting up a video link. As I did so the children also gathered round, arranging themselves in serried ranks at each terminal screen. Ben clicked a switch and I heard music, - an African chant behind an insistent beat of drums. On each screen was the same picture of a classroom of African children about the same ages as those here. The African children were laughing and jostling to get 'on camera'. The girls were wearing white 'T' shirts under pink apron dresses; the boys wore similar shirts and pink shorts. They all looked excited and very smart.

'Hello Dada Charmin,' they all screamed in unison as Dickie appeared in view.

There ensued a few moments of uproar as both sets of children were giggling and shouting over each other. Dickie held up his hands and the noise quickly abated.

'I want you to meet a friend of mine. – Matthew,' he said. 'Matthew will coming to Nigeria soon, to see you soon.'

There was more frantic waving and squeals.

Dickie's hand again reduced the volume. 'All right children, who is the moderator today?'

A gangly girl stepped closer to the video camera in Nigeria. Her face was shining, her hair carefully combed, she looked radiant.

'Ah,' said Dickie. 'Hello Oby, how are you today?

'I'm good,' said the girl.

'And your Mum?'

'She's good too,' the young girl answered, in a shy yet composed voice.

'What have you planned for today, Oby?'

As the children got down to exchanging requests and information Dickie and I moved away from the assembled children. He explained to me the principles behind the twinned schools and how a monthly interchange had become a highlight in the children's itinerary.

Every month a small box of goodies were assembled at each school and exchanged. Dickie said his charity paid the postage. I was intrigued and made a mental note to follow up this side of Dickie's pastoral care even after retirement and even at a distance here in England.

We drove home to his house. I stayed for tea and in the early evening we sat before a freshly made fire, crackling fitfully in the hearth.

The article which Paul had dubbed 'The broken society' was published in the national press a few weeks later and as Paul had predicted it caused a storm of comment from both sides of the argument. Suddenly I felt like a bystander who had intervened to save one party only to be assaulted by both.

Paul was delighted, I was uncertain how it would play out; just about every media in the world picked up on it and the storm of comment by email and letter continued unabated for days. Paul sent down emails and parcels of letters for me to analyse. After some time sifting, sorting and counting I saw with satisfaction that by far the most comments were supportive, but were more than negated by the fewer adverse comments some of which were quite vitriolic.

Jenny watched all this from the sidelines. I tried not to get her wrapped up in my business, but she did read the article and some of the comments. She said little, but I noticed that over the next few days she held my hand more than normal.

The following Friday I went to see the Rev. Charmin for our regular exchange. It was still cold, we sat indoors.

As we settled down he said, without preamble. 'I read your piece – about the broken society, Matt.'

'And?'

'Well, it was pretty forensic. I am both surprised and impressed.'

'It seemed to come together Dickie. I just wrote what I saw in my mind, I didn't try to wrap up my findings in platitudes or excuses.'

'A spade is a spade, eh?' the Reverend changed the subject. 'We talk about me, Matt, and you have learned a lot about me, my philosophy, and lifestyle, - but what about you? Are we allowed to know more about you?'

I laughed. 'Nothing to tell, Dickie. I've not achieved one tenth of your experiences. You have travelled, given your life to deprived people in Africa and here too.- Me? I'm just a local writer with a wonderful New Forest girlfriend, - that's about it.'

'Come on, Matt. What about your inner self, - your beliefs. You go to church I know. What else. Do you believe in God, - I mean *really* believe?'

'I do, evermore so.'

'Ah, - well done, Jesus Christ then?'

'Of course, Dickie. Both Jenny and I are committed Christians, but my belief seems greater than just by rote. In my head there is the vision of a unimaginable universe and I believe in a creator who bestrides place and time and that he created everything in that universe including life itself. Mind you, it doesn't matter whether I believe or not. If I didn't believe it, it wouldn't detract from the truth. It would still be true, just I would be on the outside.'

'It does matter,' said Charmin earnestly. 'You have to believe, *really* believe. That is the way to salvation, otherwise you are condemned to mortality,'

he paused and looked at me. We talked on and eventually I was able to turn the discussion back to him and his work. I told him I was hoping to complete the work on the biography by the spring of next year.

I had to travel to London often and was to make at least one trip to Africa where Rev Charmin had spent many years. I couldn't put it off much longer and the day came when I booked the flight to Lagos, Nigeria. I had explained everything to Jenny, she seemed as unhappy about parting as me.

We had taken to making our favourite walk into Brockenhurst, (well, it was her favourite walk before I came on the scene), often stopping at an hotel, where on fine days we would sit on the terrace and sip beers. On the last return walk before I was due to fly from Heathrow we were pensive, I felt edgy, the warm sun doing little to lift my spirits. As I handed Jenny down from the stile she jumped to the ground close to me, holding my arm for support. Her face was close to mine and I looked into her eyes.

'Jen,' I said. 'I don't really want to go, and,….. and well, - I love you.'

'I love you too,' she said. I took her in my arms and we kissed, gently, exquisitely. I took in her softness, her perfume, her nature.

'I love you,' I said again,

'Umm, you said it already,' Jenny murmured. 'I love you too, - twice.'

She cuddled into me. Daisy mooched around

unconcerned.

'Jen, when I get back…'

'Uh –uh.'

'Would you marry me?'

I held my breath. Holding her close in my arms I sensed that something was troubling her, but after what seemed an eternity she said it.

'Yes, Matt I will.'

'Will, What?' I said severely, trying to hide my exultation.

'Yes, Matt I will, - marry you.'

With a sense of wonder and happiness we leaned against the stile holding each other tightly and we kissed passionately. Little did I know then how short the joy was to be and the heartache that was to follow. But there, in the sun, everything I could have wished for had come true.

Several evenings later I called for Jenny; it was dark and the house was in darkness; there was no reply to my knocking. Mystified, I was wondering what to do when Daisy came round the side of the house and welcomed me.

'Hello Daisy,' I said. 'Where's mistress then, eh?' I walked round to the back of the house as the figure of Jenny came across the open grass.

'Jenny? Everything all right?' I called.

As she approached I could see her face in the gloom.

'Sorry, Matt,' she said, a bit embarrassed. 'It is such a nice evening, I was, er, well, looking at the stars.'

As I enfolded her into my arms I looked up at the heavens. With little light pollution in the forest and being a clear, chilly night, the glorious vault above us twinkled in a myriad of stars.

'Let's stay out for while,' I said. 'If you're not chilly that is?' I added.

So we wandered down to the end of her lawn, (well, rough short grass that is) where there was a bench. We sat huddled together my arm round her, gazing into the sky; we pointed out the square of Pegasus, Orion, and other familiar features to each other.

Daisy sat close by, I teased her ears absentmindedly with my free hand until she got fed up and moved away.

'Stare into the distance,' I said, 'Beyond the stars. As you stare you can pick out more and more pinpricks. Its amazing, whole galaxies, universes; worlds we can't even imagine.'

'Umm. - I can imagine, I know there is God out there, an awesome energy, across all heaven and I believe we are part of it, Matt. We will get to see it one day.'

Jenny's quiet conviction silenced me for a moment and we stared, together, into the next world, lost in our own thoughts.

One evening, late, we were returning from Southampton to Brockenhurst. At Lyndhurst Jenny suddenly wanted us to take the longer route through the forest and past Beaulieu. She insisted despite my objections.

'Turn left here,' she said.

I turned left onto the Beaulieu road, over the cattle grid, and past the cricket ground to our left. It was getting late, and the route dark; a lot more care was needed to watch out for animals on this road. It was only the next day that I learned that there had been a major hold up on the main road between Lyndhurst and Brockenhurst due to an overturned lorry. Vehicles were held up for over an hour and were eventually turned around to retrace their route.

The pending trip to Lagos, Nigeria, was even more unwanted now, I had so much else to think of. I spent as much time as possible in Jenny's company and I was moon struck happy. We talked about marrying in three months time, - on our nine month anniversary.

Inexorably the day came when I took the BA flight from Heathrow arriving at Lagos Murtala Mohammed International Airport in the evening. The temperature was still touching 26 degrees. An escalator emptied me and hundreds more directly into the customs area and we milled around trying to clear into the arrival hall.

I had been warned about requests for tips for just about anything and also to be careful not to give my luggage to anyone except my nominated greeter. Actually everyone seemed friendly enough and I had no concerns.

I emerged into the main hall and was immediately addressed.

'Mr Patterson,' Samuel Johnson came forward, hand outstretched, with a beaming smile, black face glistening. He was dressed in clerical collar and a well worn black suit. I took his hand.

'Dr Johnson. I'm pleased to get here at last.'

His beefy hand enveloped mine. 'Samuel! You've got to call me Samuel,' he said, all the while grinning delightedly.

'Matthew,' I rejoined.

'You're booked into the Sheraton, Matthew, the car's this way.'

He insisted on taking my case and we trouped off to his car parked haphazardly in a no parking area. No one seemed to mind.

The Sheraton hotel was a modern enough high building approached along an avenue of palm trees. I checked in and agreed to meet Samuel back in reception after a quick freshen up.

Over a late meal Samuel set out the itinerary he had lined up for me over the next five days. Tomorrow was to be a trip to the primary school I had seen on the video link from England. The following day was a visit to the Government Minister who had sponsored the biography deal and had produced a grant towards the costs. There then followed three days of visits to churches, a hospital and a children's care home, all of which were closely part of the Rev. Charmin's life in Nigeria. I went to bed tired but energised for the week to come.

The next morning I met Samuel in the hotel foyer at nine o'clock and we set off on the drive to the school. It was a two hour drive mostly on dirt roads, fortunately it had not rained for some time and the tracks were baked hard. Initially I was absorbed by the scenery, but eventually it became more of the same and I was glad when we approached our destination. Samuel pointed out the township in the distance and as the red tin roofed buildings grew closer, I took in the sheer basic poverty that pervaded; the dwellings were in the main unpainted and many seemed to have windows missing. It was hot.

The centre of the small town was bustling with activity, it looked like a market day, with produce set out on boxes and stalls along the street; the whole township seemed to be out, either at the stalls or sitting around on any available step. A few cars were parked haphazardly at intervals and the place was alive with chatter and gaiety.

As we slowly drove through the busy scene we attracted waves and smiles from all. The school was situated just beyond the 'high street'; outside, in a clearing, classes were being conducted in front of old fashioned blackboards. I recognised the children's white shirts and pink dresses and shorts from the video link. As we pulled up all eyes turned to Samuel and me and as Samuel approached the teachers to shake hands the children stood up, curiosity and broad smiles on every face.

Samuel introduced me to the three teachers, Helen Lambo; Joseph Kaoje and Edmund Shagari. He turned to the children.

'Hello children. This is Matthew, he has come from England to see you, and brings love and greetings from Dada Charmin.'

Unsure of what to say I just raised my arm and said. 'Hello, everyone.'

This evoked widespread giggles and waves. I was struck by the happiness and smartness of the children amidst the general ramshackle look of the surroundings.

As the head teacher escorted Samuel and me into the school we all waved again, I noticed the girl Oby, the moderator on the video link. Once inside we were invited to take a drink of water and took a 'tour' of the school; this was easy as there were only two rooms, basic toilets (no running water) and the teacher's office! I saw the two computer terminals against one wall, and the inevitable posters stuck on the walls. We spent an hour discussing the mechanics of local education and the part played by the many projects and charities that supported the people right across this vast country. We spoke of general problems, like the fact that half the country's teachers were unqualified. We touched on the special needs and the work of schemes like 'Action Aid' and the 'Change for Good' programs.

The Rev. Charmin had been a dedicated activist in helping the people of Nigeria in both spiritual and pastoral care. He fitted very closely into the well established Christian Church and took a direct interest in a number of projects such as the twinning of this school with the primary school in England.

Eventually we ran out of things to say, I had made odd notes as we talked and now we stood up to take our leave. Back into the glare of the sun I stopped in astonishment, the whole area was packed with townspeople who had come to say hello. They stood around laughing and talking; the children had broken ranks and milled around, running between the grown ups, playing.

The laughing and noise grew; a group of men began beating on drums, the crowd accompanied them with a low chanting which grew in intensity. A few started dancing and were quickly joined by a large number of both men and women; they performed a rhythmic stamping and swaying in the dust of the street. The drum beat grew louder, the chanting taken up by the whole crowd; the stamping and singing was hypnotic, the dust swirled over everything and the sun beat down on the dancers.

The scene and the noise burned into my mind; standing in this African town submerged in the primitive sound and sight of tribal dancing I was both enchanted and dazed. The heat, the beat of the drums and the stamping seemed to shake the very earth. My head began to spin as I was caught up in the mysticism of the sounds and movement.

After a while Samuel grasped my arm and we took our farewell of Helen and her colleagues; we climbed in the car and cautiously drove back into the high street, the crowds waving and dancing as we left.

The week in Lagos district passed quickly. I visited St. Peter's Church in Abeokuta; being the oldest church in Nigeria, with its distinctive white walls and red roof. I spoke to the Government Minister, I visited the hospital and the children's care home, all places that had been closely associated with the Rev. Charmin.

I ended up with copious notes made in my hotel room in the evenings, I had taken several audio interviews.

My last meeting with Samuel and several of his colleagues left an unease in my mind. The meeting was the evening before the day of my return. Five of us were sitting in my hotel room reviewing my week's experience. The room had become charged with an indefinable aura. The visitors appeared restless, they disclosed that they felt that 'Something was going to happen'.

'Like what?' I asked.

One of the party held his arms out. 'We don't know, Matthew, there just seems to be expectation, a sort of lull before the storm.'

Little more was said about this. Everyone was pleased that a biography of 'Dada Charmin' was in progress and they promised to follow up an any queries I may come up with in the months to come.

After they left, I made my usual call to Jenny and told her how much I was longing to be home. 'It's only tomorrow now,' I said, an ache in my heart. The next day I presented myself at the airport.

CHAPTER THREE

As the summer wore on I met some of Jenny's friends and became absorbed into her circle, a great proportion of who were horse people. Inevitably I got sucked into the fraternity and while I never felt that I wanted to ride I did get attached to Jenny's horse Putin.

She also came to London with me on a couple of business meetings. We would make an overnight stay of it and take in a show. She met David, Liz, Paul and a few more friends. I remember it as a summer of intense happiness, Jenny and I were kept very busy planning for the forthcoming wedding.

One evening, in London, we had gathered at David's place for supper. The meal went off well, Jenny and Liz talked animatedly about holidays, David and I discussed journalism generally. I regaled everyone with my visit to Nigeria, (Jenny put up with it yet again, but didn't seem to mind). The girls went to the kitchen to sort out dishes and coffee.

David and I sat in a companionable after dinner haze.

'You're' really hooked,' he said lazily, but looked at me carefully.

'Well yes, - Does it show?'

'Not much, buddy. I watch you look at her. You're like a slavering Labrador, with good reason mind, she is a lovely girl. Nice I mean, - all round.'

I moved uneasily. 'Is there a 'But' in there somewhere?'

'No! no,' he said hastily. 'Jenny has the same doe eyed look for you. I watched her when you were telling us about Nigeria, - she seemed, well, sort of proud of you,' he changed the subject. 'What about this biography then, how do you rate it.'

'Actually, its bloody difficult, to tell you the truth. I've set out how I want to do it,- several times in fact, then changed it all. I've got to remember its Charmin's story and not my view of his story. I've got to know a lot about the Reverend Charmin, and I think I know how he should be portrayed, - but there seems to be sense of sadness about his story I can't get my head around, there's something not clear. I suppose it will come, but I get the surreal feeling that somehow my own life is getting mixed up with his.'

The girls came back in with the coffee. Liz was still chattering on about some dress shopping. As Jenny followed she seemed tense. Her face was strained as she glanced quickly between David me. Then it was gone, she smiled and handed the coffee cups off the tray.

The following morning we travelled back by train to Brockenhurst.

'It was a lovely visit,' she said. 'David and Liz are a nice couple.'

I agreed. 'They are, and they both really like you, they said so several times.'

Jenny hesitated. 'They are going to have a baby.'

I was surprised. 'Really? Funny, David didn't say anything, or Liz come to that. Girlie confidences I 'Spose.'

'Matt,' Jenny was serious. 'I'm worried about them.'

'Worried about what?'

Jenny was evasive. 'Well, I don't know. They are both so busy and Liz leads such a hectic life, it can't be good.'

I was amused. 'Hey, Jen, I didn't take you for a broody hen?'

The subject was changed as we arrived at Brockenhurst station.

I had parked my car at her house. She changed for work and I ran her into Lymington before going on to my apartment.

It was two weeks later that David called me.

'Hi Matt, How are things,' we skated around a few pleasantries. Then, 'We're having a baby!'

'What? - well done to you both. I thought you were too old,' I joshed. 'Congratulations. Give my love to Liz.'

'I will, we only found out today, so Liz is still on a high.'

I felt a cold brace go around my chest. 'You didn't know?'

'Well no. We had no idea, Liz missed last month and decided to get a check up today. It was a surprise to both of us.'

I joshed him a bit more and we hung up after he insisted that I let Jenny know and to pass on his and Liz's love.

I sat for a long time staring at the phone. How did Jenny know that Liz was pregnant, and why was she worried? In the end I decided it was woman's intuition and that Jenny was merely responding in some womanly way to an aura thrown off by Liz herself.

Jenny and I were deep into planning the wedding. We prepared invitations and got them mailed out. The wedding itself, at Jenny's insistence, was to be a smallish affair, only forty eight guests were on the invites. Jenny was a virgin and so we were happy to go for a full on white wedding. Her dress, (as I saw in due course), was of exquisite white embroidered lace above a full gown. The lace cupped her breasts and whispered upwards to her shoulders, leaving a bare neck and daring glimpses of cleavage. An intricate headdress and long train completed the vision.

Soon after Jenny had agreed to marry me we strolled to the church to talk to the vicar of St Nicholas church, Philip Rowland.

For more than a thousand years people had

walked the path as we, to the beautiful and peaceful little church, the oldest in the New Forest, dating back to Saxon times.

Jenny seemed to have a special place in the hearts of people she knew here, especially the vicar. She had introduced me on our first visit and we had quickly got onto first name terms.

Philip Rowlands was younger than me but with a wisdom beyond his years; tall, with wavy dark hair and a calm handsome face, he was highly intelligent and seemed almost out of place in such a small church. We had got on well, and today he seemed pleased at our news.

Back at her home that night we looked at holiday brochures and decided to spend a week in Cyprus for our honeymoon. We sat round her laptop and booked the flights and a week at the Elysium hotel in Paphos.

During the increasing panic of arranging affairs ourselves, - Church service, flowers, taxis, reception and host of other tasks, I continued to work on the biography and to submit articles to various press agencies. I was now receiving commissions for specific topics, and often given strict deadlines to meet.

Just three weeks before the wedding date David called. He came straight to the point, his voice flat.

'Hello Matt. I'm afraid I've got bad news. Liz has lost the baby!'

'Oh! my God.- David. I'm so sorry, Is Liz okay?'

I struggled to find sympathetic words. My concern for Liz and David was clouded by a flashback of Jenny's concern a couple of months ago, even before anyone knew that Liz was pregnant.

I felt a frisson of apprehension and a tingle at the back of my neck.

Somehow I concentrated on David and spoke words of comfort. We were not on the phone for long, I promised to try to get up to London before the wedding.

I guessed Jenny would be home, I drove over, we sat in the kitchen.

'Jen. David called me, he and Liz have lost the baby. He was really knocked back.'

There was a long pause as she stared into the distance.

'I'm so sorry,' she said quietly, 'I'm so sorry.'

'Jenny you knew!' my voice was almost accusing. 'You said you were worried, even before they announced that Liz was pregnant!'

'I -I just guessed. They are, well, - so active there was always a chance that it would happen, I just guessed.'

Somehow I wasn't convinced. I looked at her. Her left hand rested on the table, thumb tucked into her fingers. She looked so defenceless, her face troubled, I was overwhelmed with love, I wanted to protect her, but from what?

CHAPTER FOUR

The weekend of the wedding came with a high sense of excitement. It was late summer and the days were still warm and the nights just beginning to have a chill in the air.

A group of my friends came down from London on the Friday afternoon; David and Liz; Paul and his wife Margaret; Tony Hurd (Now Doctor Hurd) and girlfriend Lesley Gardner; HH and Jessica. I had booked them all into Carey's Manor Hotel at Brockenhurst for the Friday and Saturday night. I thought they would all enjoy the Thai Spa and make a weekend break of the occasion.

Jenny and her girlfriends turned up at the hotel in the evening for a get together, while the men decamped to the Balmer Lawn Hotel for a few drinks.

My side was heavily outnumbered by Jenny's friends but introductions were made and everyone mixed in.

'Well, here's all the best,' said David over the first pint of beer of the evening. There was a chorus of 'Hear, Hear'. and soon everyone was talking at once and the party got under way. It was a high spirited evening and it was good to catch up with all my London friends..

It was a bit more difficult with Jenny's friends, most of whom were New Forest born and bred. I did get on well with Trevor, Jenny's uncle, whose job it was to give her away the next day.

Later I had a quiet word with Tony. He had news. He had got a new job and was moving closer to us, a job in Wiltshire. He and Lesley would be able to spend more time visiting.

'After I got my doctorate I wanted to do a spell away from academia, this job came up and so I'm moving next month.'

'Well done,' I said. 'Who is the job with?'

'Its MoD really, - Porton Down, not too far from Salisbury.'

'That's really close, Tony. It will be good to see more of each other. What does HH think?'

'He's okay with it, thinks it's a bit sinister though.'

'Well, Porton Down. I guess it does have connotations. I suppose any work for chemical and biological warfare is spooky.'

'Its called the Defence, Science and Technology Laboratory now.'

'That's alright then,' I said.

In a way I was relieved when the evening was over and I returned to my apartment. The big day was almost here.

The next day engraved itself on my mind as the best day of my life.

St. Nicholas church was bursting at the seams as we gathered to await the arrival of the bride. The church is very small and the announcement of her arrival at the door was soon followed by her arrival at my side. I stole a glance sideways, my heart leaping, so beautiful was she.

Jenny always looked fantastic whether in her normal bank uniform, or jumper and slacks, or in Hacking jacket and jodhpurs, - but here, now, her hair styled high, her face wide eyed and serious, her white wedding gown a creation of lace on satin she took my breath away. I felt moved almost to tears, and began to feel nervous.

Jenny, radiant, caught my mood and reaching up, quietly whispered in my ear.

'I love you Mr P.'

'I love you too, Mrs P,' I said, then felt a bolt of fear strike through me. I'm not superstitious, but we were not yet married. Would my hasty and premature words be a bad omen?

Jenny didn't seem to care, nevertheless I was greatly relieved when we were pronounced 'man and wife'. We exchanged chaste kisses in front of the gathering to shouts of good wishes as we walked over to sign the register.

Finally, at the entrance we posed for photos. The photographer wasn't satisfied until he had captured just about every combination of bride, groom and guests.

From here we were to go to Carey's Manor

for the reception. As everyone milled around preparing to leave I spoke quietly to Jenny.

'Fancy a short stroll, on our own?'

She looked enquiringly, but agreed and we strolled in the weak sun round the back of the church and into the cemetery, down the hill. I put my arm round her waist, as we walked gently as far as the place where her parents lay, we paused for a long while.

Jenny's eyes filled, I made no move to intrude. Then she leaned forward and laid her bouquet gently on the grave.

Then we turned and made our way back up the hill to the church. She squeezed my arm. 'Thank you,' she said simply.

'I wanted to show you off,' I said returning her squeeze.

The rest of the day went by in a sort of haze. I remember David making a speech, then me following. It seemed to go down well; I made the obligatory statements about taking care of Jenny for life; I also alluded to the ceremony where I promised to love and cherish. 'I had to make another promise under my breath,' I said, 'I had to promise to muck out Putin at weekends!' it drew some laughs and the day ended in good spirits.

We retired to change into going away clothes and were then seen off in a hail of rice and shouts and waves of 'have a good time'.

In fact we were going only to Jenny's house for the night as we had to be up early the next day to drive to Bournemouth airport to catch a flight to our honeymoon hotel.

Cyprus, the Island of Aphrodite, the Goddess of love. We alighted from the plane at Paphos into seventy five degree heat, a warm breeze caressed us as we walked to the terminal building. Jenny looked so carefree in a simple sun dress and sandals, her hair tied back in a high ponytail. A taxi took us to the Elysium hotel along roads lined with a riot of orilandi and hibiscus. Buildings and walls en route were covered in profusions of red and pink bougainvillea. Suddenly the stresses of work and of organising the wedding just seeped from us.

We had just one short week! The first day we lingered over a buffet breakfast then just wandered around the hotel and grounds down to the sea shore where a small hotel beach and swimming area had been created. We sat and lay for the morning on loungers, at peace, soaking in the sun. We applied sun block on each other and smiled happily, we seemed to chat endlessly. After a light lunch we tried different loungers at the poolside. In the early evening we showered and changed, then strolled onto the main road for a while and found a Chinese restaurant. We sat contentedly drinking brandy sour deciding what to eat. Everything about Jenny was a new and exciting experience. We were learning what we liked, what we felt, what pleased us, what made us angry, - there was a whole lifetime to explore our innermost feelings.

The next day we hired a car and drove northwards to Polis and Latchi. These little harboured towns consisted of no more than a street of restaurants and some souvenir shops, but it was relaxed and the warm air continued to blow over us. We drove to the Anassa hotel and sat on a wide terrace for lunch, looking down over the beach and coastline. There were few people around and we sat in almost solitary peace. Lunch consisted of a village salad, feta cheese, olives and bread. We lingered, finding that we could talk for hours about anything and everything. I could not get enough of knowing about Jenny, and she wanted to know all about my work and early life.

Jenny was a local girl who had never moved away from her roots. She was a girl of the New Forest, through and through; schooled in Brockenhurst and going onto College at Salisbury. She got a job in banking and had stayed there ever since, dividing work with horse riding and eventing. But underneath the normality was a depth I had not yet plumbed and sometimes, just fleetingly, I felt an undercurrent of darkness.

We visited the tourist areas, Limossol; the promenade along the coast, the souvenir shops. We drove to Pissouri and sat in the taverna on the beach just whiling away the moments in a haze of peaceful contentment. On the fourth day we drove to the Troodos mountains and enjoyed a different view of Cyprus, greener, cooler and serene.

Always were the typical Greek style tavernas. We lived on village salads, Kleftika Cyprus lamb and fresh fruit. Where ever we went, the Cypriots took to Jenny, she responded to their friendliness and as most spoke good English soon engaged in animated conversation.

There was a sense of timelessness about the island that captivated me, I wished we had more time, but the week passed so quickly. As we flew back to Bournemouth we vowed we would return again.

Settling to married life was easy for us. We carried on as before except that now we shared all our spare time. I let my apartment and moved to Jenny's house, (because of Jenny's horse, Putin, and Daisy the retriever).

I knew little about horses, but living with Jenny meant including Putin. I learned about 'mucking out' and cleaning 'tack'. I watched with amazement, on eventing days, the transformation of my 'Relationship Manager' into an accomplished horsewoman. Dressed in her black riding habit, gold coloured waistcoat, cream jodhpurs and highly polished boots she looked a dream. On a horse Jenny became haughty, confident and utterly desirable.

I learned something else about horses. As I grew at ease with Putin I could sense something primeval about the animal When I looked into his eyes I could imagine a wisdom going back thousands of years. I grew to love the warm oaty smell of horses and would sometimes stand at his shoulder for long moments our heads close together and I felt I was communing with a force, primitive yet knowing.

Watching Putin trot back to the trailer, Jenny rising and falling in her stirrups, I was always aroused, somehow envious of the oneness of horse and rider. On the evenings following a riding event Jenny sensed my arousal and came to me willingly and with some amusement.

When Jenny left for work at the bank, I too, would work. I had ensconced myself in what must have been the old dining room. French windows looked out over the green into the forest and the pathway into Brockenhurst.

My time was divided between work on the biography and new pieces for my agent. I also received a growing number of comments about my work from readers, by email and post. Most comments were favourable but still left a considerable number of correspondents who wrote to deride my conclusions on any specific topic and some were downright abusive.

'If you write about contentious issues you're bound to get flack,' observed Paul when I discussed it with him.

'I made a decision, when I started all this, that I would write as I saw.'

'Okay. But there are always two sides to a story.'

'Agreed, but the other side is darker. It's as if the human spirit is prevented from advancing by some opposing force. When I write about something I find the connecting opposite and lay out the logical consequence.'

'Yeah. I noticed, and that's why you draw the responses,' Paul paused, looked at me intently. 'Matt, your writing is powerful, it is forensic, but people don't like to be lectured to, or confronted with ultimatums, - the messenger is often the first to be shot, - but you are shedding light and you must continue to do what you do.'

Jenny and I settled down to married life, by the time we got to our first anniversary it seemed as if there had been no other life. Jenny continued her work at the bank; little changed for her, it seemed as if she had just added me to her collection and carried on as always, - Putin, Daisy and now me. We frequently went to London to meet agents and friends, but life revolved around my work at home and our local social life.

We would get the ferry from Lymington to Yarmouth on the Isle of Wight and have a lingering lunch at the George Hotel. We would drive to Sandbanks and take the ferry to Swanage, have a cream tea at Corfe Castle. We went to drinks parties, played tennis, cards, - and there was always the horse fraternity.

Putin and I became great pals as I went along to help, - or wait around. The horse would stand patiently waiting for something to happen, one rear leg bent in relaxation. I often stood close by, Putin would edge toward me and nuzzle me or put his chin on my shoulder, and we would stand quietly watching the activity around us.

When Jenny was not involved in horse matters we would go for long walks in the forest. We had our favourite places and as always, Daisy would accompany us, mooching along close by. She never wanted to run off, in fact she appeared to prefer the horse events, when all she had to do was to sit around the gathering point for hours on end waiting for Jenny to return on Putin. As time went on Daisy found the long walks tiring anyway and she became more reluctant to get out of the car.

'Come on old lady,' I would say as I helped her out of Jenny's land rover. On our return she could get her front paws onto the tail gate, but I had to lift her rear into the vehicle.

As arthritis and poor eye sight took their toll, the dog began to suffer ill health and seemed to lose interest in life. Tom, our local vet, tried to enhance the dog's life with supplementary diets and various applications, but old age wore on inexorably.

In our fifth year of marriage it was clear that it would be kinder to ask the vet to put the dog to sleep. Jenny couldn't bring herself to accept this and she spent several months slowly reaching the inevitable conclusion. In the end she asked me tearfully to go to the vet with her.

It was a traumatic experience. Daisy was on the vet's table, her head snuggled into Jenny's arms, seeming to have a premonition that all was not good. Jenny openly cried while I tried to comfort both.

In the end it was quite gentle, Daisy slowly fell asleep as the drug was injected. Jenny was inconsolable for the rest of the day. I discreetly moved all of Daisy's stuff out of the house.

Even months later we would still say 'Daisy would like this,' or 'Do you remember when Daisy…..'

I said to Jenny. 'We could get another puppy.'
'No!'

I was surprised by her vehemence, she quickly softened her voice. 'I don't want another dog, Matt, we would never get another Daisy.'

'Well, not Daisy I agree, but you would love it just the same, and after a year, as much as Daisy.'

'No, Matt. I am really not interested, - honest,' her face took on a stubborn set, leaving me mystified. Jenny had always loved dogs, and moved in circles where everyone owned at least one. I could see that she was unhappy so I dropped the subject.

Jenny never mentioned Daisy or dogs again.

One day in Lymington, we were emerging from the Bluebird restaurant on the quay, having stopped for coffee. A crowd had gathered on the cobbled street. Jenny and I stopped to see what the fuss was about. The centre of attention was a swan that had somehow made its way about twenty metres up the cobbled way from the harbour and was lying in the middle of the way its regal head switching side to side as it kept an eye on the crowd.

A few pedestrians were clearly nervous of trying to pass, others laughed and watched, two ladies were taking photos. Jen and I could see that the swan was distressed, and looking closer saw that it was enmeshed in some old netting discarded by a fishing boat. No one wanted to get too close.

Jenny exclaimed in alarm. 'It's caught in all that netting, Matt, poor bird!' with that, she elbowed her way through the onlookers and went straight to the swan, who on her approach tried to struggle to its feet, hissing. There were loud gasps from the audience.

Jenny, ignoring the aggressive beak, and without ado squatted close to the bird, grabbed hold of its neck, all the time whispering soothing words. The powerful bird had half risen, starting to flap huge wings that could break an arm. With her other hand she stroked the birds head and back, still whispering. The swan quietened, Jenny glanced up looking for me, her face tilted, her typical quizzical expression. I had no option but to approach.

'Matt, try to get the netting from around its legs.'

I started to untangle the netting, the closeness of the swan emphasised its size and strength. I wasn't making much headway. I called across to the onlookers. 'Get some scissors from the shop!'

After a short time someone approached nervously holding the scissors at arms length. I was able to quickly cut away the tangled mat of netting.

'Get away,' Jenny said to me.

I did and she gave the bird a final smooth and soft word and let it go. The swan stood up stretched its wings and flapped them impatiently a few times, then with dignity stalked down the cobbles to the water.

The onlookers clapped. We went back to the car park.

'I was very proud you, Jen,' I said later that day, we were lounging on the sofa at home. I had my arm round her shoulder, twizzling strands of her hair with my fingers.

'Mmm, - you cut the netting free,' she said.

'But you went straight to it, - I don't think I would've.'

'You would.'

'No, I wouldn't.'

'Would.'

'Wouldn't.'

With that we dissolved into giggles as we tickled each other and suddenly she was in my arms and we kissed, I felt her firm body arching to me.

'Jen, I love you so much,' I whispered.

'I love you too, Mr P,' she breathed.

At last the biography was published and I believed I had captured the essence of the Reverend Charmin in all aspects, - as a person, as a man of God, his beliefs, his experiences, his doubts. It was this last that challenged me. In all my interviews with him and after reading his own writings, sermons, accounts and his exaltation of the Lord I sensed sadness. I was concerned and I put it to him.

'Matt, you are perceptive and your account is without fault,' the Reverend laid his hand on my arm. 'My dear friend, you are destined to write an account much greater than my poor experience, your work for me has been but an audition,' his grip on my arm tightened, then relaxed and patted it. 'Now! Let us go into the conservatory, I want to show you my Freesias, you know they are a hobby of mine.'

With that the subject was closed, and I fretted that I still had no explanation for the undertone of sadness.

Time passed and it was with some astonishment I realised that Jenny and I were approaching our ninth year of marriage. We sat, as we often did, hand in hand, on a bench in the grounds of St Nicholas church looking down over the village. It was late summer, grass had recently been mown, the smell and the silence soothed our souls.

'Matt, I've decided to find a home for Putin,' Jenny said carefully.

I was stunned. I waited, wondering if I had

heard correctly. She couldn't part with the horse. Old Putin, now a senior citizen, was part of her life, part of her past. I too had grown to dote on the animal, he was part of both our lives.

'Jen, what are you saying? It's a joke?'

'No, Matt, Its - well I am beginning to feel that the work, -even the riding, is getting a bit of a hassle. I'll find him a good retirement home.'

'I don't believe it! - you can't! Jen he belongs with us, there's plenty of room for him to retire at home and in any case he's still got a few years of gentle riding in him.'

Jenny was silent, her face set in a stubborn stare.

'Jen! Look at me,' she turned to me, with tilted head her face set but I could see misery in her eyes. 'Why, Jen?'

'I told you, he's too much now,' she looked away. I got up and walked around. We argued some more but Jenny was adamant. We walked home in silence. At home that evening we spoke only in stilted sentences, it was our first major disagreement in nine years.

The next morning I was up early, I knew Jenny was awake but I ignored her, walking out of the house to the stable. I opened up the top half door. Old Putin clumped around, then came to greet me, his large head came over the door and he nuzzled my shoulder.

'Hello, old boy,' I took in the oaty smell, the calm impassive face. We looked eye to eye, a wave of emotion swept over me and I hugged the old head to me. 'Putin, old boy, everything's going to be alright,' I said, with tears in my eyes. 'I don't understand it, - I just don't understand it,' we stood that way for a long time, I drew comfort from his closeness and returned to the house.

I made a cup of tea and took it upstairs to Jenny, She stared cautiously from beneath the bedclothes.

'Jen. I'm sorry! I've been a right heel. I didn't mean to upset you, I had no right to get onto you like this,' I put the cups down and held her in my arms.

'S'okay,' she said, holding me tightly so I couldn't see her face, then she cried. Huge sobs, I could feel her body wracked with grief. She cried until long after the tea had gone cold, then just held onto me.

Two weeks later, we trailored Putin over to Fordingbridge; Trevor had agreed to retire Putin at their working farm and training stables. Jenny had insisted on a monthly payment towards the horse's keep. We offloaded Putin, who stood around quite unfazed. Trevor was in the yard as we arrived, he strode over accompanied by a stable hand, who then led Putin across the yard toward the stable block.

Putin clopped sedately beside the hand, about half way across he suddenly stopped and despite gentle coaxing turned his head and looked back at us uncertainly. For a long while he stood looking back, I could feel the tension rising in Jenny beside me and we both nearly lost our composure. Putin turned away and continued his walk to the stable. Without any goodbyes to Trevor, Jenny fled to the car.

The next month was fraught as Jenny fielded incredulity from her horse loving friends; we re-organised our life without the early morning chores, or the weekend eventing. I did not interrogate Jenny any more about her decision.

It was two months later that two awful facts hit me. One, Jenny was psychic and two, she was ill. The first I should have learned over the nine years of marriage. I berated myself mercilessly. How could I have missed it? Was I so wrapped up in my own business that I was insensitive to the nuances of Jenny's behaviour? How often she had steered our course to avoid mishaps of a minor nature. How she was not surprised when she received news. I now remembered dozens of occasions when she did or said something that was later borne out, but I had been too blind to notice.

But the illness was something else. Jenny had foreseen this! This why she had retired Putin! She began to feel tired after a days work. She was breathless walking up the hill to St. Nicholas church and suffered frequent headaches.

I was beside myself with anxiety and remorse.

Her doctor sent her (us) to Southampton for tests. There followed more tests, we travelled back and forth to Southampton, we were directed to the Portland hospital in London, then finally received the consultant's verdict. It was devastating. I could not take in the consultant's words, he spoke of ratings and metastasis.

'I can't dress it up Jenny,' he said. 'There are palliatives, little else at this time.'

After an hour we stumbled from the room. Jenny had received the diagnosis and the options of treatments, but nothing could hid the fact that she had a very short time left. At home that night we sat close together on the settee, we talked, and talked on into the night. Only when Jenny fell asleep in my arms did I gently carry her to bed.

I returned downstairs to my office and connected to the internet. I could not accept the consultants words, - 'Only palliatives! - it is best to get your affairs in order, - probably three to four months, - of course there is always the chance.... etc etc'.

I spent all night looking through hundreds of web sites, I did not believe the number of sites dedicated to the subject, diagnosis, hospitals, clinics, pharmaceuticals, alternative therapies, support and care organisations; it went on and on. I devoured page after page. Eyes pricking with fatigue I finally lay my head on the keyboard as dawn was breaking and slept.

Late in the morning I came to as Jenny appeared in her pyjamas. She looked at me solemnly through her beautiful blue eyes, now shadowed with tiredness and emotion. There was still the tilt to the head, the quizzical look and my heart went out to her.

'I love you Jen,' I said.

'I love you too Mr P,' how many times had we said these two sentences to each other over the past ten happy years. Now I felt anger and helplessness rage within me.

'Jen, I've been looking at the internet, there's so much out there, I don't think we should leave it here, there must be an answer.'

'Mr Edwards is a leading consultant, Matt. He knows the score.'

'Yes, he may be, but we ought to get a second opinion, Jen. We owe it to you. I want to fix up another appointment.'

Jen said nothing, her hand rested on the settee back, thumb tucked into her fingers.

'Look,' I said desperately. 'Let me just try and get another expert to confirm, - there is a chance that he'Ll know something different, - later technology or something.'

Jenny smiled weakly at me, and wandered into the kitchen. I could hear her clattering about with breakfast things. Over breakfast we did get round to discussing the subject again. Jenny was going into work later and would hand in her notice. I was to get a power of attorney arranged. I said I was going to call Mr Edwards.

Slowly we picked up the threads of daily routine. While Jenny was away I did some shopping, called into the solicitor, got home and called the consultant.

'Its not that we have any doubts about what you told us,' I said. 'But I would really like Jenny to talk with someone else as well.'

Mr Edwards was not fazed, he even recommended a top man, Mr Evans, at the Cancer Group in London and said he would send the files to him. He then gave me a number to call and fix an appointment.

I cleaned the house top to bottom so that Jenny would have nothing at all to do when she returned. I spent the rest of the day on the internet printing out articles and semi planning visits to experts in Europe and USA.

The next day was grey, we went to St Nicholas church. I took the car so that Jenny would not have to walk up the hill. We sat on our bench overlooking the village and chatted gently. Jenny seemed to have recovered some of her spark, but I sensed the fragility of her spirit. Later in the week we went to London by train and met Mr Evans. His observations were exactly the same as Mr Edwards's.'

We said little on the way back, but at home I pointed out the wealth of chances elsewhere.

'There's a clinic in Germany…,' I started.

'No Matt! It really is a waste of time. Two of the top people in UK have looked at the tests. I don't think I have the energy to trog round the world looking for the silver bullet. If there was an answer it would be here, -- on the internet,' Jenny waved a hand to the office. 'Besides, I know……,' she stopped suddenly and went to move into the kitchen.

'Jen, wait! What do you mean, 'You know?'

'Nothing, Matt. I'm just getting tired, that's all.'

So we left it, but my mind continued to try to put it all together. The next day I contacted a number of names I found on the internet and tried to elicit information.

I got very little help, only offers of appointments or steers to books and articles.

I called Mr Edwards again. He had received the file back from Mr Evans in London.

'There's got to be something we can do,' I said. 'Where is the leading edge research going on, - can we sign up to clinical trials for new procedures?'

'This country is at the forefront of research Mr Patterson, if there was a breakthrough we would know about it. Yes, of course there is a lot of advance research, especially into DNA engineering and the like, but we're ten years off yet. Its a sad fact that once the problem has metastasised we are powerless.'

'I can't just leave it, I've got to do something, Mr Edwards, - I'm pleading with you. Please tell me about someone somewhere in the world, or some procedure that has any claims to beat this, orthodox or not.'

We spoke on for a short time, there clearly nothing the consultant could say or do to help. I stormed out of the house and walked aimlessly for a while, then, from habit I suppose, made my way to St Nicholas's church. I entered through the porch into the calm and intimacy of the Nave and stood for a long time, unseeing, eyes blurred with tears, only the desperation of the situation filling my being.

'Matt!'

I started. Philip Rowlands stood before me emerging from the vestry.

'Oh! - Hello Philip, sorry, I didn't see you, I was wandering by really, - I just don't know what to do.'

The Reverend Rowlands was sympathetic.

'I'm glad you feel able to drop in. We missed you both last Sunday. How is Jenny?'

'Weak, tired, - but she is holding up well to all the consultants discussions. We're very depressed by the total inability of the medical profession to come up with any solutions. I have been talking to a neurosurgeon in Austria, but Jenny is adamant she does not want to shop all over the world, she does not even want to go into hospital at all.'

Philip Rowlands came close and put his arm round my shoulder.

'Matt, I know it's awful for you. Try to remain strong, for Jenny's sake.'

'You're right,' I said. 'Although Jenny has taken it all very calmly, sometimes I get the impression she is comforting *me,* and that hurts; I feel inadequate, I should be doing something to help *her*.'

'You are Matt, you are. Just stay by her. Jenny is a strong person with special gifts.'

'Sometimes I feel she knew , she seems to be - well I don't know, sort of psychic.'

Philip smiled gently. 'Let's just say that she's a girl of the New Forest,' he changed the subject and said he had tea in the vestry and would I join him.

I followed him across the small aisle, a sudden idea and urgent desire came to me.

'Philip,' I said. 'A few friends are coming down from London this weekend. Could you arrange a special prayer for Jenny at service, - I mean would it be alright?'

Philip agreed he would make special prayers on the Sunday service and I ran home filled with adrenaline. At least I could do something. I didn't mention anything about the plan to Jenny.

I called every person that Jenny and I knew as friends, even acquaintances, I asked and pleaded with them to come to Brockenhurst and the service on the coming Sunday. I was moved by the warm response from just about everyone I called. 'Yes they would come'.

Jenny mooched about the house and, - if the weather was fine, in the garden. After giving up her job and with no Putin to fuss around she seemed at a loose end. She never queried my surreptitious phone calls. In the evening sitting on the sofa she would look at me with her quizzical gaze, her face showing signs of strain, but she smiled and I felt her love radiate out to me. I wanted to hug her all the time and often made excuses to go to the kitchen for something to do, just to hide the tears that came unbidden.

I became sure that Jenny knew what I was doing, but she said nothing and Sunday came. I was totally unprepared for the scale of the event. I wanted to drive to the church, to save Jenny the long walk up the hill. As we drove along the long narrow road we arrived at the little gravel car park. There, cars parked on every inch of space and crowds of people making their way up the road and the few steps to the porch. Jenny evinced surprise at the activity. One of the church wardens had taken on the role of car parking attendant and beckoned us forward. Somehow they had got permission from the big house for the private gate to be opened and allowed parking on the grass verges of the long drive. We made our way back to the church, people greeting us, - well, Jenny really, with smiles and well wishes. It was clear that there was nowhere near enough room inside the church and people spilled out around the grounds.

As we breasted the few steps to the porch Jenny abruptly stopped in consternation! There by the porch looking down at us, his old head tossing enquiringly, stood Putin! I was stunned. Somehow the old horse had been coaxed up the steps and now stood patiently waiting, ears pricked and I'm sure knew who was coming.

Jenny left my arm and ran forward to take the old horse's neck in her arms. A ripple of applause went round the gathering congregation. I could see Jenny's shoulders heaving as she sobbed and sobbed. Everyone left her alone to gather her composure and some minutes later we entered the packed church.

Philip held a very moving service and at the appropriate point turned his attention to a prayer for Jenny.

In the days that followed Jenny and I fell into some kind of routine. I had become exhausted in my quest for help. I still scoured the Internet, I badgered MacMillan Support and all the charities I could find. I held long discussions with the Reverend Charmin, and with Philip, but all to no avail, there was no advance on the advice we had already been given.

Jenny grew more tired and increasingly tormented with headaches. She asked me for pain relief pills more frequently. I sat with her for hours on end holding her close to me. I prayed to God to let me take some of the pain, but it didn't work.

One day Jenny asked me to go to St Nicholas with her, it was a habit we had dropped over the weeks, so I was a bit surprised. It was grey and slightly raining. I made her wrap up well and helped her on with her water proof riding trousers and jacket, finished off with an old water proof Stetson. We drove to the church and made our way slowly to 'our' bench where we sat for a while quietly. We looked down through the drizzle and greyness to the village, it was silent save for the rain dripping from the trees and memorial stones. We were cosy inside our waterproofs, I held Jenny close and looked into her face, I wiped off a raindrop that had fallen onto her cheek from the brim of her hat. I loved her so much, I could see the pain and weariness in her eyes and my heart ached. I felt the presence of the souls that had gathered in this place for over a thousand years, they waited behind the headstones and the trees, I imagined movement from the corner of my eye as they gathered closer, I heard the soft drum of the rain and I sensed a holding of breath.

Jenny spoke in a whisper. 'I've always loved you Mr P.'

I had to lean close to hear.

'My darling Jen, I've adored you from the moment I first set eyes on you, and I always will. Somehow we're going to come through this together.'

She smiled, the old quizzical smile. 'Yeah, we will, Mr P.'

We were silent for a long while then she whispered, 'Matt, I'm so tired. It's time now. - Time to say goodbye.'

I held her even closer, 'No! No Jen, I can't say goodbye to you, ever,' my voice broke as I cried in pain.

'Hush Matt, I am just going on ahead a little bit, please say goodbye!'

' No, Jen I can't, I can't.'

We sat holding each other close, I sobbed like a baby. Eventually the sobbing abated, and we were quiet. Jenny whispered again her voice was almost inaudible.

'Say goodbye, Matt.'

'I can't, Jen.'

'Matt. Say it.'

I gagged trying to get the words out 'Goodbye my darling,' I whispered into her cheek.

I felt her sigh, as if contentedly. Her hold

relaxed and as I looked into her face I knew she had left me. I felt a wail of anguish rise through my body and my loud cry echoed around the grounds. I held Jenny for an hour, tears and hopelessness washing over me, then numbness. I pulled my mobile phone from a pocket and summoned help.

I shut the door of the apartment and closed myself into oblivion. Till now I had been able to mange; to run on auto pilot, but now, everything was done. Everyone had paid homage to Jenny and, one by one, left. I was now alone and I began to come apart. I cried until my body was wracked with pain. I couldn't cope, - just couldn't cope.

I railed at the medical profession for their inability to help Jenny, but most of all I railed at God. Why Jenny? Why had he deserted us? My thoughts ranged back over the years, the attendances at church, the belief, the sure knowledge that God was there and that we were part of his plans.

Jenny and I weren't just 'Best friends' as kitsch anniversary cards fashionably announced; we were soul mates, Jenny and I, we shared a deep, often unspoken, even not understood, spiritual bond. We knew that our souls were a microscopic part of an awesome scenario played out over the unimaginable distances and time of the cosmos.

As the night wore on I remained beyond despair slumped in the armchair. It was in the early hours that I roused from a doze of exhaustion, my mind instantly, but drowsily, playing back the event of Jenny's passing. I had a sense of not being alone, there was a presence in the room, benign, comforting; so much so I accepted it and remained lethargic as thoughts ran uncontrolled in my brain.

My personal situation had to be placed in the context of eternal life; the physical life I had with Jenny was in any case transitory, we lived this life in preparation for the next. The voice in my head spoke gently, authoritatively.

'This life is but an evening gone. You will live forever, with God, and be master of all universes. Jenny will be with you again, you will reign with God's Grace, and you will be awarded the final power, mastery of the final dimension, - time! Be steadfast, seek always the way of God.'

And so, the voice still murmuring to me I slept. Utterly exhausted I slept for twenty four hours.

The days and weeks passed as I struggled to cope with the practical tasks and emotional backlash of Jenny's death. She had been laid to rest beside her parents in the burial ground of St. Nicholas church. I sold the house, and moved back into my apartment. Paul gave me space and held off requesting articles for publication. I sat around the apartment brooding. I responded grudgingly to calls from friends, and more often than not ignored calls left on the answer phone.

I would visit St. Nicholas church frequently, sitting on 'our' bench and with the tears came memories of special moments Jen and I had shared, at home, with the horses, on our annual holidays in Cyprus. I stared across at the hundreds of graves of New Zealanders, buried here during the first world war, and thought of the men and women lying here so far from home. I thought of the futility of life. My mind cried out 'Why?' - But there was no answer.

On occasions Philip Rowlands would come and sit with me.

'How do you do your job?' I asked him one day as we sat overlooking the village. 'How do you square the joys of birth and marriage to the anguish of death?'

'Death is not death to the dead,' he said, 'it is a transition, - painful to bear for those left behind. They are going on, we will follow.'

His words triggered a flashback. 'Oh? Jenny said something like that to me the day she died. She said she was going on ahead a little.'

'She was right. We believe in the resurrection of the spirit, Matt, and life after death. Jenny is there and time is a dimension God controls, for us is immutable, but in time we will be rejoined.'

'I don't believe it Phil. You and the church in general pump out the Christian rhetoric. It means nothing. Why did Jenny have to die so young. We prayed, Phil, we really prayed. *All of us*! You had a hundred people here only a couple of months ago and we all prayed that Jenny would not die, - but she did. Our prayers had no effect at all.'

'It did have some effect, Matt, but not always

what you expect. God moves in mysterious ways, but his agenda is cosmic. There is a plan for Jenny, and for you too. It's just bigger than you comprehend. You'll remember these words one day and be comforted.'

We talked on for a while then stood and moved on, he back to the church, I to my car and drove back to my apartment.

Trevor would call and invite me across to Fordingbridge. This was one invitation I usually accepted because I would visit Putin, we would stand as always, his head over the stable door and resting on my shoulder. I felt we communed. Putin gave me something spiritually, I could not begin to explain, but perhaps stemming from a lineage of thousands of years. But time was beginning to tell on the horse too, he was arthritic and weak.

I had little concept of time and spent the days and months in a sort of anesthetised routine; doing little. I could find no solace in the company of the friends that Jenny and I had cultivated. Jenny and I as a twosome had enjoyed company, but without her I was the 'odd' man at the party. I continued to denigrate the medical profession and the church for their failure to help Jenny. Gradually I received fewer and fewer calls from friends we had known, although I did keep sporadic contact with Tony, Jessica, David and Liz.

Paul called from time to time wanting me to produce work for one publication or another, but I showed little interest and he too stopped calling.

It was a year later that Trevor called to tell me that Putin had passed away. I suppose we were not surprised as the horse had had a good innings, but it was a break with a connection to Jenny and I was deeply depressed.

I drifted, not rising until mid morning and dreading the emptiness ahead. At forty, I looked at the years stretching in front of me, bleak and without purpose. I frequently wondered if I would be better out of life altogether, and worked out several scenarios to die. I began to lose touch with David and Liz and saw them infrequently. I did stay more in touch with Tony. He was closer, at Porton Down, and I still felt a bond with his mother Jessica.

Periodic discussions with the Reverend Dickie Charmin and Reverend Philip Rowlands saved my life, tipped the balance and kept me from making the final act.

I needed something, I don't know what. Something to pull me out of this suicidal depression. The past two years had seen me lose the woman that I loved beyond all reason, I had alienated friends, lost any credibility with my agent. In the first year after Jenny left I had written a number of long articles railing against the medical profession and the church. Paul sent them back, at first with helpful criticism, then after a time without comment. I stopped writing for publication, but continued reams of uncoordinated papers. Slowly this too stopped and I languished, exhausted and dispirited. I spent a lot of time reading, I was in a wilderness, I tried to think of a positive role, but could not conjure up enthusiasm. I was at the lowest ebb.

CHAPTER FIVE

Thanks forever to Mandy, a nine year old girl I saw in the park. She was the image of my Jenny and took my breath away. As I watched her walk and skip beside her mother, engaged in animated conversation I couldn't believe her, it could have been Jenny!

It was Mandy that brought me to my senses, rekindled curiosity, made me ashamed of the shadow of a man that I had become, - I knew now that Jenny would be frantic with worry about my decline and that, for her, I had to rejoin the human race.

I discretely followed Mandy, (I learned her name a few weeks later), and her mother to their home, skulking around their street for an hour, feeling conspicuous, somehow guilty, yet my emotions were a riot. How could someone look so much like Jenny? I contrived to be in the park at the same time over the next few days; it was three days before I saw them again. As Mandy skipped along holding her mother's hand I was again filled with wonder, yes, she was still a diminutive version of my Jenny. I tried to pretend I was in the park on a mission of my own, - I was surprised how conspicuous I felt, - male, forty years old, on my own and trying not to be obviously following two younger females.

Was I 'stalking' them? I felt furtive and a bit ashamed, but I had to watch and bask in the vision of Mandy, - animated; happy. She looked like a young Jenny, laughed like Jenny; blonde hair, like Jenny's, tossed back every minute or so. It was incredible, how many times had I watched Jenny with exactly the same mannerisms? I longed to find out if Mandy had other similar characteristics, A very slight lisp to her speech; how she held her hand in repose, with her thumb tucked under her fingers, a sort of quizzical lop sided glance when she made a point, - there were many such cameos etched on my conscious, - and I hurt.

I saw Mandy and her mother several times after that first blinding encounter. I found out where Mandy went to school, where she and her mother would go to shop. But always I kept a distance, ever fearful of accusations of impropriety, but a few days later I did literally bump into them by accident, and that night I slept the best I had for two years.

I had taken to shopping at the same supermarket, but careful not to use the school leaving times, so that I wouldn't be faced with Mandy and her mother. On a Wednesday I was shopping at lunchtime, my mind on auto pilot.

As I rounded an aisle I physically bumped into Mandy's mother. I stepped quickly to one side..

'Sorry,' I stammered, off guard and confused.

'Sorry,' she said good humouredly, and as I stepped to one side, she did the same, so again we faced each other.

'Sorry,' she said again, and laughed, making slight 'rugby' side to side evasive movements.

'No, its my fault. I was not thinking.'

I warmed to her laugh, and relaxed. Mandy watched with some amusement. Then the moment was over and we passed on our ways. I walked down the aisle, completely forgetting what I intended to buy; it was only as I rounded the other end of the aisle, inevitably we met again. This time we smiled as acquaintances.

The next day I woke up for the first time in two years with some interest in the day to come. I decided that I needed a reason to get up in the mornings, - a project perhaps; an expedition, or even a role in some life testing experience.

What I got, a couple of weeks later, on a cold October night at the Bournemouth International Centre was a blinding revelation of things to come; exultation coursed through my body and my spirit soared like an eagle.

It was unbelievable; after two years of depression, hardly caring whether I lived or died, I had received a sudden and overnight jolt to my system. My psyche, roused from the depths began to rise to the here and now.

It didn't actually happen on that one night, - but the course was set; and for the first time since Jenny died, I had a purpose, I had been blind but now I saw.

In my mind I knew that the unimaginable events to unfold and my role in them was preordained, even from childhood. I was destined to be the chronicler of the most awesome story ever told.

The night of revelation came about as a result of my determination to 'pull myself together'. Over the past two years my family and friends had tried to sustain me, but in the face of intractable sorrow, had slowly, one by one, withdrawn. I realized that I was lonely. Yes, - I began to get up on time and shaved, toyed with a breakfast of tea and toast. I made half hearted attempts to start a clean up operation on the flat, but then what? How do you fill your day when two years your life has been on hold? I walked, I watched TV, I tried to shop, I even tried to go to a pub for some company. But always I was on the outside, disinterested and alone; getting back into society was going to be a hard call.

I was looking through the local paper and saw an article about an address that was advertised for two weeks hence. The lecture was to be on a Friday night at 6.45pm; the title intrigued me: *'Man and the Cosmos.'* I had always been interested in astronomy, perhaps I would go along for something to do. I lost interest and dropped the paper on the side table, already overflowing with old papers and magazines.

Later, I went to pick up the TV times from the disorganised pile of magazines on the table, the article about the address again catching my attention. This time I read the passages.

The lecture was to be presented by a man called Christian Fellowes. I knew of him, his name cropping up years earlier while I was involved in writing the biography of the Reverend Charmin.

Fellowes was leading a revival of creationism, now sweeping North America and much of the world. His latest big event was in Alaska where he drew almost all the population of the State in a fervour of Evangelism not seen since the days of Billy Graham.

He had almost the complete African continent mesmerised to his cause, and had adherents in every part of the globe.

Now he was in England; he had based himself in Salisbury, only fifteen miles from where I lived! I read that from here he planned to visit a number of provincial towns, beginning in two weeks time right here in Bournemouth. I was intrigued, several banner headlines, culled from a number of publications stood out from the page:

'Fellowes: Creation and evolution are not mutually exclusive';

'Fellowes slams the flat earth society';

'Christian Fellowes: The case for Intelligent Design';

'Religious leaders stand aside as Fellowes rewrites creation'

- and so it went on. Christian Fellowes, it seemed, had the capability to stir up passions in the scientific, political and religious world in such a way that all regarded him as a maverick, a seeker of notoriety, a general stirrer up of accepted views.

Following my commission, some twelve years ago, to write a biography of the Reverend Charmin and during the course of nearly two years work I had read numerous news articles about Christian Fellowes. He was an evangelist with a world wide following. He preached creationism and intelligent design, and seemed to irritate most of the scientific establishment.

A prominent Atheist derided his views, and published his own books, expounding reasons why God did not exist. To which Fellowes had commented dryly that believers in God had absolutely no doubt about the subject, whereas this leading light of atheists hedged his bets and added the word 'probably' to his belief that God did not exist, thus adding uncertainty to his convictions.

Christian Fellowes's band wagon rolled on and every venue was overbooked as the curious and the committed turned up to hear, and often scorn, his views. Now, he was appearing in Bournemouth, only twenty miles from where I lived. I was intrigued enough to finish reading the article, then my normal daily disinterest took over; I exchanged the paper for the TV times, wandering off to seek something to fill the evening.

The evenings were the worst part, well, - except for the days, or the small hours. I hated waking before dawn, the bed beside me empty, my life empty. But now I had decided to pull myself together, so what next? I didn't know, yet something inside me was stirring; I was restless, I felt a portent of something very important, - yet my days seemed to drift on without note; only the remarkable meeting with Mandy and her mother had excited me.

Two days later, I contrived to be at the local supermarket where I knew Mandy and her mother would be, doing a shop after school. I watched Mandy skip and walk beside her mother and I was entranced. Funnily enough she did not pick up her mother's looks, - you wouldn't say, automatically, from their looks that they were mother and child, yet the bond was clearly a mother and child relationship. I wondered about the father and turned away confused; sad and yet energised.

Back in my apartment I dropped the daily paper onto the table. There it was again! I would have sworn that the article about Christian Fellowes would have been buried under two days of riffling through the papers and magazines. Yet here it was, on top, staring up at me again, I noticed that the lecture was for Friday evening. What was I doing that evening? – as if I had anything to do anyway! A 'normal' evening would be to moon around the apartment thinking about what to do, then sink into an arm chair and unseeingly watch TV. I made a decision and called the booking office, credit card in hand.

'Can I have a ticket for the *'Man and the Cosmos'* evening please,' I asked the pleasant sounding woman who had announced that she was the 'Booking office'.

'I'm sorry sir, the event is well overbooked.'

This came as a shock, I hadn't even thought about that eventuality. Now that I couldn't go, it seemed imperative that I did.

'Oh! Er - is there a cancellation list?'

The woman chuckled. 'There is sir, that's well oversubscribed too.'

Suddenly, I really wanted to get a ticket.

'Is there ANY way I can get an admission?'

The 'Booking office' sounded almost sympathetic. 'There's just too many applications sir, some have been block bookings.'

I seized on this. 'Block bookings? What do you mean, - for example?'

'Well, two schools have made a block booking, - a themed hotel weekend I know, two churches. Oh! and the Evangelical Fellowship made a block booking.'

'Evangelical Fellowship, Who are they?'

'I don't really know Sir, they've got a place out at Rookes Green, taken over the old Baptist chapel.'

'I'll try to get a ticket from them.'

'Do you want their number?' the ever helpful voice asked.

'Yes, thanks very much.'

I was given the number, the home it seemed, of one Mary Conway, a luminary of the local branch of the Evangelical Fellowship. I called the number.

A woman answered, her voice warm, helpful. It was Mary Conway.

'Hello,' I said, 'my name is Matthew Patterson. I wonder if you have a ticket to spare for the BIC on Friday?'

'Matthew?' she sounded startled, there was a long pause. Then, cautiously, 'I don't know you?'

'No, actually not. I don't – er, belong to the *Evangelical Fellowship?* But the booking office kindly said you might be able to help me. There are no tickets left.'

'Oh! I see, - no room at the inn, so to speak!' a slightly breathless giggle. 'I have been asked to dispense tickets, - but normally these are for our Followers.'

'Followers?'

'Well, yes. The people who attend our branch of teaching are called Followers.'

'Well, I don't 'Belong' but I do need a ticket and I will of course pay for it.'

I felt old anger near the surface. For nearly two years I had blamed God for Jenny's death. And, turning aside from years of church attendance, decided there wasn't a God anyway and just carried on with despair instead.

'You could come along to one of our meetings.'

'Yes, I could.'

'Well done,' her voice was breathless, as if she had a lot do and was busy. She had seemed alarmed at my acquiescence and her reaction to my name puzzled me. She sounded as if she sort of expected my call, then was surprised when I did. 'Okay, I will have a ticket for you at the box office, before the lecture, say 6.15? see you there,' she rang off before I could ask about identifying ourselves.

I arrived at the Centre exactly on time as instructed. The front reception was a sea of people milling around, a typical pre theatre crowd. Groups stood around talking animatedly, people crowded up the wide stairs to the mezzanine. I gazed around for Mary, the dispenser of tickets, how would I know her? It was hopeless, I didn't realize the reception would be so vast. Those already with tickets crowded the officials, gossiping good naturedly, waiting to get through the Foyer. I tried to imagine what Mary would look like and where she might stand. I watched long queues at each ticket kiosk as people waited in vain for cancelled tickets.

'Hello, are you Matthew?'

I turned to see the woman who had arrived breathlessly by my side. She carried a handbag and brown envelope.

'Yes I am, - you must be Mary?' I smiled, which was easy, she was an attractive thirty something, with long auburn hair and bookish glasses. She wore a long coat, and long university scarf, boots, - no hat.

'Good. Here you are then,' she fished in the envelope for a ticket and, about to hand it to me, held onto it and paused. 'Have you been to one of Christain's presentations before?'

'No,' I said. 'I've read about him over the years, sort of evangelical preacher, isn't he?'

Mary looked around, anxiously, busy, - she had more tickets to dispense. She looked back at me through her bookish glasses. Her eyes were magnified and startlingly beautiful.

'Here you are then.'

The ticket was finally in my hand. 'The seats are not allocated, you can sit where you like,' she said, then saw a 'Follower' across the foyer and was about to rush off to dispense another ticket, but called me back as I turned.

'Keep me a place, I'll sit by you.'

Then she hurried off, long coat, scarf, big brown envelope and handbag all waving around her animated role as the dispenser of tickets.

When I finally got into the auditorium it was filling rapidly. There was a lot of noise as people chatted; some standing by their seats, most sitting in readiness. I saw a few seats about ten rows back and to the right of the second aisle. I chose a seat, and mindful of my duty as keeper of Mary's seat I put my coat on the seat beside me, settled down and looked around.

The soft lighting ended at the stage curtain, which was red, and, I thought, perhaps a safety curtain. From each side of the stage and adorning the walls along the auditorium to nearly as far back as my row were projection screens, continuous from shoulder high to ceiling.

There was a pre-theatre buzz about the

assembled audience, I felt it creeping up on me, an anticipation, and yes, some excitement. I reflected that I hadn't felt excitement for two years, I was not certain that I could take it, and wondered if I should have sat closer to an aisle so that I could slip away if necessary. It was too late now anyway, most the seats were filling up, and at six thirty five a discreet buzzer sounded. Five minutes to start time. Mary suddenly arrived, still looking harassed, I wondered if it was her natural persona. She plonked down beside me and set about distributing her (and my) coat, then scarf and handbag.

'Did you get a programme?' I asked seriously.

Her eyes met mine through the heavy frames; I noticed the set of her chin and the smooth line of her cheek and decided that behind the bookish, nervous energy she was a very attractive lady; not married.

'What do you mean, programme?'

I grinned. I wasn't used to it, but it seemed to come OK. 'Just joking,' I paused. - 'No room at the inn? A joke.'

There was a moment of incomprehension, then a smile that showed perfect teeth. 'Ah, yes, - well.'

We both had to stand to let a couple past, then the rearranging of coats, etc. The auditorium was by now full and the fidgety rustling began to subside. There was a sudden last minute clearing of throats, then a dead silence charged with anticipation.

The lights faded and a spot light came onto centre stage, a man dressed in a dark suit and tie entered from the wings, and walked calmly to the lit circle. He scanned the auditorium, a slight smile on his lips.

'Ladies and Gentlemen,' he raised his arms in welcome. 'Good evening. My name is John Waterman. In a moment Christian Fellowes will address you, but first allow me to introduce you to tonight's topic.

Many of you will be aware of Christain's international work on the subject of our creator. He and his disciples around the world are preparing us for the revelation and retribution that is fast upon us.'

He paused, his chin lifted and he stated: 'God created Heaven and Earth and all that is in it. - Yes he did.

Did he create everything in six days? No, probably not. Gospel writers in the biblical days wrote to the limits of their comprehension, or illustratively for the benefit of illiterate peoples.

But what about evolution? Didn't man evolve from the prehistoric mud? No he didn't! As Christian Fellowes explains. Evolution and creation are not mutually exclusive. God created life those millions of years ago and life evolved, preparing an environment for the conception of God's spirit into man, ergo the spirit of man was created and born into Homo sapien. The physical has continued to develop and is even today evolving. What do we mean by this?

Man can develop three things, his physical being, his intellect and his soul. Of these, great advances have been made in the first two, but the development of the soul has been sorely neglected. Man has not invested as much effort and time into learning about his soul as he has to external phenomena.

Our creator has watched the choices we make with sorrow; soon he will return to this planet to examine our balance sheet. Christian Fellowes and his disciples have for some years been preparing the world for the return of Christ, the examination of accounts and the revelation.'

Waterman stopped, mused, then said.

'Tonight is different. There will be no sermon, no address regarding the creation of man, - nor the revelation to come. Instead Christian wishes to set out the explanation of the beginning of time. He will show you the grandeur of the heavens, and lead you into the cosmos inhabited by God, from which the immaculate creation of everything springs and into which man will aspire.

You will see God's workshop, the crucible out of which all things emanate.

So, the topic tonight is *'Man and the Cosmos,'* in this topic we are going to make use of theatre videos that will run from that screen there,' - He raised his right arm to indicate the huge wrap around screens that rose from shoulder height to ceiling. His raised right arm continued to indicate them as he slowly pirouetted round to his right taking in the stage and then changing to his left arm to continue the journey round to the right hand walls, again to about ten rows back.

He paused and scanned the audience calmly. 'What you will see are true scenes, not computer images! We have taken liberty in one area only; we have enhanced the huge grey bodies that you will see later, they would be invisible as they emit no light whatsoever, therefore the bodies have been made grey to be visible to you.

With that, Ladies and Gentlemen I am going to welcome Mr Christian Fellowes, and I hope you enjoy the evening.'

John Waterman held his hand out as a tall man, dressed in an open necked shirt, sports jacket and light coloured trousers emerged from the wings onto the stage. He wore longish hair, greying at the temples. His patrician features were set in a fairly gaunt face. There was a sudden noticeable rise in tension as he was recognised by a large number of the gathering. He paused to survey the packed auditorium, his intense gaze swept past me and I could see, - even feel, from where I was, a powerful radiance.

He didn't speak for some time, perfectly at ease as he scanned the crowd. When he did finally speak, his voice was vibrant, warm, relaxed.

'Good evening. Thank you all for attending. I see we are again blessed by some eminent colleagues,' he nodded to a bald headed man in the fifth row, - 'Professor Reeves, - Welcome,' he gave another nod. 'Dr Cooper, NASA jet Propulsion Laboratory,' his gaze shifted to a tall bearded man,

- 'Dr Johnson. Washington University. We *are* well represented from the USA tonight.'

His eyes alighted on a heavy set man with a shock of grey hair.

'Ah, Dr Kirkpatrick, we have not met. I am honoured that so eminent a physicist from the LHC Project attends my presentation.'

Again his eyes travelled the audience pausing on individuals and smiling their names, 'John Noble, - John Nelson,' he went on to greet another six or seven people by name.

'Thank you for attending, even though I am aware your views do not accord with the truth of creation. That you attend again is reward enough. - but this presentation is not for you, as you well know. It is for the general public,' he held out his arms waist high, palms outward. 'I am presenting this evening for you all. If this is your first attendance, welcome, you will be enlightened.'

His eyes turned to an elderly looking man, about level with 'our' row, the other side of the auditorium, too tall to be obscured by the person in front of him.

'Bishop Stanton, - I am indeed honoured.'

I looked across at the discomfited balding man addressed, who had patently expected to observe anonymously, but was now thrust into the limelight. I was surprised that Christian could identify and remember all the personalities; my natural thought was that he had a back up team researching and feeding him information, but at the back of my mind was a frisson that Christian

Fellowes himself sensed their presence.

He went on. 'I see there are also a number of media people here, I welcome you too, but I regret the usual sound bites taken out of context that seem to find their way into your reports. Tonight is more, - physical, I will watch your reviews with interest.'

Tension and expectancy was growing in the audience. Christian looked around the packed hall. There were a number of journalists, academics and scientists, drawn by a mixture of controversy, scorn, his charisma and the topic; they were clearly in a mood to ridicule his theorems. There were also, apparently, a few incognito religious figures. By far the majority of the audience were devoted followers; the remainder were people drawn from a wide range of interests and the frankly curious, – and me.

Christian continued. 'This evening I shall explain to you that there *IS* a creator who has designed what we are, - more importantly where we are going, we shall address these topics in the context of the cosmos.

The evening will be presented in a very visual form, first the cosmos, then after the break I'll talk about what we have seen and why God created man, please settle back; think carefully about what you see and hear.'

With that, the stage plunged into darkness, the auditorium lights, which had been glimmering, went out as well. The blackness was all encompassing. Then, as the assembled crowd gave a collective sharp intake of breath, a soprano note filled the theatre, and in a growing eerie glow on centre stage, Christian had gone and was replaced by a figure of a woman, dressed in a flowing white Grecian dress, tied tight and high below her bust line.

The stage curtain had gone, she stood centre stage bathed in a soft glimmer, except for her there was darkness throughout the assembly, - the stage receding into blackness.

Then she sang! The purity of her voice stirred my soul. Unaccompanied, her words, possessed by the mood of the song, were at times plaintive, then sorrowful, emotion slowly evolving to exultation. She sang a hymn pleading the inadequacy of the human spirit, glorifying God, expressing awe at the eternity of the universe, and finally exalting in the arrival of the grace of God into the human spirit.

It was moving! It was beautiful, as was she. She was tall, blonde hair tumbled to her shoulders; her face, barely visible in the glow, was nevertheless clearly of classic beauty.

In the closing verse of her song, a myriad of pin pricks of lights appeared on the backdrop of the stage and all the way along the sides of the auditorium. The glow around her faded and she slowly dissolved into darkness while at the same time the points of light all around the stage grew in size and strength. I suddenly realised we were looking into the night sky. An intensely dark background and the whole panorama of stars and constellations surrounded us on all sides. Staring into the distance it seemed as if I could see forever.

The planetarium effect was electric. I could hear subdued murmurs from the assembly. I stared at the planetarium effect, recognising the Plough, and the constellation of Aries; the haze of the milky way swathed across the backdrop and around the side screens. The magnificent sight seen typically on cold dark cloudless nights, but often dimmed by light pollution.

Then Christain's disembodied voice. I felt Mary beside me jump.

'Ladies and Gentlemen you are looking at the October night sky, seen from the northern hemisphere; it is what you would see outside this hall now, if you had a clear night and an uninterrupted view.

With a telescope you could see a trillion stars, worlds bigger than our sun, and stretching far, far away, - beyond the understanding of man. Yes! - We can measure stellar distances, but the distant stars tax even our light year convention.

Our closest neighbour star is just over 4 light years away, and this is the closest! *Think* about this, think about the unimaginable distances even beyond this, - and marvel.'

Christian paused. There was enough glow

from the myriad of 'Stars' for me now to see his silhouette standing on stage to one side. His voice was firm, relaxed and convincing. I could sense Mary next to me, wrapt in the atmosphere.

Christian continued to talk for another ten minutes or so about the nature of the universe and the configuration of stars, constellations. Then he stopped.

There was a pause, the back of the stage exploded with a roar into a gigantic ball of flame.

The audience erupted with shouts and I heard a woman scream. It took a few seconds to realise that the explosion was in fact a depiction on the back screen. A ball of fire filled the back of the stage sending spumes off in all directions and around the side screens, leaping out along the side of the auditorium with a continuous deafening roar.

Exclamations and nervous laughter rippled round the room as people reacted to the shock. I could feel hot air blowing down on me, looking up in the devilish light I saw what looked like air condition ducts spewing hot air. All part of the theatrics!

Mary had clutched my arm and pressed against me. I could see her face transfixed, staring with alarm at the stage. The noise and fire continued for a few minutes while the audience regained composure, then slowly the noise abated, but the ball of chaotic flame continued, a cauldron of light, heat and energy.

Christain's calm voice came clearly above the muted noise. 'Ladies and gentlemen, - we have arrived at a star! Here is the womb of creation, the giver of life. Our universe contains billions of these 'creators' spread over billions of light years and millions of them have solar systems, - and some of the systems have *life*. Yes, - Life! This is not a theory it is a fact.'

As he spoke, the fireball diminished first to a more orderly inferno, then with the sound also dying, to a sullen red glow, at the same time getting smaller and smaller. The 'planetarium' of heavenly bodies re-emerged, the red ball grew smaller, more yellow and merged into its place as a 'Star' in the myriad of lights around the stage.

After the inferno it was darker, peaceful, silent. The hot air had stopped blowing.

Christian spoke, his form again ghostly visible in the glow of the 'Stars' his voice was encompassing, clear, it seemed to surround us.

'The universe around us is awesome, but what of the distances beyond our universe? Despite the ability of the physicists to give vast distances a measure, the immensity is beyond our comprehension. This is our universe, the place where we live!

But this story is not the end, nor even the beginning of the end. What happens when we travel through the universe?'

With this, the lights on the screens grew larger, closer, giving the impression that we were travelling forward. We began to speed past the 'Stars', - galaxies came and went ever faster the whole backdrop and side screens a mass of lights and spiral displays. Then, looking into the distance ahead, the lights grew more sparse, bigger distance between the lights. Now there was more darkness than lights and still the impression of hurtling forward, now into darkness. Fewer and fewer 'Stars,' until there was none. There seemed to be a low sound of a primeval wind, a cold air blew down from the ducts and everyone collectively shivered. I could sense we were still rushing forward but there was nothing to see.

Christain's voice came over the sound system, the surround effect made him seem close.

'We have left our solar system, left our galaxy, left our universe and are speeding into the cosmos.

But wait, - what do you see ahead, - now! To the right.'

We all strained our eyes to see. A small light twinkled intermittently, then, as the cold air blew down on us the light grew in strength. It began to look familiar! The shape was that of our universe.

Christian read our thoughts. 'No, - this is not 'our' universe, - it is another universe altogether. The distance from our own universe in billions of light year terms is so great the noughts would fill an A4 page. You can see over twenty five universes.

Your mind has already lost the capability to take in the immensity of what you see, but you *have* to believe it, you have to *feel* it. Be frightened of its awesome infinity.

I spoke of a light year. Four light years take you from our earth to the nearest star in our own universe, 24,000,000,000,000 miles! A universe comprising of billions of stars taking up over 90 billion light years of space, and this, ladies and gentlemen, is only a small fraction of the unimaginable distance to the next universe, again a similar size to our own, with a trillion stars, solar systems and yes, *Life*.

'We have one last vision, before we take a break.'

Christian appeared at the front right of the stage in a dim, soft glow of light. 'And now I present to you the most awesome fact you can imagine, a concept you will take with you to the end of your days on earth,' he paused. 'How immense is what you have seen? Immeasurable, yes, - but where does it end? Watch closely.'

The universes began to move towards the audience, we were again moving forward, the 'cities' of lights coming towards us, more rapidly and yet more rapidly, disappearing off the ends of the screens in a blur. This time it was the universes that slowly thinned out and we stared again into blackness. Again we had the sensation of moving at unimaginable speed; then the sensation left us and we were drifting.

After the lights and movements it seemed even more black. It was cold, I could sense again the cold air. There was a very soft moaning, as of wind over desolate landscape and a soft sound theme, - portentous, frightening. The audience tensed, and I too felt my nerves taut waiting for the shock I knew would come. I felt Mary clutch my arm even more tightly, her hand had found mine and I was held in a vice like squeeze.

'We have moved on,' Christain's voice, calm, but close, made us all jump. 'We are no longer in the universe, nor the universes, nor the cosmos, - we have entered the *VOID!* Here there is *nothing!* There is no life, there is no temperature, no galactic gas, just an emptiness, a void. We have travelled unimaginable light years from our universe, -from the cosmos. You cannot even begin to comprehend the vastness, not just ahead, but all around, for 360 degrees there is nothing, nothing, nothing - save the small light dot behind us representing the totality of the cosmos, and the hundreds of universes that we saw.

The emptiness goes on, - not for an age, but for *eternity.* This is desolation in its ultimate form. There is no beginning, no end. The void is forever, forever in distance forever in time. In this cold black void there is emptiness, - nothing. There are no dimensions, not even time exists here.

But God does! This is the firmament of God. But look ahead!'

Straining our eyes into the blackness, a huge sphere became visible in the merest of glows, drifting slowly towards us, off on the right and moving gently toward us and centre stage. It was grey, it looked somehow sinister. The portentous theme had picked up a beat and we all tensed.

The massive body, grey, featureless, grew nearer, menacing, larger until it filled the whole back screen. Then it slid past, silent as the grave, moving off the side screen and we were beyond it, the foreboding sound dying away into the distance.

'Where now?' Christain's voice continued in the total darkness. 'We travel on, faster than light, tomorrow, next year, next century, we just travel on and on and on,' his voice faded.

In the absolute silence we watched occasional massive bodies appear like vast whales in murky water to slide harmlessly by. We saw tentative lights in the distance, growing stronger and passing by, sometimes on the right sometimes on the left. We could see the lights materialise into distant 'cities' of lights, then grow small again as they receded behind us. More darkness, more massive bodies and in the extreme distance, more lights in a haphazard parade of celestial wonders. In the darkness we watched, each wrapped in our own thoughts, trying to absorb what we had seen. My own feeling was one of sheer and utter loneliness, vast unimaginable black distance occasionally interposed with many universes each of myriads of stars, throwing out heat, light, life, only to recede and leave us still travelling in the cold stellar void.

I began to look forward to seeing the halo of light in the distance, moving towards us, materialising into a city of lights, then stars and constellations. I suddenly longed to be part of the life of the light and feared the encroaching dark again. Long minutes passed. It was silent, the audience made not a move, not a cough, each deep in their own thoughts, watching the procession of bodies as we moved forward.

'How far can we go? How long do we travel?' Christain's voce was magisterial. 'We go on forever, - the void is infinite, without end. There is no end, there is no beginning, God reigns supreme over eons of time, eternity of space, - what a pathetic creature man is! - perched precariously on an insignificant planet and a mere speck in the grandeur of the cosmos to even question the existence of a creator.'

There was silence as we watched the drifting scene, then. 'Look again. Behold.'

Straining our eyes, another huge sphere became visible in the blackness, again drifting slowly towards us, off to the right and moving gently toward us and centre stage. It was grey, sinister. The undertone had picked up a beat again, the audience waited nervously.

Christian spoke. His voice was more powerful, more triumphal.

'Welcome to God's crucible. Here is the Creator's material. A whole universe in one massive, - unbelievable - world of matter. I know what the physicists say! - *You Dr Johnson!* - I know what you want to tell us. That a body of this mass cannot exist, the gravity of mass this size would be untenable and the body would explode. You are right, - but not for the reasons you think. There are celestial laws that transcend those of the physics and science of this world.

In the void are an uncountable number of these massive bodies, inert, dead, drifting for eons, silent, their tentacles of gravity reaching out like a blind person scouring the dark space around them.'

The huge ominous sphere had drifted onto the left screen. Christain's voice was imperative.

'Look! There is another body, - there -on the right!' we strained our eyes to see; a grey global outline was just discernable on the right hand screen.

'These massive bodies drift in the void, forever, in eternal loneliness. Their mass is immeasurable, the dimension of gravity is unbearable, nothing escapes from the body, not even light. You only see them against the blackness because I have illuminated them for visual effect. They drift. Their tentacles of gravity reach out over trillions of light years, but encounter nothing; any remnant of long dead stars, any particle of matter, gas, even light has long since been swallowed by the all pervading gravity. Then slowly, - over millennia, a massive body drifts within several trillion light years of another massive body. At first their attraction is tenuous, almost indifferent, but enough to cause the drift to stop and - slowly, - inexorably, - the mutual attraction of gravity begins to pull the bodies nearer together.

Look! - You see them moving now.'

We had already noticed that while the grey body on the right was continuing its slow drift to the back screen, the body on the left had halted its drift off and was now slowly drifting back towards the centre.

Suddenly I could see what was coming! Most of the audience had also understood the implication and there were intakes of breath, murmuring and a tension of unbearable anticipation. Mary was practically cutting off the blood supply from my arm, as I too, felt every muscle in my body stiffen.

Christian spoke into the tension, his voice amused at the alarm. 'Ladies and Gentlemen, you are privileged to be the first ever to witness the work of the creator, - the birth of creation, another universe, - in astrophysicists terms - a new 'Big bang'.'

The huge bodies were now moving at an increasing rate towards each other, I held my body rigid, I could feel Mary shaking against me. Without warning the two bodies flashed across the screens and snapped together. A deafening clap of thunder that hurt my ears, screeching, roaring, white light as the bodies crashed into each other at astronomical speeds. The whole of the back screen was a torrent of light, thousands of globs of liquid fire hurtled off the back screen and raced round the side screens and off the end. The globs were spinning, throwing off catherine wheels of liquid matter. The whole stage and side screens were a mass of explosions, writhing fire and a deafening cacophony. We were in hell I thought, caught up in a virtual reality, my mind lost all sense of where we were, what we were doing. Some of the women in the audience screamed, holding their hands over their ears, their eyes tightly shut.

The inferno from Hades went on, and on, my mind becoming numb from the noise and intense light. I became frightened, tears welled into my eyes.

Then, slowly, the noise abated, the scene pulled back and suddenly, like the sun bursting through cloud onto a green meadow, we saw across the screens a magnificent array of a multitude of stars and galactic spirals. Everything became serene and ordered. A crucible of new life had been born!

The view looked remarkably similar to our view of the sky at night, but this universe was an immeasurable distance from home, even by the astrophysicists measures. We sat for a long time in silence, wrapped in thought. A lot of the audience understood the immensity of space, but never had our insignificance been brought home so vividly.

'Only when we join God in heaven will we understand. He is the controller of physics and of time.'

The auditorium lights slowly illuminated; Christian stood centre stage.

'Shall we take a break?'

His words released pent up emotions, the audience heaved a huge collective sigh; a babble of discussion broke out. In the journalist's ranks mobile phones and Dictaphones sprang into life, but his continued presence on the stage pervaded the auditorium with an overshadowing aura.

He stood relaxed, his gaze ranging over the audience. I noticed his eyes were compelling, sometimes brooding, I may have imagined it but as his attention ranged over the audience and his gaze swept passed me, I felt intense warmth.

I took in the transition back to everyday audience; people getting up, some dazed, a number talking animatedly and leaving the auditorium for the interval.

I turned to Mary, 'Shall we take a break?' I glanced at my arm with amusement, where Mary was still hanging on grimly. She noticed, and with a self conscious laugh, disengaged her grip.

'Sorry,' she said, 'The noise made me jump.'

'Me too,' I said. We got up and joined the queues to get out to the foyer and bar.

I got us each a drink and we managed to find an unoccupied corner to stand.

'Cheers,' I said, looking around at the throng. 'Well, that was something, wasn't it. Absolutely realistic.'

'It *was* real,' Mary said seriously. 'As John said, it was not computer graphics.'

I was sceptical. 'I agree Christian Fellowes needed the theatrics to make his point, and it seemed real, but he couldn't possibly have got scenes of the universe that didn't come from NASA or somewhere. The deep field scenes must have been graphics.'

Mary said nothing, her face composed, serene, as she sipped her drink.

'What do you think then,' I persisted, 'do *you* believe in the Christian Fellowes version of creation?'

Mary looked surprised. 'Well, yes of course. I 'Spose I'm a dreamer really. I love to look into the night sky, and in my thoughts I can travel on into space, like the experience we've just seen, - well, - not so violent. I think of all of that and of nature and I know God is there somewhere – I just don't know how to understand it,' she paused. 'And you, - do you believe?'

Standing so close I was acutely aware of her lips and her eyes. I was astonished at the co-incidence that she, too, studied the night sky as I had done all my life, - as Jenny had. Did I somehow attract people who stargazed? I could empathise with the dreams; the wonder, the questions.

'I, - I used to,' I sort of muttered, then a wave of emotion swept over me, 'Yes, I do, - still.'

'Still?'

'Things have happened, Mary, I don't really want to talk about it tonight.'

'S'okay, Matt,' she let it drop and told me a bit about her job as a researcher. I was greatly intrigued comparing her experience in commercial research with my work in the Civil Service in the old days.

Before we could get too engrossed, the bell went and we filed back into the auditorium. In the queue ahead of us was an untidy man explaining in a loud voice to anyone that would listen that the whole visual effect was a farce.

'For one thing,' he said, 'Even if there were such collisions, we wouldn't hear anything. For one thing the distance is too great, in any case sound couldn't travel because space is a vacuum and sound only travels in air,' he looked to his companions, a sort of self satisfied leer on his face.

We arrived back in the auditorium and everyone settled back into their seats, with the usual getting up again to let people past; the rustle and fuss subsided as conversation slowly died, there was an admission that the first part of the presentation had been very visually effective. Everyone was eager to discover what the second part held in store.

The stage curtain had been raised, there was more light on stage, although the back screen remained in darkness taken up completely with the sight of the night sky. Again I recognised the positions of the stars and the glow of the milky way. There was a lectern front centre.

As we settled, the soprano who had enchanted the audience at the beginning of the evening walked onto the stage. There was an immediate spattering of applause. She walked gracefully to the side of the lectern, not acknowledging the audience, her face serene. I could see, now, in the better light that she was, indeed, beautiful.

As the audience subsided into silence, she began to sing, her voice pure, her emotion controlled, she sang of the Grace of God, how great were his works, inspiring and awesome. As before, I could feel the hairs on the back of my neck tingle with emotion in response to the purity of her voice and the import of the song. As the song ended there was a stillness, a hush of awe. Then a smattering of applause died away in some embarrassment, but the auditorium was now charged with anticipation.

During the interval Christian Fellowes had sat in a dressing room reserved for him and his close followers. He sat amongst them, lost in thought. He heard the bell for the second part of his presentation; heard his soprano, Faith, begin her song. Her voice uplifted him and he stood and made his way to the wings, beside the back drop. From this vantage point he could survey the audience, their faces visible in the half light of the auditorium.

He scanned the crowd his senses picking up a kaleidoscope of emotions. In the 'noise' of average interest, he could sense the areas of disbelievers; or of rapture. He could detect one or two areas of exceptional feeling. His eyes paused for a moment on a man he knew as Matthew sitting on the left of the stalls, he had been expecting him. Matthew sat next to Mary whom he knew as an enthusiastic member of a group of evangelicals. Christian felt a kindred aura around Matthew, but something about him troubled Christian and his gaze moved on.

An aide stepped quietly to his side, a notebook in hand. Christian spoke to him in an undertone as Faith's voice soared into the theatre.

'Yes, we can invite him in,' he said and turned his attention to Faith; the man next to him stepped silently away.

From where he stood Christian had a three quarter view of Faith's shoulders, bare; smooth; the folds of her white dress gathered below the breast line by a golden cord, As the final notes of the hymn ended, She paused, smiled and walked off the stage as Christian walked on. As she passed, their eyes met briefly.

He strode to the lectern, his manner alert, smiling.

'My friends, we have spent some time considering the cosmos. The 'Big bang' was the beginning of time for us, in our universe. But time has a different start point for other universes, many of which existed long before ours, - and some after. Out there, - ' Christian gestured with his hand, throwing his arm forward at shoulder height. 'Is a vastness beyond our comprehension, not just light years away, nor even billions of light years, - but forever. Do not be beguiled by the scientist's vision of a finite universe. Throughout the void there is eternity, whole universes spangle space as the stars above us spangle the night sky, and the creator is King of all....But...' Christian paused dramatically.

'There are *two* ultimate powers! The Creator and the dark power of Satan, the destroyer, the Antichrist. This is the way it is! Those of you who have attended some of my previous lectures will know that in the immaculate concept of creation, every part is finely balanced, intricately engineered. For every positive there is a negative, for every condition there is an opposite. Even as in creation, awe inspiring and good, there is the opposite power of despair and destruction.'

Christian paused, suddenly relaxed, his eyes roaming across the audience, just for a second his glance caught the man, Matthew, next to Mary, then moved on.

'So what about man? Where does he fit into the whole galactic system of creation?

Among *all* the signs of immaculate design, of impeccable engineering, of breathtaking physics, there are those still who believe that man crawled from the primeval mud and evolved by trial and error into what we are today!

Is this what we have come to? After untold millions of years of evolution, ten million years of creation, after two thousand years of teaching, to reject our creator without a second thought! Our whole planet is littered with clues left by God for us to see, why do we not see! - Why? It is because our soul has not developed, and we cannot comprehend.

Can we *really* believe that on that day, billions of years ago, swarms of the descendants of lobefin fish struggled from the sea onto land, resting for a while, blinking in the sunlight! Then, although given identical conditions, all went their own way and evolved into millions of different species, birds to butterflies, ants to lobsters, hedgehogs to cows, and yes! Dinosaurs into monkeys and man. All this by accident of evolution, - survival of the fittest.

Given the identical conditions how did they go a million different routes. When you think about it, - *really* think about it and about your inner self, can you deny our creator?'

Christain's eyes focussed on a balding man near the centre isle. *'Doctor Blake?'* his mild query carried undertones of a challenge.

'Er, well, - we um,' was all the discomforted man could say before Christian moved on.

'Yes, there is evolution. Life on this planet has been evolving over billions of years, each species changing, adapting from inception and is still evolving. These millions of life examples, including man, evolve physically and intellectually from century to century. Man today is not the man of ten thousand years ago.

So where does this leave us regarding the creation of man? We are two entities, the physical and the spiritual. Yes, God created the physical form to provide a womb for the spiritual.

Our soul he created in his image. It is only by nurturing the soul and acknowledging our creator can we enter the kingdom of God. Only then will we control the fourth dimension, - time, and understand the true *why?*

We, you and I, are children of God. We were created and placed on this planet into an environment which already existed, created earlier by God, and evolved over billions of years.

Our soul he created in infant form and as infants we reside in man as a child in the womb.

Man has developed his ability to discover, to dissect and learn, but in evolutionary terms his alter ego, - his soul, has remained in the primeval mud; he makes little effort to prepare for the Grace of God, to learn the ways of creation. He leans close to evil, until soon the creator will abort civilisation, as he has done many times before, and start again.

My friends, there is a spiritual being existing within your physical form that is you, but it is still an infant, unable to survive without the physical vehicle to transport it,' Christian paused, his powerful presence holding the audience's attention. Then he dropped a bombshell!

'True man, - image of God, is not evolving. - he is incubating! What if man was conceived into an evolving environment, waiting to be born into the kingdom of God.'

There was a murmur from the assembly, people shifted in their seats.

Christian went on to speak for nearly an hour on the spiritual persona; the true self that was born and waited, through generations, to be exalted into the kingdom of God. Of how God the creator was, himself, the synergy of all spiritual human endeavour here on earth and on countless other worlds.

He spoke of the antichrist; out in the dark void, another supreme force lurked, evil and decay, a natural balance to good, - destroyed many millennia before, now slowly gathering strength again.

Christian summarised the evidence for creation, exhorting his audience to learn of God's purpose and to seek redemption.

'The clues are all around you,' he concluded, 'Don't be found wanting when God returns to exalt his people. God bless you all. Goodnight.'

The theatre lights came on and the fire curtain lowered.

We filed out of the theatre into the foyer. As I shuffled forward with the throng my mind was still taking in what I had seen, what I had heard. I had an overall sensation of utter loneliness in which were glimpses of something exciting, powerful beyond measure, and too, with disturbing undertones of an evil waiting in the shadows. What did it all mean. Was Christian just a showman, skilfully weaving a mystical world. Was he just playing with our minds, or…?

Mary was following as I created space in the queues. Once in the foyer we paused, people were milling around, some leaving through the front entrances to waiting taxis, or going round to the car park at the rear. But many hung around in the foyer animatedly discussing the experience in a sea of chattering, and yes, there were some thoughtful expressions.

'Whew!' Mary exclaimed when we had found a space. 'What do you think then, Matt.'

That she spoke and used my name with a relaxed familiarity after having just met me somehow warmed me. I had spent two years in a fog of depression and anger; I had forgotten how to be sociable.

'Umm. Yes I was inspired, sort of excited I guess.'

I didn't tell her that Christain's words had penetrated into my psyche. I caught a faint glimmer of awakening, a pattern that included some concept that Jenny's death was not the final curtain. I needed to be alone to think it all through.

Mary looked at me questioningly. I could see that she was still fired up with Christain's powerful images. As she looked at me with an earnest expression I was taken again by her beautiful eyes behind bookish glasses and the up tilted chin. In the hard light of the foyer I could see just a whisper of down on her cheek. Her long coat had fallen open. She wore a black long skirt and red blouse, the top button gaping slightly to revealing a hint of white lace.

Suddenly I was getting into uncharted territory. But as I was about to ask how she was travelling home, John Waterman, the man who opened the address, joined us, a friendly smile on his face.

'Hello Mary, did you like the evening,' he asked, sort of addressing us both.

Mary responded immediately, her breathy voice excited. 'It was very effective.'

'Good,' the man smiled, looking at me quizzically.

I didn't want to show the inner excitement that was awakening within me and I pondered Mary's turn of phrase, 'it was very *effective*'. I also noted that John Waterman and she were acquainted.

I responded carefully. 'Well, yes I did. I was sort of inspired. There did seem to be quite some disagreement about Christain's theories from some sections of the audience.'

I told him about the man rubbishing the cacophony of colliding worlds.

Waterman nodded, listening carefully. 'Not theories,' he said quietly. 'Most of the scepticism comes from the scientists and astronomers in the audience. The man you speak of is quite right of course. Sound travels in air, not a vacuum, but he chose not to apply the full rationale. The collision of two black holes releases energy on a scale totally beyond the comprehension of man. The energy blasts away from the collision at the speed of light and greater. It comprises galactic sized storms of material and particles oscillating at all frequencies. Sound is merely a by product which is modulated on some of the energy. Our depiction demodulates the sound component for the human senses. Scientists and atheists rarely agree among themselves and always disagree vocally with Christain's explanations - but they still attend his meetings,' he smiled broadly. 'I'm John by the way.'

'Matt,' I said, then 'And Mary.'

John glanced from me to Mary. 'Yes I know Mary,' he hesitated, 'Look would you like to come back stage and meet Christian?' then added hurriedly, 'He likes to get feedback from these do's.'

I felt odd. I felt that somehow the whole business was drawing me into something, I didn't know what, but I was intrigued enough to want to meet Christian.

We three trouped off. John led the way through a service door and subterranean passages until we were backstage. There was a long corridor, people were hurrying back and forth, presumably packing up the paraphernalia of the theatre.

John paused at a door and entered. It was an ante room with two doors on the opposite side. We walked across the room and he opened one of the doors. Turning to us he beckoned, obediently we entered into the inner room. It was sparse, a typical theatre multipurpose room, part store, part dressing room. There were enough chairs for us to sit facing a small desk at which sat Christian Fellowes. He stood up to welcome us. I was aware of a distinct feeling of power that emanated from him. It was his eyes that dominated his presence; they conveyed amusement, warmth, yet could suddenly burn with compelling intensity. They say that eyes are a window into the soul,- in Christain's case they were a window into a force that made me uneasy, and a force, I fet, would penetrate sheet lead, so intense was it. His voice though, was warm, friendly enough.

'Hello, come on in, take a seat.'

There were four chairs arranged loosely in a group. Mary bunched her chair closer to mine, I didn't mind. I sensed she felt the force of Christain's personality and was suddenly nervous.

I had never been so close to a power that I could feel so clearly. Primitive senses within me murmured in a frisson of alarm.

Christain's words, however were disarming. 'Thank you for taking the time to come backstage. I would like to get your views about the evening Do you have a question you would like to ask, or a comment?'

I did not reply immediately and I could sense that Mary was waiting for me to begin before she added anything. I had a feeling that we were not here for innocent fact finding, but that some deeper motive was working below the surface. I remember, in the auditorium, when Christain's gaze had swept by me and for second caught my eye, the intensity unnerved me. I felt he had read my soul and that somehow I had evoked a chord in him. I was sure he already knew the answers to the questions he posed.

I spoke carefully. 'Mr Fellowes, two years ago....'

Christian Fellowes interrupted me. 'Christian.'

'Uh, - Christian, two years ago an event occurred in my life which traumatised me. I have never really recovered. Before then I knew with all my heart, - and logic too, that God created heaven and earth.

That he created man. What you have presented this evening has evoked all these old passions. For two years I have been in a wilderness, I did not want to know. But tonight, - well tonight I feel I have received a very visual and powerful message about the 'World' inhabited by God, - a message from the creator which transcends the Christian message, that encompasses all who seek the true God whether through Christ or another route.'

Christian smiled. 'Is there another route? You're right. You cannot understand the immaculate order of the universe, its immensity, nor the existence of man here on earth without acknowledging God. Christianity is merely the record of the presence of Jesus Christ who lived two thousand years ago and proclaimed God the father; and to set out the path so that all man could be exalted into heaven. So, yes tonight was a Christian event but it was a call to all who seek God's salvation, Christian or not.'

Mary asked hesitantly. 'I was trying to understand the identification of the soul as separate from the physical and how it can be separately developed.'

'The soul is you, Mary,' Christian said gently. 'the attractive young lady I see is a vehicle protecting and nurturing your soul because it cannot yet exist alone. Like a baby in the womb, your soul has not reached its term, it is not capable of separate existence. You must learn how to look inward, to think of yourself as the knowledge within you. You have to believe, *really believe*, that the inner you exists as an entity. You have to believe so much, so passionately, that it hurts, that what you practice becomes reality and slowly your soul will manage to exist in its own right.'

Christian glanced at me, his eyebrow raised, inviting a question. I did not ask. He looked at me directly and I felt his power wash over me like a warm tide. He smiled.

'Matthew, you are not unknown to me. I know of your circumstance, I know you completed the biography of Bishop Charmin, and that you know the Reverend Samuel Johnson, - as do I. I also know of your abilities as a journalist and writer, your reputation goes before you.'

As he spoke, I reddened with some embarrassment. Christian continued.

'I also know that below the hurt, you are committed to God and would serve him should he show you the way.'

I nodded, the conversation bringing back memories and I began to feel miserable. Christian seemed to be aware of this and finished up our meeting, saying he would like to invite me to another, more private, meeting soon.

As we took our leave he placed his hand on my shoulder and in a quiet aside, unheard by John or Mary, said. 'You have been hurting I know, Matthew. Jenny is with God's Grace, she will appear to you soon.'

I was dumbfounded. How did Christian know so much about me? How could he say this? I was torn between anger and fear. I more or less stumbled from the room, Mary supporting me.

'Are you alright Matt?' she asked with concern, shaken by my sudden loss of co-ordination.

Outside, at the rear of the theatre, I gulped in huge breaths of air while Mary looked on with worry. After a while I regained control and offered to drive Mary home, which by now I had learned was in my direction. We did not talk much, each deep in our own thoughts about the evening. It was now late and I dropped Mary off at her house.

'Would you come to one of our Evangelical meetings,' she asked as she got out of the car. Her earnest face looked into the car window at me, very close.

'I'm not sure Mary, I'll give it some thought. I've got your number, I'll call you?'

As I spoke I looked behind the bookish glasses into her brown eyes, they were unfathomable and somehow desirable. I felt ashamed and unfaithful.

I had experienced a lot this night and I needed to be on my own to evaluate it all.

It was midnight by the time I got back home. I was tired but still trying to understand what had gone on. Slowly the adrenaline ebbed away and my routine sense of lack of self worth came back in the cold emptiness of the apartment.

CHAPTER SIX

Christain's event at the Bournemouth International centre and the evening in Mary's company had unsettled the morose routine I had become accustomed to. I spent the next day reliving the events and in the evening I drove to St Nicholas church. Sitting in the dark I stared into the night sky, it was clear, the stars shone brightly and as I stared I could see more and more, further and further, even faint glows impinged on my eyes and I saw the heavenly firmament in all its glory. I wanted to be there, visiting, to see and to experience. I tried to imagine myself travelling forward as in Christain's virtual images. I wondered what was really out there, beyond there and beyond 'Beyond there'.

I remembered, too, vividly, stargazing with Jenny, sitting close together on the bench in her back garden. How we gazed into the heavens, murmuring to each other. Somehow I felt closer to her, and I was comforted.

Was space really infinite, going on forever? I

could well imagine that, but then on examination tried to come to terms with the concept of space 'never ending'. Surely everything has a beginning or a boundary? If so, what lies over the boundary. If we came back to where we started it implied a sphere, and all of creation lay within the sphere. But what was outside the sphere? I gave up and went indoors, more intrigued and more curious than I had been for years. It was a good sign that I could recover and do something. But what? I needed was a stimulus, a project.

The next day I went to the supermarket. Mandy's Mother was there, Mandy must have been at school.

'Hello,' she said with a friendly smile.

'Hi,' I tried to be relaxed and respond to her friendliness. I had two years of catching up to do in the 'Being sociable' department, I was curious and wanted to stay talking.

'No work today?' I said conversationally.

'Day off,' she said succinctly

'Mmm. House work then?'

''Fraid so, always things to do before Mandy gets home from school.'

'What time does your husband get home?' it was a clumsy line and Mandy's Mum knew it.

'No husband,' she said, amused, 'He's been gone over five years.'

'I'm sorry,' I said, discomfited.

'No worries. We're used to it, Mandy and me. Life's fine.'

It was a line lightly given, but I detected a note of strain. I felt suddenly glad that there was no husband, but sorry for her too.

'Oh,- my name's Matt,' I said taking the bull by the horns.

'I'm Kate,' she responded.

Chatting to my new friend Kate close up I had time to study her. She was tallish, with dark tousled hair to her shoulders. She was attractive; a straight nose and high cheek bones. Nice brown eyes that looked directly at me as she talked. We exchanged a few more words, then looking around as if for inspiration, agreed that we 'must be getting on'.

I arrived back at the apartment with a new spring to my step. There was a message on the answer 'phone. John Waterman, would I please call back.

I remembered John, the admin chap who chaperoned Mary and me into Christain's dressing room. Intrigued I called. The phone was picked up almost immediately.

'Ah, Matt, thanks for calling back. I, uh, wanted to check that you enjoyed the 'event' and meeting Christian afterwards?'

'Well, yes I did. In fact I have been intrigued ever since. There are things I never even thought about,' I was being honest, but mystified as to how John had got my telephone number.

'Good. Good. Um, - Look, there is a meeting next week at Christain's place. Only a few close associates. You would find it educational I'm sure.

Why not come along and join us? We would like you to come.'

I felt both flattered and cautious. Why would Christian and his cohorts be interested in my presence? Was I ready to take on socialising yet?'

John sensed my hesitation. 'Its not too far to travel Matt, and oh! - Mary is coming too.'

In the end I agreed to go, after all I didn't exactly have a full diary. John was suitable pleased and, I sensed, somewhat relieved. I was to turn up about six next Wednesday evening. There was supper at eight, dress casual. John seemed to want to add something, but in the end we rang off, looking forward to seeing each other.

I decided to call Mary, I still had her number from the 'ticket office'. The phone was picked up almost at once.

'Hel-lo.'

The warm, breathless voice immediately evoked her image in my mind. I wondered if she wore the bookish glasses at home?

'Hi Mary, Matt here. I was just talking to John he's invited me to Christain's and said you were going too?'

'Well, yes I am, John said you were coming.'

'Have you been there before? I mean what's the form?'

'Well, yes. I've been lots of times. We have an evangelical meeting there every month. But next week is different. I think there is an extraordinary meeting.'

'But why invite me, Mary, I mean, - I don't know

them or anything. Can you tell me something about Christian, other than his lectures?'

'There's a lot to say,' she hesitated. 'Look, would you like me to explain a few things to you, I mean you could come over here and we could talk over a coffee or something.'

'Yes, I would like that, if it's not too much trouble.'

'Absolutely not. If we are to go to Christians next week, we ought to meet soon. Would tomorrow be okay?' her breathy voice made the invitation warm and I felt a nuance of pleasure.

I checked her address and the following evening drove to her house arriving, as agreed, at about 7pm. Mary opened the door to me, not at all the bookish girl I carried in my mind. Her brown eyes sparkled behind heavy framed glasses, She was wearing a cerise shirt over black palazzo trousers. The top buttons of the shirt were undone revealing a glimpse of white lace cupping firm breasts. My admiration must have showed.

She blushed, gently laughing 'Matt, you found me then. Come on in.'

She lived, she informed me, with her parents, but had the luxury of a sort of granny annex, with its own bedroom, kitchen, bathroom and living room.. The annex was built out on an 'L' shape and I could just see the corner of the main house, where I presume her parents were settled.

The living room was simply furnished in modern taste and distinctly decorated with feminine softness. One corner of the room was arranged as a small study area. A laptop and phone sat on a desk, a corner shelf was haphazardly overflowing with books. There was a largish coffee table in front of a settee and arm chairs. I could see that Mary had not made any particular attempt to tidy up; papers lay on the table; a jacket lay over the back of one of the chairs. The casual appearance of the room made me feel comfortable.

'I'll get us a drink, take a seat, what would you like? Coffee, a glass of wine?'

I smiled at the hurried, busy sentence.

'Do you drink wine?' I asked.

'Oh yes. I have some white, will that do?'

'Sounds good to me, thanks.'

I sat on the armchair without the jacket over its back while Mary disappeared into the kitchen to reappear very quickly with a tray, two glasses and an opened bottle of Chablis.

Mary curled up on the chair facing me, one leg tucked under her on the seat. She didn't seem one for strained silences.

'Matt, I'm so pleased you agreed to go to Christain's. Tell me what you think of him?'

I looked across at her over my glass of Chablis. She looked comfortable, sort of wholesome and an air of suppressed excitement. I thought back to the event, Mary in her long coat and scarf, busy organising her ticket distribution, then later clinging onto my arm as the heavens crashed around us. Then Christian; on the stage, his presence dominating the hall.

'To be honest, I didn't know what to expect. The whole effect was very visual, and Christian put forward some strong views. Somehow I could believe in him. But there was some under current that made me feel uneasy. He emanated a powerful charisma, I caught his eye once or twice and felt he was looking into my soul,' I stopped, feeling a bit foolish.

Mary nodded, she seemed to consult within herself, making a decision.

'You're right, Christian wanted to make it as visual as possible because many people cannot project their mind's eye into something called 'forever'. The distances are so awesome and people have not developed their consciousness in order to really, - really get their mind around it. Christian is special, Matt, when he caught your eye he was indeed looking into your soul.'

I stared at her, 'You seem sure about that.'

'Well I would be,' she said simply, 'I sort of work in the field.'

'What do you mean, - work in the field?'

'I do research for the local Evangelical Federation. Not paid of course.'

'Look Mary, I'll be honest with you. I'm out of my depth here. Who is Christian, what is the er, Evangelical Federation, why am I invited to this meeting? I mean, - I just got involved by chance. I was at a loose end and saw the advert in the local paper and went along. I've had a pretty difficult couple of years and was just really looking for something to do. I am, - or was, a journalist, I……'

Mary broke in. She could see that my composure was thin. She gave me a reassuring smile.

'Let me say something about our Evangelical Group. We're part of a worldwide group of Christians who follow a particular doctrine. No church buildings, no clergy in robes. They operate in local groups, of course we need a place to meet, often community centres, or hotels or conference halls.'

I interrupted. 'You said 'We', Mary, - you are, uh, a practising Evangelical Follower?'

She made a moue. 'Well, yes I am. I was going to tell you anyway. The point is that our group is very Christian. We adhere strictly to the testaments, especially the new testament. Christ really happened. He did instruct us to obey the ten commandments, and he has promised to come back on earth, and we expect it fairly soon.'

She paused, eyes shining behind the heavy framed glasses, her lips parted, waiting to continue once her thoughts caught up. I looked doubtful.

'You really believe Christ will return?'

'Oh, yes. The second coming. There will be a judgement then for sure.'

'Okay, where does Christian fit in, - is he an Evangelical Follower?'

'Christian is different, he seems to have his own close followers and has never said he was a member of the Evangelical Federation, - in my hearing anyway, but a lot of what he teaches is directly from the bible. Strangely, he has a lot of different people around him, different faiths too, I know he had a group of Muslims at his place a few months ago. He seems to be more than 'Christian faith', he preaches about God the Creator; he acknowledges Jesus the son of God, of course, - and other prophets too.'

We talked for over an hour. The wine was superseded by coffee and sandwiches. I enjoyed talking with Mary, her uncomplicated breathy words fell easily into my consciousness and I relaxed more than I had for years. We discussed mundane things, daily routine. I learned that she had never had a real boyfriend, which I found incredible, - I wondered if the heavy spectacle frames made her look too studious for some. In my eyes she was a very attractive young woman, and behind the glasses were deep attractive eyes, looking into them I saw energy, intelligence, yet also an innocence that beguiled me.

'By the way,' said Mary, 'You know that Christian expects us to stay over don't you? So bring an overnight bag.'

'What! No, - John didn't say anything at all about staying. I don't believe he meant overnight.'

'He did,' Mary was emphatic. 'Christian has weekend house parties. John must have assumed he'd told you, or forgotten.'

'Well, I don't know,' I said doubtfully.

'Look. Just bring your overnight stuff along, then you are prepared if needs be.'

We moved onto other things. I told her about my work as a writer and I told a little bit about

Jenny. She was a good listener and I felt the weight of depression lessen a little as I spoke.

'I'm glad you told me,' she said quietly. 'I knew you were hurting, Matt, - its etched on your face and in your soul. Look, I know it seems stupid to say, but things will be okay, I promise. What's happening isn't an accident, Matt, Its ordained.'

Talking about Jenny had brought thoughts of past happiness back, and despite the relief in talking, I felt an ache for what had been.

'How can you say that?' I said bleakly. 'How can anything be okay again?'

Mary paused for a long while, maintaining a steady look into my eyes.

'Matt,' she said at last. 'I knew you are a writer. When you called me for a ticket, I had been waiting for a 'Matthew' to call. Then when you did call I was caught off guard,' she stopped, looking away for a moment, before returning her gaze. She went on. 'You are going to write an account that will ignite the world, it will the most important writing ever discovered or published.'

She softened her voice, but it was a bombshell nonetheless, 'And Matt, *you will be with Jenny again*.'

I stood abruptly, anger and uncertainty flooding over me.

'Mary! What the hell are you talking about! I really don't need this!'

Mary looked away, her face contrite. 'I'm sorry, Matt. The last thing in the world I want to do is to upset you.'

Slowly the anger faded and we reverted to 'Safe' conversation. We even shared laughter at anecdotes and the evening passed more pleasurably into night-time.

Eventually it was time to take my leave. Mary came to the door and we arranged to travel together to Christain's place. I thanked her for the sandwiches, told her I had enjoyed the evening. We stood uncertainly for a moment, in the end I kissed her cheek gently and left.

The evening with Mary had unsettled me. The next day I drove to St Nicholas and sat in the church for a while, its intimacy and tranquillity calming my nerves. I walked down to 'our' bench, Jenny's and mine. I sat for the rest of the day, stiffness and cold unheeded.

I sensed the spirits, interrupted and dispersed on my arrival, slowly gather again, edging closer, a protective blanket. So spiritual was the place I could almost hear the soft murmurs. I acknowledged them, those New Zealanders, far from home, the Squires, the New Forest dwellers, the snake catcher and of course my Jenny and her parents.

Quietly, Philip arrived at my side and sat. He produced a flask of hot tea and two cups. His pastoral care, gently administered, had over the past two years saved my sanity. We sat wordlessly, sipping the welcome hot drink.

I eventually broke the silence. 'Phil, what about life after death?'

'What about it?'

'Well, I mean, is there life after death? Do we all experience it? How does it work?'

Philip said nothing for a moment, I could feel he was assembling his thoughts.

'Yes, Matt, there is life after death. The spirit leaves the mortal body at death and is exalted into God's presence. God is the synergy of all exalted spirits, time is no longer a dimension and the spirit can exist everywhere and anywhere at the same time.'

I fidgeted for a moment. 'Will I see Jenny again after I die?'

Philip smiled. 'The answer is not straightforward Matt. Yes you will, but not in the form of man and woman, - the spirit is without form. You will exist in harmony with Jenny forever.'

'What about the non-believers?'

'The real non-believer, the atheist, - his spirit has nowhere to go at death and stays in limbo until absorbed into the dark force of evil.'

'Christian Fellowes speaks of the opposites, positive and negative; light and dark, opposing forces, everything in balance.'

'Well, it's a scientific fact I suppose. Where there is imbalance there is stress, whether in energy, spiritual or material manifestation.'

We chatted on for a while then we wandered gently up the hill to the church, he to the vestry, I to my car. I felt better but Philip's words had aroused many questions in my mind. Why was everyone telling me I was destined to write something important, that I was on a journey; -

the Reverend Charmin, Jenny, Philip, Mary, (Who I had known but for two weeks!), even Paul, my one time agent. The whole business mystified and exhilarated me. I was coming out of the abyss of despair and journeying to the project I needed, I wasn't to know at that time my very life was to be compromised, but my imagination was fired up and I began to feel the stirrings of normality. I thanked God for Mandy, she had evoked the drive in me to do something.

CHAPTER SEVEN

I picked Mary up at her house and we drove towards Apsley Manor, beyond Fordingbridge on the Salisbury road. She had brought a small pink duffle bag which I placed on the back seat beside my battered holdall. Mary was trying to be nonchalant, but I could sense a suppressed excitement and nervousness. We kept to small talk as she directed me off the main road onto a series of very minor roads until we reached a wall that ran for half a mile before reaching a massive pair of closed iron gates. A sign proclaimed that the gravel road within ran to Apsley Manor.

'This is it,' said Mary un-necessarily. 'Pull in close to that pillar, there's' a key pad.'

Mary couldn't reach the keypad from her side. 'Key in1643,' she said. I did and the gate duly swung silently open. The road ran for about a mile and then through a small thicket to reveal an impressive stately home style of property. A wide gravelled area lay in front of the building. We swept in a circle round the front of the house and joined a group of cars parked on grass to the right of the house. I suddenly felt nervous, what had I let myself in for? What could I have in common with Christain's friends?

Steps ran up either side to a large, iron studded front door which opened as we reached it, John stood there a friendly smile on his face.

'Hello Matt. Welcome to Apsley Manor. Hi Mary,' he shook my hand then greeted Mary with a peck on her cheeks. 'Come on in and meet the others.'

We crossed a wide hall and entered a huge drawing room, in which stood a number of people in groups of two or three, drinks in hands, animatedly talking. The noise level was high and no one seemed to be aware of our arrival. My apprehension was quickly dispelled by the normality of the scene and when a waiter appeared with a tray of wines I relaxed and smiled at Mary.

'Here we are then,' I said holding up my glass. We touched glasses.

Looking around I counted about fifteen people. Christian was across the room talking to two men, one an African.

'That's Doctor Samuel Johnson!' I said, surprised. 'I met him in Lagos, he chaperoned me around for a few days a long time ago. Small world!'

Mary scanned the group, counting.

'Uh, well, ten of them are close colleagues of Christian, then there's three people who look after arrangements, and some staff I 'Spose.'

'What do you mean, look after arrangements?'

'Like John for instance, - sorts out the venues for Christain's lectures, organise the equipment and stuff.'

'You mean theatre props?'

'Yes, I….,' she was interrupted by John.

'You two Okay?'

We nodded. I said. 'There seems to be an international feel to this crowd.'

John laughed. 'You're right, Matt, perceptive as always. Let me point out who's who. Those three nearest us,' he indicated two men and a woman in relaxed conversation, 'the balding chap is Andrew, an American, Los Angeles. The other man is Peter, he's from Russia. The lady in the sari is Sybil, from India.'

At that moment the lady in question caught my eye, and smiled at me across the room. Older than me, I guessed. The two men followed her gaze and nodded.

'On the right there,' continued John. 'The Tall man with the goatee is Marc, he's from Germany, the man he is talking to is Simon from Pakistan. The oriental looking gentleman talking to the fair haired giant is Paul Yu, China. The big guy is Philip from Australia.'

He paused for a moment, then.

'Those two are John Rosenberg from Israel and Yvonne from Brazil.'

Our eyes dwelt on the couple. The man was tallish with luxuriant curly black hair. He had a heavy face and a prominent hooked nose. But it was the woman that held the eye. She was tall, shining raven hair falling to her shoulders. She was elegant and devastatingly attractive.

'Over there, you know of course, is Christian talking to Samuel….'

'Yes,' I interrupted, 'Doctor Samuel Johnson, I know him. He chaperoned me around Lagos for a few days some years ago.'

'Look Matt,' said John seriously. 'We shall soon be going in for supper. There are just a couple of, well, - protocols we observe, so don't get caught out. I will show you where to sit, then we stand until all are assembled. Christian will be at the head of the table. Take your lead from him. There is bread on each side plate. Everyone will pick up the bread and hold in both hands in front of them. Christian will say a short thanksgiving and then we all tear the bread in half. Put the left hand piece back on the plate and hand the right hand piece to your neighbour on your right, taking the piece from the person on your left. Take a bite and place the remainder onto your side plate. Do not eat any more, - at all. Then everyone will take up the glass of red wine in front of them. Taking your cue from Christian take a sip, pass it onto the neighbour on your right, and take the glass from the person on your left. Take a sip and place the glass down in front of you. That's your wine and glass for the evening.'

He looked anxiously at me. 'Is that Okay?'

'We don't eat the bread, - at all?'

'Only the one bite.'

I struggled to remember the rationale for the breaking of bread and taking of wine, distinct from communion. John took my arm.

'Come and say hello to Christian, I know he is looking forward to talking with you.'

Christian and Samuel Johnson greeted us with smiles and outstretched hands.

Close to, Christian again overwhelmed me, I felt vunerable.

'Matt! I'm so pleased you accepted our invitation,' he indicated Samuel Johnson. 'You've met Samuel, of course?'

'Yes, we met in Lagos. Hello Doctor Johnson,' we shook hands all round.

Samuel Johnson's round face beamed. 'Samuel.- you must call me Samuel, - please! We are all friends here. Its good to see you again Matt; we haven't met since the finished biography, it was good work and a great success.'

I made a dismissive gesture.

'No,' said Christian. 'Accept the plaudit, Matt, it was a first class effort. Your other work too, - it's well thought of.'

I struggled to make small talk with two people I didn't know very well. After a while John took Samuel off to meet another guest. Christian looked at me, as if assessing something.

'Matt, - at the lecture. The things I spoke of. They resonated with you?'

'Well, yes they did. I thought you uncovered a number of truths which lay dormant.'

Christian nodded. 'In what way?'

'I believe what you were saying was important, but the majority of people deliberately bury it because they can't get their minds around it.'

'Do they want to?'

'I think yes. But there seems to be a force out there obscuring the way.'

'What do you mean by a 'force'.'

'Well, I don't know. I guess a combination of laziness and greed. Maybe fear too, in some cases. Also people tend to ridicule things they don't understand, a sort of defence, but there's something else, deeper, more frightening - I can't put a finger on.'

'Try.'

I hesitated. 'Evil,' I said at last.

Christian looked appraisingly, seeming to confirm his thoughts about me.

'Matt, tonight is a special night for us, after the supper we are having a meeting, - I want you to attend.'

'I know little of what you do, Christian, I'm not sure what I can bring to the table, so to speak.'

'That is so. Matt, but you notice things, you have an extraordinary ability to write powerful yet accurate accounts. I am sure You'll find something 'to bring to the table'.'

Suddenly, I thought I knew where all this was going.

'You mean you want me to act as a sort of chronicler for the group?'

Christian smiled. 'Ah, Matt, I see we are going in to supper,' with that he took my arm and guided me towards the dining room.

The guests crowded into the dining room milling around the table looking for their seating arrangements. Mary beckoned me, 'Matt. You're sitting next to me.'

The supper table was a large truncated triangle. Christian sat at the head and everyone else was distributed on the other three sides, four to a side. Mary and I were on the bottom side, facing Christian. Mary sat on my right and on her right was the German, Marc. On my left sat Samuel.

The table was set simply but elegantly, bread already placed on side plates and red wine poured.

It was only then, when we stood quietly waiting for a lead from Christian that I realized there were thirteen for supper! It shouldn't have mattered, but I felt a tinge of apprehension run up my spine and I gave an involuntary shiver.

Christian, seeing we were all assembled, picked up his bread and held in both hands across his chest. I watched everyone else and carefully followed suit.

Christian spoke clearly, his deep voice vibrant with sincerity.

'This bread represents the body of our creator. We take this in acknowledgment of him.'

Christian then tore the bread in half, placed the left part on his side plate, and offered the other to the diner on his right, at the same time, with his left hand, he took the bread from the diner on his left. We all followed suit. Christian then took a bite from the bread and placed the remainder onto his side plate. I watched carefully and followed. Everyone seemed to accomplish the routine with practiced ease, as did Mary, I noticed.

Christian took up his wine, we all followed.

'This wine represents the blood of mortal man. We take this in supplication.'

He sipped the wine and passed the glass to the diner on his right, who took it with his left hand and after taking a sip placed the glass on the table in front of him. We all carefully copied his example.

'May God forgive us and guide us,' Christian concluded. He gestured for the guests to be seated.

The solemnity was broken as everyone began to talk. Waiters appeared and placed soup before us. No one touched the bread.

The supper of roast lamb garnished with rosemary, served with new potatoes and a selection of vegetables proceeded with good bonhomie.

On the left of Samuel, around the corner of the triangle, sat the Brazilian, Yvonne. In an unguarded moment I caught her looking at me speculatively, we exchanged smiles, my own libido in confusion.

I engaged Samuel in small talk to divert my thoughts.

'Amazing to meet up again after all this time,' I said.

Samuel laughed. 'Amazing? Well yes I suppose it seems that way. Do you believe in ordainment Matt?'

'Fate you mean?'

'No. Not fate. I mean a higher level that guides and motivates us.'

'God? Well yes of course I believe in God, but I hadn't thought about an ordained path.'

'God is watching us, Matt, he knows we are here, and will guide us to eternal life, - if we want it.'

'Many would disagree with you, - atheists.'

'Then they are damned,' Samuel said quietly. 'They may enjoy this physical life; for all that, the end is the end for them, there is nothing more. They have no anchor,' he paused. 'Anyway enough of this, you have not known it Matt, but I have been aware of your trials since those days in Lagos, I am happy that you are with us tonight.'

We broke the sombre mood and chatted about more social matters and the meal progressed enjoyably.

After the desserts John stood and suggested that coffee be taken in the study which was a large panelled room, with soft easy chairs placed randomly but focussed toward a huge open fireplace. A log fire was burning fitfully, its aromatic scent filling the room. A coffee table was placed within easy reach of each chair and on which sat coffee cups. Christian sat near the fire his chair turned to face the room. The guests sat in casual order around the room, chatting amiably. It was a cosy relaxed atmosphere, although I did sense an undercurrent of excitement, of anticipation beneath the surface. Coffee was served, and as the guests fell silent, Christian spoke.

'My dear friends, we are gathered here at my request, some of you have travelled a considerable distance, thank you for your diligence. I have a lot to say, but before I begin, I welcome Matthew to our number, we are now complete. We are ready to move forward in the service of our creator.'

At my name, everyone had looked to me, smiling and nodding in welcome. I acknowledged the welcome and had expected to feel some embarrassment, instead I felt only a surge of enabling energy from the assembled guests. Adrenaline coursed through my veins as I settled down to understand what was going on.

As everyone sat enjoying the ambience, Christian claimed attention.

'My friends, throughout the world the message of God is beginning to be heard with clarity. A wind of change is blowing. The word is proclaiming the creator in language of today, in the technology of today, in the science of today.

Hundreds of millions of ordinary people feel trapped by a hedonistic world, - trapped in the resulting retreat of civilised behaviour. They see the increasingly unGodly exhibition of envy, of crime, sodomy, greed and fornication.

Men that sow their seed as animals, as animals they become.

The Godly long for leadership in terms they understand; fearful of evil, they look to you and your ministries, ladies and gentlemen, to bring them safely to the Grace of God.'

He went on to speak for a short time. After which a debate ensued as disciples informed the meeting of events and feelings in their own dioceses and the night wore on to its companionable conclusion. As the gathering broke up Mary waited in an ante room while I went to the car for our bags.

When I got back Christian was talking to Mary, he turned to me, smiling.

'Matt, thank you for your input this evening.'

'I enjoyed it,' I said. 'it was enlightening, and, - well stimulating.'

'Would you like to do your work from here? Your own work as well of course. I feel you would benefit from the facilities here at the manor. John will make arrangements for you. Have a good night,' he touched our arms and went back into the drawing room.

It was surreal! I was being drawn into a situation that I felt was outside my control. No one had said directly what I was expected to do, and yet, at the back of my mind, it seemed to be accepted that I would write the story of Christain's movement.

Guests were making their way to the stairs.

Mary led the way up a wide staircase to a large landing with an ornamental stand and two armchairs. A corridor extended in both directions, we turned right 'These are ours,' she said, stopping towards the end. 'You have this first one, - I'm there,' she added indicating next door.

We paused, uncertain of how to say goodnight. In the end I told I her I had really enjoyed the evening and her company. I leaned forward and gave her a friendly peck on the cheek.

'Goodnight Mary, - oh! what time do we get up?'

'Lets meet in the dining room at, say, seven thirty?'

'Seven thirty it is then. Good night,' I leaned forward and kissed her cheek again.

'You already did that.'

I let myself into my allocated room with a softness and a perfume lingering in my senses. It wasn't Jenny's perfume.

The next morning I called my one time agent Paul Kneale.

'Paul? Matt here, how are you?'

'Matt?' he paused. 'Hi there, long time! Are you in town?'

'No. But I'm planning to come up in the next week or two. Can I come and see you?'

'Yeah, of course, it will be good to see you.- Business?' he added cautiously.

'Well not this time, but I am hoping to get back into things before long.'

Paul brightened considerably. 'You bet. Just let me know and I'll free up time.'

We chatted for a short time, ending on good terms. The day felt better, perhaps the clouds were beginning to lift.

CHAPTER EIGHT

I stood in the supermarket pondering the merits of various ready meals. I thought of trying something new, wandering along the shelves I almost bumped into Kate, hardly recognising her. She looked pale and haggard, almost unkempt.

'Kate!' I said in surprise.

She looked through me before finally focussing. 'Hello, Matt. I can't stop,' she moved quickly towards the checkout.

'Hey! - Kate! Hang on, what's wrong?' I strode alongside her, catching her arm. She snatched it away before stopping and looking at me with haunted eyes.

'Matt, Mandy's in hospital, - she's had an accident. I'm going to her now, just dashed in for a few things to take. I must go.'

'Mandy!' my strangled cry brought Kate up sharply. I felt a lead weight in my stomach and panic rising. 'What happened, Kate? Tell me. I'll come with you!' I dropped my half filled basket on the floor and helped her through the check out. We hurried to her car.

'Mandy's in Southampton hospital. She was knocked down by a car last Wednesday,' Kate's face crumpled. 'Matt, she's in a bad way.'

'For God's sake, Kate! Why wasn't I told.'

Anger and fear filled my voice. I had lost Jenny, - now Mandy too? Mandy was the re-incarnation of Jenny in my eyes, it was she that had pulled me out of my stupor, and now she was in danger and I hadn't known!

Kate looked at me strangely. 'Why should you have been told?' she said, then her voice gave out and she burst into unrestrained tears. I caught her to me and held her close, her sobs now muffled in my chest.

' Because I'm your friend Kate. Mandy's my friend. I love you both, I need you.'

Kate pulled away, staring.

'I'm sorry,' I said hurriedly. 'I didn't mean it like that! I meant, -well, we're friends aren't we? Friends are to help. I'm coming to Southampton with you. When are you going?'

Kate's personal misery took her thoughts and she said no more. We drove both cars to her place. In the kitchen we made tea, then she disappeared to tidy herself up.

I had not been inside Kate's home before; it felt strange, as if I were in a privileged place I had no right to be. I wandered into the living room, looking around I thought what a difference a woman's touch made to a home. The room was warm and comfortable, unlike my austere apartment which was functional only. Here, small unnecessary things were dotted around, drawing a picture of her in less traumatic times relaxed and enjoying her home. There was lots of evidence of Mandy too, - a jumper discarded on a chair, hair ribbon and brush on a side table. There was a child's easel in the corner and boxed games beneath. In the kitchen too, I had noticed childish drawings held on the fridge door with magnets, a satchel hung on the kitchen door.

I felt panic rise in me again, desperation. Images of Mandy swam before my eyes, then became Jenny, then Mandy again, the two faces, happy, flashing alternately, looking at me coquettishly, heads tilted identically, wisps of blonde hair falling over their faces. Hopelessness and fear tore at my nerves, I made a dash for the front door, crashed outside and stood in the cold air, heaving great breaths of air.

Slowly as the world returned to normal. Kate appeared at my side. She stared at me uncomprehendingly. 'Matt, are you all right?'

'Yes, I'm fine,' I muttered, making a show of retrieving keys from my pocket. 'Shall we go in my car? I'll bring you back after.'

The trip to Southampton was made in silence, each of us lost in our own miseries. At the hospital we circled the hospital car park three times before I could find a parking space. We hurried across the road to the main entrance. Kate knew the way to the ward. Mandy was in an intensive care unit. We stood for a moment staring through the glass looking at the small girl lying inert, tubes and wires snaking from her to a large monitor system on a trolley. A nurse appeared and told us to go in and stay by Mandy's side. The monitor screen glowed with several coloured lines of pulses, an audio alarm beeped softly in the background.

Kate and I held Mandy's hands, they were cool and limp. A doctor arrived, probably warned by the nurse that we were here.

'Mrs Tatman, Hello, I'm doctor Mailer,' he moved towards us.

Kate nodded, her voice anxious. 'Where's the other doctor, Doctor Whitely?'

'I'm doing night shift Mrs Tatman. Doctor Whitely will be back in the morning.'

'How is Mandy, Is she going to be alright?' Kate's voice trembled, she was holding it together with difficulty.

Doctor Mailer glanced at me, then back to Kate. 'Mandy is weak, Mrs Tatman, very weak but she's fighting.'

'Is she better than yesterday?' Kate's question was a plea.

Doctor Mailer remained silent, busying himself scrutinising the monitors and we knew our answer!

'We're all working to pull her through,' he said eventually.

We sat at Mandy's side throughout the night. There was no sign of change, no movement or flicker. I wandered away several times to get plastic cups of coffee and to find the toilet. Kate sat throughout, her face stiff, lost in worry and grief.

It was light, with signs of increased activity in the corridors. Then doctor Whitely arrived. Kate and I looked up, we were drooping with fatigue; with his arrival adrenaline bucked us up. He had a file with him which he examined while walking in. He looked at the monitors, and held Mandy's arm for a moment.

'She could be like this for a long time,' he said. 'She has severe internal trauma. I'm afraid her vital signs are weakening.'

'But she'll get better?' Kate asked, willing the doctor to admit improvements.

'Mrs Tatman, of course we hope for improvement but you must also be prepared for the worst.'

We heard the words without taking them in and after a while the doctor left. Kate and I sat in silence, there was no change in Mandy. I held her slim hand and tried to pour my will into her, but tiredness dimmed my efforts.

'We ought to go home for a rest and some clean clothes,' I said.

There was no response from Kate who sat dully staring at her daughter.

'Look, Kate, lets go home and get a bath and change. Mandy's okay here for a short time.'

I put my arm around Kate and eased her, unresisting, from her chair and we returned to the car. The car park fee was prohibitive.

At Kate's house I took charge of matters, ran a bath, instructing her to get her dressing gown, take the bath and I would fix a meal. I rummaged around in the unfamiliar kitchen, I could hear Kate moving around in the bathroom above while I prepared an omelette with bread and butter. When it was ready to cook I laid the table and waited for Kate to reappear.

After twenty minutes there was no movement and I began to worry. I went upstairs and knocked on the bathroom door.

'Kate? Breakfast is ready, - you coming down?'

There was no response. I went along to the bedroom, knocking on the door, in case she had bathed and was dressing. There was no response to my knock. I cautiously opened the bedroom door.

'Kate?' The room was empty. Kate must still be in the bath. I ran back to the bathroom, knocked more firmly on the door.

'Kate? - you okay?' There was no response. I knocked loudly. 'Come on Kate!'

Still no response. Suddenly I had visions of Kate harming herself in despair. I tried the door it was unlocked, I opened it without looking in the room.

'Kate! Come on, time to get out,' I said loudly. After a moment I peered round the door. Kate was in the bath, her head lolling to one side, her mouth close to the water.

'Oh, my God!' I shouted, and rushed forward grabbing a towel, holding it up in front of me as I ran trying not to see her naked body. Spreading the towel I laid it on the water to preserve her modesty and cupped her head in my hands.

'Kate! Kate! Come on.'

Her eyes flickered open, 'Umm, What's happening?' her voice slurring from heavy sleep. Relief poured through me. Clearly the fatigue had taken hold and in the hot water she had fallen into a deep sleep. Now I felt embarrassed to be kneeling against the bath.

'You fell asleep,' I explained. 'I couldn't wake you up, and, - well I got worried you had hurt yourself. Look, I'm sorry. You get out and I'll start the breakfast.'

Kate was coming round fast. She looked at me then down at the towel floating on the water, then back at my face. There was no censure, just an assessment. I looked into her eyes, trying to project caring innocence. She began to sit up.

'I'll leave you to it,' I said hastily and left, closing the door firmly after me.

I had cooked the omelettes and made coffee when Kate appeared in the kitchen. She wore a red soft jumper over black trousers, had applied make up, her hair was brushed and despite tiredness showing in her eyes she looked good.

I didn't know how to comment on the bathroom intrusion so I said nothing and busied myself serving and pouring coffee. To my relief Kate said nothing either, and any embarrassment was averted. We discussed Mandy and the hospital visit as if the situation had not arisen. Later that day we visited the hospital. There was no change in Mandy's condition. I stared at her for ages, drinking in her serene face; suddenly I shivered, there seemed to be a sharp drop in the room temperature, I turned away, tears misting my eyes.

Over the next few days Kate spend most the day and evenings at Mandy's bedside. I visited every evening. During the day I drove to Apsley Manor where Christian had given me the use of the library to work; it was a huge room lined on three sides with book filled shelves. A wide bay window looked out into a large walled garden. A large oblong table took up the centre of the room; it was here I would sit with John and discuss the role and activities of the Christian Follower movement. I was there on the Saturday, it was coffee time, eleven days after the accident. I sat at the large central table, papers scattered over its surface. I was well advanced in working out the sequence in which I wanted to record events. I had indexed the contact numbers and addresses of all the disciples and had tentatively fixed up visits to two of them. Tiredness and worry sapped my concentration and I was almost asleep when I felt a change in the atmosphere, as if the air was charged with electricity, I came to quickly as Christian entered the room.

'Hello, Matt,' he indicated the papers. 'You are busy. We all appreciate what you are doing,' he came and sat at the table.

'Good morning Christian,' I said. It had never seemed appropriate to call him Chris, and I had not heard anyone else do so. 'Yes, I've started on some of the background. I have arranged to visit Marc next week to get a feel of work 'on the ground' so to speak.- Just a two day visit.'

Christian nodded. 'I trust you are receiving co-operation from everyone?'

'I am, John is very helpful here and all the, - uh, disciples, are anxious to provide information and support,' I hesitated. 'I find Simon is a bit difficult...,' I paused. 'He doesn't seem to want to co-operate, something about him unsettles me,'

'Christain's face darkened momentarily, then he smiled. 'Your perception always surprises me, Matt, - but he is well liked by everyone.'

'I know, that's what makes me uneasy, it must be me.'

Christian smiled again. 'You write as you find, I have every confidence in your judgement,' his tone changed, he became serious. 'Matt there's something on your mind,' it was a statement.

I tried to make light of it.

'Who's being perceptive now? Well, yes, I am very anxious about a young friend of mine, Mandy. She's in hospital, she was knocked down by a car; and desperately ill. I'm frightened for her,' my voice cracked.

Christian looked at the lines etched on my face, the tiredness.

'Yes, I know. You have a special relationship with this young lady, - her likeness to your wife Jenny.'

I was astounded, how did he know? I guessed John must have ferreted out my personal business and informed Christian. But talking about it brought the memories of Jenny flooding back, and the anxiety for Mandy tore at me. I nodded wordlessly.

Christian stood and placed his hand on my shoulder. I felt warmth and a power soak through my tired muscles. I was afraid.

Christian sensed my feelings. 'Don't be afraid, Matt. You are being sorely tried, and events can sometimes overwhelm us. Please! - Stop work now, - leave your papers on the desk and go to the hospital immediately, I am sure that Mandy is recovering.'

Suddenly I couldn't cope with all this, I just couldn't cope. I stumbled to my feet, as I got up it seemed natural to grasp Christain's hand in a high five clasp. We stood for a second he supporting me, his eyes burning into mine with compassion and power. Then he turned and left the room.

I collapsed back onto the chair. My mind in a turmoil; before I could collect myself John entered the room.

'Leave this Matt,' he said quietly, nodding to the papers spread over the desk, 'They will be alright here, no one will touch them; the room will not be used until you return.'

I don't remember the drive to the hospital except that I phoned Kate, She was at home having lunch and preparing to visit Mandy later in the afternoon.

'Kate, I am on the way to the hospital,' I didn't want to alarm Kate, I just told her that I was leaving early today and calling into the hospital. Please would she come as well.

Kate was at Mandy's bedside when I got there, she looked up and imperceptibly shook her head. No change. We fell into the routine, I held Mandy's hand for a while, went and got coffee, came back, sat and looked at the little girl, pale and still.

By ten o'clock that night we were again drooping with fatigue. We had been sitting there for nearly eight hours. The doctor had visited twice. He had taken us aside and warned us that we should prepare for the worst. Kate and I and Mandy held hands tightly, wrapped in misery.

The corridors had quietened down as the night routines took over. My head drooped, I was half asleep, with just the steady audio monitor beeping quietly in the background. Kate just stared into the distance lost in her thoughts.

'Mummy?'

Neither Kate nor I reacted, then, for the second time,

'Mummy?'

I jumped as if I had been electrocuted. Kate's head shot up as with a cry she leaned forward, one hand holding Mandy's hand, the other cupping her cheek.

'Mandy, my darling, Mummy's here,' Kate laughed and cried in confusion.

I had leapt from my chair and after reaching for Mandy's hand, I heard whispered the weak but sweetest words.

'Hello, Matt.'

Letting go of her hand I rushed to the alarm bell and then out into the corridor to hurry the medical staff along.

Doctor Mailer arrived, he fussed around Mandy and the monitor, looking bemused, until he announced at last that Mandy was 'fine', adding that she would be in hospital for some for some time yet, but the worry was over, so we eventually departed leaving a little girl very much of this world.

The next morning I spent thinking deeply about what had happened. Before lunchtime I drove to St Nicolas church. It was open and the Reverend Rowlands was in the vestry. I sat in the nave for an hour. I tried to address God, to thank him for his mercy. Images of Jenny reappeared in my mind. Why couldn't she have been saved? It was all too much to take in.

I then I drove to Apsley Manor. As I talked with John, Christian came into the room. I went before him. My voice choked. 'Christian, I, - I don't know what to say.'

'Say nothing,' said Christian placing his hand on my arm. 'God already knows your thanks.'

Three days later Kate and I collected Mandy from the hospital. She was weak, but in good spirits. Kate and I walked on air.

It was a few days later, I had been invited round to supper, (In fact I seemed to spend as much time there as at my place). We had an early supper so as to include Mandy. I was sitting in an arm chair reading the paper, Kate fiddling about with something on the table, Mandy was sitting at her little easel, doodling with coloured dry markers. There was desultory chatting.

Mandy said. 'Mummy?'

'Yes dear?'

'Who was that lady sitting with me in the hospital?'

'It was me, darling, I came every day, because I wanted to be near you.'

'No, Mummy, the other lady, who came when you went home.'

I caught the conversation, turning my head, suddenly alert.

Kate stopped what she was doing and cuddled Mandy. 'I'm sure it was me, Mands, you were probably too sleepy to understand.'

'No, Mummy. This other lady sat with me all the time you were out, she told me stories and kissed me.'

I had sat up, uneasy, my heart began to pound.

'What was the lady like?' I said conversationally.

'We-eell, she had long blonde hair like mine, she was very pretty.'

'What else, Mandy, I said urgently, 'Did she tell you who she was?'

'No she didn't, but we laughed because when she sat with her hand next to mine on the bed we both had our thumbs tucked in, it was funny.'

I leapt to my feet, feeling sick, I stumbled to the door and out into the garden and the street. For two hours I walked, my head hunched into my shoulders, oblivious to the cold, trying to understand what was going on. Eventually I realized I had walked all the way to my own street.

It was dark by this time, and I had no coat and no car; it was blowing a gale and raining fitfully. I let myself in, the place felt cold and uninviting; by now I had grown inured to this and set about making a mug of coffee. I put the table lamps on in the living room, trying to soften the ambience and turned up the heating thermostat.

I was still mulling over the recent events. What had Christian meant when he said 'It wasn't time yet'? Time for what? Was he really responsible for Mandy's recovery, or was it just a co-incidence? And what about Mandy's visitor? She described Jenny, but had no way of knowing about her, I had never spoken to Kate or Mandy about Jenny. It must have been a dream and the likeness just another co-incidence.

My mind in a turmoil I tried to summarise my situation in all this; was I merely a writer being asked to chronicle the events of Christain's disciples? Or was there something else?

Was I a follower of Christian? Was this doing anything for me? Or was I just fooling myself into escapism; a withdrawal from the real world, brought on by two years of defeatism. And too, there was something about the way Christian sometimes looked at me. When he was scanning a group his eyes sometimes paused on me. I could feel the intensity of his gaze, just for a brief second, but I noticed that sometimes when I caught his glance there was something uncertain in his eyes, as if he was trying to assess something. Sometimes I thought he was about to say something, then the moment would pass and his gaze move on.

I was still pondering these feelings as I crossed the living room, coffee in hand. Suddenly I shivered as the room, as yet still un-warmed by the heating system, took a further sharp drop in temperature and static seemed to fill the air, I could almost feel the crackle dancing on the corners and edges of the furniture. I stopped mid stride, a stab of fear jolting my body.

Breathing! - I could sense breathing, - and perfume! A perfume that had been burned into my consciousness for ten years.

Suddenly I knew, - I just knew! I could feel my heart pound as if it would burst from my body and fear mingled with an illogical hope. There was a need buried deep after two years but now suddenly surging to the surface,

'Hello Mr P.'
I leapt as if I had been electrocuted, dropping the mug and coffee onto the floor.

IT WAS JENNIFER'S VOICE! - Not ethereal, not dis-embodied, just her normal warm voice with a hint of lisp and using her favourite diminutive name for me. It was not possible, NO, NO, NO! Jenny had been dead for two years. This macabre illusion just could not happen.

My voice was hoarse, I dare not look round, I whispered, 'Jenny?'

Christian had said that Jenny would come to me. Emotion welled up, I was totally unable to react. A sob convulsed my body and I sank to my knees on the floor, covering my face with my hands.

'Jenny!' Through my fingers I exclaimed her name in anguish, two years of pent up despair wracked my body. I did not know what to do, where to look or what to say.

I felt, or imagined, some slight movement of air behind me, a gossamer touch across my shoulders. I toppled off my knees onto the carpet and lay in foetal position, gasping for air between sobs.

'Jenny, I love you so much' I sobbed, 'Want to come with you, want to be with you.'

Where there was cold was now warmth, it settled around me; I heard Jenny's soft whisper in my ear, endearing, comforting, healing.

'Not yet,' her words soft, *'It's not time, there are still things to be done. I love you too and you will come to me, I promise.'*

I grew warm and comfortable, my sobs subsided. We were together, Jenny and me. I spoke to her, she spoke softly in my ear and we stayed through the night together. I dared not move or look up lest it all ended. My loneliness and fear was slowly replaced with joy and resolve, I felt life pumping into my body and I knew then that I was a Follower of Christian.

We whispered comforts to each other through the night. I was exhausted, our whispered conversation slowed and then stopped. We lay together, spoons, warm and one in mind and spirit. My thoughts ranged over the good times until exhaustion took over. I fell asleep, awaking as dawn light took over from the lamps. I was lying on the carpet, still curled up and feeling cold and stiff. The nights extraordinary events flooded into my brain.

I sat up with a start, urgently calling Jenny's name. But even as I did, I knew she would not be there. A moment of panic and loss was quickly replaced by wonder and joy. I knew now that I had found what I was to do with my life, I would join with Christian and place my life in his hands and I knew that Jenny would be with me, - all the time.

CHAPTER NINE

I could not do or think of anything else for three days. I mooned around the apartment, my mind going over and over the events of the past weeks. Where was it all heading? I slept all hours. A phone call from Kate inviting herself and Mandy over for tea brought me back to near normality.

As I opened the door Mandy came into my arms without any inhibition.

'Hello Matt,' she said excitedly. 'Mum says I can go to school on Monday.'

Kate stepped forward and gave me a more chaste, but nonetheless warm, kiss on the cheek. We spent a pleasant evening together and my world returned to an even keel.

The next morning I returned to work at Apsley Manor. As I drove, I mentally reviewed the sketchy ideas I had. Following recent events it was clear I needed to know more about Christian. Who was he? Where did he come from? I knew he was known world wide for his evangelical preaching. More than that, he postulated the existence of an infinite universe and the presence of a creator. He was viewed with caution by both the scientific fraternity and clergy alike.

Christian was unfathomable, often I felt his power, noticed his sometimes sombre moods. He was not the sort of person I felt would unburden himself to me on a man to man basis. He was a man who preached biblical gospel in a modern language. He spoke of the creator, he was a creationist. He spoke of evolution in terms of intelligent design. His public orations raised his audiences to fever pitch excitement, an evangelist par excellence. But in the private gatherings of his disciples he was stern, technical and unforgiving. I did not know how to approach learning about his past. I had once broached the subject with John who sidestepped the issue and I believe probably didn't know anyway.

The solution came to me as I entered the library. I could hear singing from the depths of the manor, - the drawing room I believed, where I had very first met the disciples. I knew Christian and John had gone up to London to prepare for a major rally. (To which I was also going).

I walked back into the reception hall, through an ante room and quietly entered the drawing room. I paused in the doorway and listened. Faith stood alone in the room, an arm resting on a piano, looking out into the grounds, singing *'Amazing Grace'*. She sang the words with heart wrenching feeling and clarity. She sang gently but still her voice rose and fell filling every nook of the huge room.

The room had been re arranged, now sparsely furnished with a few occasional tables and chairs. A suite of overstuffed easy chairs ranged around the huge open fireplace, in which a log fire burned. The view out through the French windows took the eye along a rosary, past a central fountain and onto the gardens beyond. The scene before me was enchanting.

I had a three quarter view of Faith, her hair was, for the first time I had seen, tied back in a high pony tail. She wore cream trousers, jumper and a brown gillet. She was no longer the enigmatic singer, confidant of Christian; more just like the girl next door. Nevertheless her voice penetrated my inner soul.

She could not have heard nor seen me, and continued singing until the final lines:

> *'The earth shall soon dissolve like snow,*
> *The sun forbear to shine,*
> *But God, who call'd me here below,*
> *Will be forever mine.'*

Then she paused, not looking round.
'Hello Matt.'
Could she have seen my reflection in the glass? I didn't believe so, yet she knew it was me.
'Hi! Umm-, Sorry I didn't mean to barge in. We haven't really met before. I wondered if you could spare me some time?'
She turned, her smile friendly, assured.
'You want me to talk about Christian,' it was a statement.

'Well, actually yes. I was hoping I might ask you a few questions.'

'I knew you would, - come.'

'Have I interrupted your singing? I mean I can come back later.'

'Not at all. I have to sing everyday to exercise my voice, sort of like an athlete in training. I mustn't do too much though or else it will be strained.'

'I think you have the most beautiful voice I have ever heard,' I blurted, then stopped in confusion.

Faith laughed and as I looked into her eyes I caught the fire so typical in Christian. As she held my gaze, I felt warmth spread through my body and an exhilaration I could not explain. As I looked away in consternation my sub conscious registered a warning. Suddenly I realised that Faith, too, was unfathomable. Who was she? What was she to Christian? And why is this dark cloud seemingly ever present on the periphery of my consciousness?

Faith motioned to the chairs by the fire, logs burning aromatically in the huge fireplace. As we sat, a servant entered with a tray on which were cups, coffee cafeteria and biscuits. I wondered about the timing.

I wasn't sure whether to engage in small talk before launching into a quiz about Christain's life. 'You know I'm putting together a record of events for Christian?'

'Not a record,' Faith said quietly. 'A gospel, Matt. A story of good news. It will be used by our disciples to teach and guide the people in the short time left to us.'

I was silent, digesting the import of Faith's words. She set out the cups and poured coffee.

'I'm out of my depth, Faith,' I said frankly. 'I don't understand what's happening, ever since, - well ever since,' I paused again, unable to put into words what I wanted to say.

'Ever since Jenny went on?' Faith said gently. 'You have been through a testing time Matt, with two years in the wilderness. You have not been found wanting. God is close to you, even now here in this room and he has been with you all along. The day is growing close.'

'What day, Faith?' my voice was rising with frustration; did everyone know my business, about Jenny; my despair? 'Can we start at the beginning? If I am to set down the overall 'raison d'etre' of Christian and his followers I need to know more about Christian. Who he is? Where he is from and what his aims are?'

'Christian is an emissary, Matt, here amongst us. It has been long foretold that one day the creator will call the human condition to account. That day is now.'

'That has been said many times, Faith, why now?'

'Look around you Matt, the clues are everywhere. The human condition is on a downward spiral again and...'

'Again?' I interrupted her. I had learned in my journalistic career that often, in order to collect all the sequences for an account I needed to interject, to bring a conversation back to a baseline that I could take off from or make a point that might otherwise be overlooked.

'Well, yes. Civilizations have been destroyed many times before by God in retribution, going back as far as the flood and before. The world is scarred by the remains of quite advanced civilizations, long disappeared without present day explanation.'

'Like the Egyptian, Babylonian, Mayan and others.'

'Yes. Many others. All fell into hedonistic ways, the soul was neglected.'

'And you believe we, today, are about to, uh - disappear?'

'Yes Matt. It's not a question of belief. It will happen whether or not one believes it.'

I was startled by her emphatic statement.

'Why?' I asked. 'Why now, what is triggering this?'

'To answer this Matt, you need to understand, - really understand, the whole concept of creation and the meaning of life. You see, mankind is repeatedly taking the wrong turn at an early age in its social evolution. We are not here merely for our own pleasure. We are a link into a greater, much greater, scheme. We develop and nurture the physical and intellect, yet totally ignore what God intended.'

'Which is what?'

'The divine soul. A fragment, tenuous, drifting throughout the void of the cosmos, collected into the human condition at birth, to be incubated and protected by the physical until mature enough to exist without form. In synergy, God himself.'

We were silent for a while, then I said.

'Can I go over that again? You are saying that God exists, - all powerful in the cosmos, without form and is the sum of all human spirit?'

'More than the sum, Matt. God is greater than this. God exits in part within us, a fragile astral embryo relying on our physical persona to house us. But remember, such fragments exit throughout the cosmos, - which teems with astral life. It is the synergy of all this which is the source of God power. It is this power which is truly awesome and which can tear worlds, even universes, apart. Equally God is a force for love and creativity.'

'So our human role is what, - exactly?'

'You must wait for Christian to explain this, Matt. I am not a teacher and although I follow God, I do not have the depth of knowledge to teach others, - save by example. I do know that there is another force, equal and opposite which is vying for our souls; this force is evil and destructive.'

'Whew! I hear what you are saying, - but getting my mind around it, well I don't know where to begin.'

She smiled, diffusing the deep thoughts by pouring coffee for us both.

I could now see that Christian postulated a divine soul that existed in every human, a metaphysical that required development every bit as much as the physical. The real person is not the body, which is just the vehicle, - but the 'I am' within. It is this that sorely needed development, but was overlooked in the pursuit of earthly gratification and intellectual attainment.

Faith was telling me that the second coming was now in progress. The thought sent a tingle up my spine, I had a million questions.

We talked, Faith and I, for the whole day, relaxed, in front of the fire.

As the day ended I thanked Faith for her time and company, but my next words evoked a startling response.

'Faith,' I said, 'It has been an illuminating day talking with you. I have learned a lot, - you really are an angel.'

At these words Faith looked at me sharply, her eyes blazed with a piercing energy and held mine for a second. Then she relaxed and smiled.

'Matt, you truly are amazing.'

CHAPTER TEN

Later that week, arriving at Apsley Manor I found Mary sitting at her place in the library with a visitor. They stood as I entered.

'Good morning, Matt,' Mary said smiling. 'This is Jeffery, he's at Apsley today and I wanted him to meet you.'

The man came forward amiably and we shook hands.

'Jeffery Bowman,' he said. 'I've heard so much about you, it's good to actually get to meet you.'

Jeffery looked a couple of years younger than me; dark hair cut short, he wore smart jeans, open necked shirt and a sports jacket.

'Jeffery is co-ordinator for the Hampshire and Dorset groups,' Mary explained.

'Ha! Jeffery,' I said, 'Good to meet you. You can explain all that to me, - if you've time.'

I indicated to a chair and we sat at one end of the huge table.

'Sure,' he said, 'Although Mary can fill you in on most of it. She has been an able researcher for the groups and knows her way around.'

Mary went to the sideboard where coffee had just been quietly delivered and brought back three mugs of coffee. I noted she knew how Jeffery liked his.

We chatted about generalities for a while. He told me he had started out as a lay preacher, and had spoken at a number of different faith meetings. Then he learned of Christain's teachings, went to see him and never looked back. Christain's message was bringing a consistency of teaching to a number of local faith groups.

'It was fantastic,' he said, 'Now we were teaching people about God in today's language. - I don't mean dumbing down at all, it's just that suddenly everyone is looking again at the bible and relating the message to today's world, and the word is spreading like wildfire. It has become relevant; reading the bible suddenly became fun, investigative; Groups discuss bible stories and how even today, over two thousand years on, they hold up.

We also found that by using the same dogma as scientists we could 'prove' the existence of God and creation. Our church meetings became exciting, overflowing and splitting off into second groups, it became exponential, two, then four, then eight.

The big thing is, Matt, the meetings became places of hope, community forces. Atheists have nothing to offer mankind. No one is under any illusion about the state of the broken society and the coming of the revelation. Christian has been instrumental in putting into place a teaching that is bringing in as many people as possible into God's fold before the retribution.'

Jeffery paused, enthusiasm emanating from every pore. Mary glanced from him to me. In my mind's eye I pictured the groundswell of renewed vigour around the world. I could see how evangelical fervour could harness the force for good and Jeffery's experience, even at local level, demonstrated this.

'I'm impressed Jeffery, I would like to come with you to a selection of meetings and get the feeling at ground level.'

'You're on,' Jeffery pulled a well thumbed diary from his brief case. 'Okay these are the next two weeks meetings within twenty miles of here.'

We picked out two venues and I noted them down, we fixed times.

Mary looked at me, her eyes shining behind the thick frames.

'Can I come with you, Matt?'

The weeks flew by as I worked hard at Apsley. My social life was now improving and, although I was becoming approachable, Jenny remained in my heart, and accompanied me everywhere.

I had in my mind now a clear picture of the way I needed to present the account of Christain's message to the world. There would only be a brief account of his early years, concentrating more his message of creation and the creator; the role and purpose of man and the imminent and final revelation of God. I had the connectivity I always sought. I had anyway a feeling that global instability in politics, social life and economics were sure clues; the story was compelling and urgent.

I wanted the account to motivate and to encourage people; to explain Christain's interpretation of the bible in today's scientific world; to warn of the reckoning to come.

Christian himself had vetoed accounts of his early life as being distractions from the word, and that the account should confine itself to his teachings. So it was that I made a very short reference to Christain's early days from a few snippets that were a matter of public record and some I collected when we first discussed the project.

Christian was orphaned at birth, found barely twenty four hours old, lying in the nave of Bath Abbey, wrapped in a shawl. From there he was hurried to Bath General Hospital maternity ward, checked over and cared for. There was no indication of his parentage nor his nationality. The police made perfunctory enquiries, but lost interest under pressure of work. It was left to Social Services to pick up the case and to foster out the new baby until, and if, the mother was located.

From what little I could glean from local archives it seemed that no clues were available to help the authorities. In those days, forensic science was non existent, or in its infancy. A county wide check was made on hospitals in case a distressed woman was admitted and could be linked to the baby, but days and weeks went by without progress.

The shawl that wrapped the baby was sent to Nottingham for detailed examination in an attempt to determine its origin. The experts could not find a match to any specific area or weavers, but more oddly, they could not identify the material it was made from. There was an animated discussion at the time and recorded in the archives about the source of the wool. After a while the whole thing died away. The experts decided it was wool of a rare breed from foreign parts.

Christian was fostered to a local couple, since deceased, and attended schools in Bath until his fifteenth birthday. He left school and there is no record of his youth until he turned up in Australia working in an orphanage. He was then twenty five. I was fortunate to discover a small clipping in the Bath & Wilts Chronicle & Herald which led to Australia, which recorded his Foster Parent's pride that their care home fees were taken care of by their foster son in Australia. There was no further information or lead.

CHAPTER ELEVEN

It was Saturday; I was to travel to London early on Sunday to attend the international rally being held at the Wembley Stadium. I took the opportunity to relax in the apartment. I called Mary, who was travelling with me. I sensed a warmth to me and excitement in her voice. I arranged to pick her up at her house then drive to Brockenhurst to catch the first train. It was going to be an early start; I just hoped there would be no delays or route diversions.

I called Kate and checked that all was well, - she knew I was going anyway, but the contact was comforting. Mandy demanded to speak to me and I spent a few minutes discussing the merits of having a dog, or a horse, or a dog and a horse.

Then, in the quiet of early evening I made my way to St Nicholas' Church for my never missed commune with Jenny.

'It is beautiful here,' I said to Philip. We were sitting on 'our' bench, - Jenny's and mine. The forest was having one of its wet, gloomy days. It was not raining but the trees dripped water drops onto the ground and mist hung over the village below. 'You can hear the silence,' I added, and meant what I said.

'You're right,' concurred Philip. We chatted for a while, then he took his leave and walked up the hill to the church. The silence and damp closed round me as I sat. The spirits did not wait long before I sensed their approach, with soft sighing and murmuring. My mind became abruptly alert! There was something different. The murmuring, usually soothing, comforting, seemed agitated. There was an anxiety in the sounds. I became uneasy. For so long now I had at first imagined, and now accepted the presence of souls that had dwelt in this place for over a thousand years. At first I was an intruder, but slowly grew at peace in this place. I tried to understand the atmosphere, and suddenly I knew I was being warned! Something was to happen, the spirits knew and they were concerned.

As soon as I connected with the thought the tension eased and the crowding spirits pulled back. I sat alone.

After a while I stood, and stretched the stiffness from my body. Before I walked up the hill I stopped where Jenny lay. I knelt on both knees, the wet soaking through my trousers, I lay my hand on the mound above her.

'I'm here, my darling,' I said. 'I love you so.'

A whisper of a sigh filled me, and there was peace.

On Sunday morning I called for Mary before dawn and got us to Brockenhurst station for the 07.31 to Waterloo. On the train we sat opposite each other and as we settled in I was able to look directly at her, seeing the excitement and the shining eyes behind her heavy framed glasses. She looked, and was, an intrinsically nice person. I was glad we were travelling together. Having promised to get a coffee on board the train, in exchange for a hurried departure from her house, I was annoyed to find that the buffet car was closed.

'How British,' I said in frustration. 'A ten car train, fairly full and we are locked in for over two hours without any refreshment!'

'We'll get one there,' said Mary, completely unfazed, and continued to glance at the scenery streaming by. I contented myself with watching Mary. My thoughts ranged over the catastrophic two years since Jenny died, how I had plumbed the depths of despair, lost my friends and self esteem until I hardly cared if I lived or died.

It was the Grace of God that had sustained me, I now realized.

I always had an inherent love of Christian values, a belief in the creator, consolidated during ten years of marriage to Jenny. Personally, I wasn't sure about the efficacy of the established church in instilling knowledge and belief, but Jenny had always been a regular church goer and I just fell into her routine after we met.

It was the grace of God, too, leading me to Christain's meeting and me now sitting here opposite Mary.

I suddenly realized that for the first time since Jenny left I was at peace and enjoying the company of this intelligent and attractive woman.

Mary looked back from the window, and caught me staring at her. She raised her eyebrows in query, I smiled and glanced away, embarrassed.

At Waterloo we transferred to the underground system and arrived at Wembley Park station at just after eleven o'clock. The rally started at two o'clock but as we made the ten minute walk to the stadium we were already merged in hundreds of people streaming to the venue. Mary linked her arm in mine; I didn't mind. Outside the stadium more people disgorged from National Express coaches arriving from over forty towns and cities across the country.

It was my first visit to the stadium, and I was awed by its size and design. The Triumph Arch dominated the distant view while close up and inside represented much more than a football stadium, more like a grand hotel concourse or large corporate foyer. There were people crowding everywhere agog and excited, clearly it was the first visit for most of them as well; an air of festival and good humour abounded.

As we approached the reception area Mary produced two large yellow encapsulated identity cards on a cord.

'Put this around your neck,' she instructed, 'It will get us to Christain's management suite without too much hassle,' she was right. There were ushers every metre or so, identified by a red identity card slung around the neck, red armband and carrying clipboards. Most also held walkie-talkie handsets; some glanced at our identity cards, others made a show of taking hold of them and giving a cursory glance, but in the main we were left to wander. Once inside we walked around for a while taking in the public areas and restaurants.

'Shall have a coffee before we find Christian?' I volunteered.

'Umm.'

I knew her well enough by now to know that this meant 'yes, okay'.

It was interesting just to sit and watch the crowds milling around, mostly in family or social groups. There was a wide racial representation, European, American, African, Asian, young and old, male and female, many with children and teenagers.

Eventually we moved on and found the huge conference room that Christian had taken as his dressing room and office. It was arranged with a number of large tables, each with six to twelve chairs. The noise level was high, full of people standing or sitting in groups. Many were Christain's aides, - the 'ushers'.

On one wall was a large media screen with a view of the arena; the stadium playing surface now covered and sporting a large raised platform towards one end. Technicians were testing the sound system. Around the stand a sea of people forming choirs and bands were tuning up. On the terraces an ant hill of activity as over eighty five thousand people were gathering, talking and settling into seats. The din was good natured with an air of pre-stage anticipation. There was just one hour before the first speaker was due to appear. I drank in the scene and wanted to join in the preparations on the stage, - first I ought to see Christian and check in.

He was standing near a table at the far end of the room surrounded by a number of people. I recognised Marc. Samuel was there, and Sybil. Several ushers were earnestly consulting their mill boards and wrist watches in turn.

Samuel was talking animatedly to Christian, who looked up while I was still half way cross the room. A thin smile of welcome crossed his otherwise sombre face as our eyes met. Unexpectedly, I felt a compassion for him; I was sure something was troubling him and as I approached I had the urge to embrace him and to infuse my own feeble strength into him.

I detected a softening in his eyes, as if he knew my feelings and the moment passed.

'Hello, Christian, I'm here,' I said unnecessarily. Then I looked at Samuel, Marc, and Sybil, greeting them in turn.

Samuel grinned at me, his round face shining with perspiration.

'Hello, Matt,' he said in his rich African tone, 'I'm about to go down to the stage to check on the preparations, - would you like to come along?'

I glanced at Christian and received an imperceptible nod. So Samuel and I, with an attached usher, made our way to one of the tunnels reserved for the performers. Mary was nowhere to be seen.

As we came out into the arena I was staggered by the effect. The stadium was breathtaking, now almost full with its complement of eighty five thousand people, a sea of colour and movement, - and the background noise from eighty five thousand voices animated and loudly chattering as they sought to be heard.

It seemed like a mile across the covered ground to the stage through sections of people now identified into choirs and groups. I was later told that twenty two different singing groups were assembled, each distinctive in club or choir regalia. I passed a group of young girls, - the 'Songs of Praise' choir of the year, all jumping up and down excitedly. They looked so happy and each one beautiful regardless of look. I imagined their parents were up in the stands looking down on them with pride.

The stage was approached by full width steps on each side. Near the foot of each side were bands; a brass band; an orchestral ensemble and near us, as we approached, an African gospel band. They recognised Samuel and greeted him with high fives and back slapping, huge grins splitting their happy faces.

On the stage, some five feet off the arena surface I got a full panoramic view of the whole event, as I turned, slowly taking in the panoramic view of the colour, the sea of faces, the noise, the anticipation; I was exulted .

Samuel was staying to prepare for his opening of proceedings in thirty minutes time. I took my leave to return to the 'management suite', as I put my arm around his shoulder I felt the heat and sweat of his body, the tension and anticipation of his role evident at close quarter.

Back in the conference room, the speakers had left to join Samuel on the platform. I could see them on the media screen, walking through the crowded arena to the stage and beginning to form up behind a lectern from which sprouted a number of microphones. In the press boxes, TV companies from around the world were making their final count down. Christian was due to appear after the first hour, he would stay on stage for one and a half hours; and then the finale.

As I joined Christian and John, Mary detached herself from a group of ushers and came to my side, handing me my notebook. Christian glanced from her to me, and to the notebook.

'Still at work?' he asked gently.

'Well, yes,' I replied. 'I can absorb most things as I go about, but occasionally I make a note to check on something later. I've just been to the podium with Samuel, the atmosphere is electric.'

Christian smiled, but I could see he was pre-occupied, almost withdrawn. I guessed it was something to do with building himself up for his entrance, so I spoke instead to Mary and we drifted off to another table to sit and watch the media screen. As we sat, we saw that everyone out in the stadium arena and the stands were assembled and the proceedings were starting.

A man I had seen with Samuel stepped to the front of the staging. The African band and choir opened with a full bodied refrain of the hymn: *'How Great thou art'*. The crowd settled, many singing the words. Then the man on the stage began to sing, his rich baritone voice filling the arena with sound, and was picked up by a score of TV cameras; the powerful picture and words, beamed around the world, fell on ears of rapt audiences in every country:

Lord my God! When I in awesome wonder
Consider all the works thy hand hath made,
I see the stars, I hear the mighty thunder,
Thy power throughout the universe displayed;

After the initial verse, the massed voices of over eighty five thousand souls took up the praise, acknowledging God the creator.

Then sings my soul, my Saviour God, to Thee,
How great Thou art, how great Thou art!
Then sings my soul, my Saviour God, to Thee,
How great Thou art, how great Thou art!

The power and glory of the words roared around the great arena, the huge sound absorbing into the senses. I watched the orange and black robed choir swaying side to side, commitment etched into faces glistening with sweat. I saw the speakers on the stage, with Samuel at the forefront waiting for the hymn to end when he would begin his address.

In the conference room the talking had subsided as we watched the proceeding get under way.

Suddenly there was a loud noise of raised voices at the door and a grim faced man strode into the room followed by about twenty people, including a number of agitated ushers, and some uniformed policemen; four men were in army uniform. The grim faced man was in charge, he stopped in the midst of everyone; the entourage behind him stopped and grouped around him.

'Who is in charge of this event?' his eyes swept the room, voice loud, imperative. He wore a grey suit, his steel grey hair brushed back. His body language told me he was used to being obeyed.

John moved from the table at which he, Christian and two others were standing.

'I am the organiser. Who are you? And what can we do for you?' he said pleasantly.

The man nodded and strode forward, entourage following. He stopped face to face with John.

'My name is John Hawker, Superintendant Metropolitan Police, - and you are?'

'John Waterman. What's this all about?'

'I'll be blunt, Mr Waterman. There has been a bomb threat received concerning this event. We are going to evacuate the arena and buildings - *now*! I want you to assist us in getting this done as quickly and as orderly as possible,' John Hawker spoke with authority, his head jutting forward.

There was a collective gasp and exclamation as a frisson of concern rippled around the room. Mary and I moved closer to the group.

Alarm had spread over John's face.

'You can't evacuate, - where did the information come from? I mean how do you know its not a hoax?'

John Hawker barked.

'Hoax or not Mr Waterman, a threat is a threat and we have a contingency for this. Now, please, just do as my men here instruct and all will be well. First We'll evacuate all non essential personnel from the concourses. There are uniformed police to direct evacuees. What we want you to do is to ensure the show goes on as we start to move people from the rear of the stands and work forward. This way we avoid panic.'

Christian spoke from behind John, his voice quiet but emphatic.

'Mr Hawker, of course there will be panic. There are eighty five thousand people in the stands. Some old, and many children. The word will spread like wild fire once you start to evacuate, and no measure of control will guarantee safety.'

Attention immediately moved from John to Christian. Irritation showed in John Hawker's eyes.

'And you are?'

'I am Christian Fellowes.'

Christain's name was clearly known to John Hawker, and as the two men faced each other there was subtle change of dominance. The Superintendent's voice more conciliatory.

'We have every reason to believe the threat is real, Mr Fellowes. It is necessary to act. I know this is a big event for you, but Health and Safety rules have to be obeyed, you cannot be responsible for the people's safety.'

'But I *am* responsible for the people's safety,' Christian said simply.

'Mr Fellowes, my role is to get everyone out of this building as smoothly as possible, so that experts can search for explosive devices. Now we either do this with your co-operation or I remove your team here and we manage without you.'

Christain's next words stunned us all.

'They do not need to search, Superintendant, I know exactly where the bombs are.'

'*What!* What the hell do you mean?' John Hawker practically exploded. The police with him became even more alert and closed in so that Christian was loosely boxed in.

'Explain yourself Mr Fellowes. What are you talking about, what do you know?'

All eyes were on Christian.

'Gentlemen,' he said calmly. 'There are three explosive devices in this stadium. One is in a carpenter's tool box under the central stage...' he held his hand up in a stop gesture as two of the entourage made to leave the room. 'Wait, - there are two more both in service trolleys under the stands north and east sides. They are designed to be remotely triggered by radio when I go on stage.'

The room erupted in confusion as everyone talked at once. I noticed that two of Christain's ushers had appeared and stood, barrel chested, at the door.

Christian continued, the talking suddenly hushed again to hear his words.

'The devices are safe, Superintendant, they will not detonate. I will address the people, there will be a finale, we will leave, the people will leave, and you can then get your army team to attend to the bombs.'

'Impossible!' Hawker snapped. 'There is no way that we can allow the event to continue in such a case, especially if you are right about the number and location of the devices. How do you know so much about them?' he added suspiciously.

'I became aware of them just thirty minutes ago, by then the stadium was full, I did not know the location or intention until a few moments ago. By then the opening addresses had been made. The sensible thing to do, is as I have suggested.'

'*Sensible!*' Hawker's voice rose in a derisive bark. 'Do you know what you are playing with here Mr Fellowes, - there are thousands of lives at stake here!'

For the first time a glimmer of humour appeared in Christain's eyes. He stood erect, calm. I could sense the power of another world in his demeanour. Hawker must have felt it too.

'I do, Mr Hawker, every soul in the world is at stake.'

Hawker paused, uncertain. Christian continued.

'There are over eighty thousand people trapped in this arena, Superintendant, if there is any move to evacuate there will be pandemonium. Any wrong move and the scene will be seen by a billion people around the world watching this event through the TV networks. Please consider my proposal.'

Hawker looked thoughtful.

'How did you know about the planting of the devices?' he asked, the atmosphere calming.

'The people at this event are in my care, they have my protection. I need to know.'

'That doesn't answer my question,' snapped Hawker regaining some composure. 'How do you know they are safe? Have you seen the devices, - touched them?'

'No, I have not seen them. I just know they are rendered safe - for now! I am going onto the stage, immediately above the bomb in just under one hours time. I shall be safe and therefore everyone will be safe.'

An anguished cry wrenched the air.

'*NO!* Christian, you can't!' I realised with horror that it was my own voice and every head turned to me. In confusion and embarrassment I continued. 'Christian, you can't risk your life.'

Christian looked me with compassion, and I detected a fleeting sense of love. I was devastated.

'Fear not, Matthew,' he said. 'My time is not yet, God's work remains to be done. I am safe my friend.'

I vaguely noticed that Mary had snuggled her hand into mine.

Everyone tried to speak at once. Superintendant held his hand up.

'*Silence!*' he shouted. 'Mr Fellowes, I and my team will confer, over in the corner there, and I will give you my final decision of what we are to do.'

Christian inclined his head and the people of authority moved off into the corner where they huddled together in conference.

Christain's people grouped closer to him, as if in protection. His face was sombre as we all watched the huge media screen with the muted sounds of the stadium.

Samuel had finished his address, I saw that Marc was about to go to the front, meanwhile the 'Choir of the year' were singing the new hymn currently sweeping the world, 'B*ring me home';* the words, poignant and powerful were lead by a soprano her words supported at first softly by the massed choirs, then their voices in crescendos seemed to rise and envelope the singer in a tide of emotion.

An usher increased the volume slightly. We could feel the mood in the stadium ratcheting up as eighty five thousand voices joined in the singing. The sound reverberated around the stadium, an avalanche of emotion, love and sincerity. I noticed Faith had unobtrusively moved onto the side of the stage, her rendition, in only thirty minutes, would herald the arrival of Christian. A cold fear welled within me

There was activity from Superintendant Hawker and his entourage, he crossed the room to Christian, voice raised over the media sound.

'I've some questions for you,' he said to Christian. 'What makes you believe the devices will not be detonated?'

Someone reduced the media volume.

Christain's voice remained calm, conversational.

'God has sent me, Mr Hawker, to proclaim his salvation. The work is not complete, therefore I am unassailable. I am safe, the people here are safe.'

I could see that Hawker had problems absorbing this simple conviction. I felt my face redden as I interjected.

'We are not suicidal, Superintendant. All the people here have everything to live for. What Mr Fellowes says is true, everyone on the stage will be comfortable with the decision, I too will be accompanying him.'

I don't know why I uttered the words! A few months ago, maybe yes, but the urge to die had lifted and I had no intention of putting myself in harms way. Was I so utterly captivated by Christian and his message? My brain, spinning along trying to cope with unfolding drama, registered the fact that Christian was manifesting a deep spiritual understanding that Jenny and I had embraced before she died.

Hawker looked uncomfortable.

'I too, am a practising Christian, Mr Fellowes,' he said. 'I am aware of your ministries around the world, your beliefs about creationism and I tend to go along with you, but I cannot allow any risk to the public.'

'It is not a belief, Superintendant, it's the fact, and there is infinitely more risk to the public by trying evacuate them in an emergency.'

Hawker turned to the army officer.

'Major Turner?' The officer, in working army uniform, had been following the conversation quietly. He spoke in a relaxed confident manner. 'I could agree with Mr Fellowes. If we start to poke about in this hornet's nest there could be a catastrophe. If the perps see us making moves to evacuate they could detonate by remote, - anything could happen.'

Hawker made his mind up.

'All right, Mr Fellowes, we'll soft pedal the threat until the stadium is clear. Meanwhile we'll secure the perimeter and prepare three disposal teams.'

'Any idea who or where the perps are?' asked Major Turner casually.

Christian nodded.

'They will wait for a mobile phone message that I am on the podium and then they will attempt to detonate the bombs simultaneously by remote radio from outside the complex. When it is unsuccessful they will flee the area.'

'Christ!' the officer said, then looked apologetic. 'Sorry, Sir, but you're pretty laid back about all this, seeing as you'll be on top of the bloody thing. You should join our mob.'

Christian smiled.

'Take the time to listen to the message, Major, your bombs are but a irritation in the global scheme of things to come,' he turned to leave to make his way through the tunnel to the arena, then paused. 'Oh, - one word, Major. Please ensure your disposal teams treat the devices as armed and active.'

Superintendant Hawker nearly had apoplexy

Christain's followers trouped after him towards the tunnel. Mary and I too. Mary seemed to have appointed herself as my P.A. and stayed close to me.

As we approached the back of the stage I felt tension in the air around me. Clearly many of the followers were also nervous of the outcome, and although I showed nonchalance, my heart rate increased as we stepped onto the stage. I thought of the large toolbox of high explosive under our very feet, primed and just waiting for the signal from a lunatic fundamentalist to blow us all to smithereens. My thoughts turned to Jenny and her image was suddenly very strong, in the background I fancied I could hear again the warning sighs of the spirits of St Nicholas.

Faith was at the front of the stage, her soprano voice soaring above the orchestral strings. She sang a hymn of indescribable beauty that I had not heard before. As the music and her voice stirred the soul a swell of 'amens' were wrenched from eighty thousand throats.

Then, to thunderous applause and rapture, Christian stepped forward. The shouting, the cries and applause reverberated around the great arena without let. He waited patiently, then held his arms out at chest high, palms open and waited a moment while the adulation subsided, he then waited some more in silence; the vast arena became silent, there was not a cough, not a movement; one would have heard a pin drop. Finally he lifted his head and spoke to the waiting audience and to the world wide TV cameras.

'God created the universe. He created the earth. He created man. How great is God that he is in eternity omnipresent? But you know this! For over two thousand years you have been told, you have read and learned. Some have experienced. Yet how little we have heeded God's instructions, - his entreaties.

Time and time again God has forgiven, letting us start again. From the flood, the rise and fall of civilisations, from war and famine he has redeemed us.

From the beginning when God created the earth and all on it, he slowly build an environment in which man could live and flourish. From small beginnings of just a handful of humans there are now five billion people inhabiting this world. This you know. How few of us ask 'Why'? - Why are we here? What does God want of us? We make little attempt to understand these questions.

I will tell you why mankind is on this planet and what God wants of you.'

Christian paused, his gaze slowly sweeping the vast sea of faces. Then he began to orate. For nearly two hours he spoke to an enraptured audience. His voice sometimes calm and reassuring, other times rising in anger and scorn.

All this time I stood, at first conscious only of the bomb below my feet, then as Christain's speech took hold, I was spellbound by the story he told. Every concept I had of creation and Godliness was extended in a vision unimaginable to the material mind. He spoke of God's purpose, God's instructions and how God's revelation was almost on us. There was not a sound from the massed audience as they drank in every word, every gesture. As the address progressed, the crowd's wonder turned to shame, then to fear and finally to a silent plea for help.

Finally, Christian closed his address. The crowd roared in applause, clapping and shouting amen.

Samuel stepped forward and summarised the day, repeating Christain's exhortation to the watching masses to learn about their God, to learn how to develop their spiritual side, to ask God for help and forgiveness and to prepare for the judgement day about to dawn. He called on the grace of God to descend on those watching and all mankind.

The choirs joined to sing closing hymns and the event was over.

People were unhurried in their exodus from the venue, they did not want to leave; chattering; still with awe and tinged with apprehension.

In quiet corners, the authorities waited with impatience for the word to go.

At the height of Christain's address, a short

distance away, in Engineer's way, four men in a blue cavalier car pulled out and headed north along Fulton Road, unknowingly passing through a police cordon. The observer, a trained officer of the anti terrorist group, Metropolitan Police, caught a view of the driver and front seat passenger. He called forward and a mile later two police cars pulled across the road in herring bone formation. The blue car had time to stop, but instead roared forward and slewed into the police cars with a thunderous crash of metal, bursting into flame. Within seconds, before the fire could take hold, security forces were dousing the flames with extinguishers. Armed police in full assault gear rushed forward to surround the car. An army land rover was rushing to the scene, siren blaring. Immediately the whole area was covered in uniformed police and security officers, shouting orders and clearing space around the vehicles.

Two officers wrestled with the smashed car and dragged out the four occupants. Two were obviously dead, the two rear passengers were alive, injured; they were pinned to the ground and quickly searched, as were the dead bodies. Two mobile phones were recovered.

'Sir!' shouted a police officer, who was routing about in the car. A plain clothes man ran over, clearly in charge. 'There is a mobile, - in the front well,' he stooped to carefully lift it out.

'*LEAVE IT!*' Roared a commanding voice. Major Turner ejected from a land rover at a run as the vehicle screeched to a halt.

'Right! Back away all of you. This is a bomb scene until I release it!' he ordered the man in plain clothes. 'Those mobiles,' he pointed to the phones recovered from the passengers. 'DON'T touch the keys. Just lay them in the well with the other phone and keep away,' he turned to two army men in combat gear who had followed from the land rover. 'Jones, - Partridge! One each side of the car.'

The two soldiers took up positions, their faces stern, eyes focussed and scanning the scene.

Major Turner beckoned an armed policeman forward.

'Nobody comes near this car, understood. *No one!* If they do, - shoot them! - Clear?' The tension in his voice eased, and he smiled at the men, then turned to the civilian, hand outstretched. 'David Turner, Ordnance. Sorry about the theatrics, but there could be a bomb on the end of those phones.'

The man took the proffered apology. 'Inspector Blake, Met. No problem, We'll look after this lot.'

Major Turner nodded to his men and the land rover took off in a hurry back to the stadium.

We had all returned to the management suite from where we were dispersing. John was staying on with a team of ushers to complete the administrative tasks and to thank the choirs, musicians and followers for their inputs. Christian was in close conversation with Samuel, Marc and Sybil.

Mary hooked up with me and we set off for the underground back to Waterloo. As we walked Mary and I talked about the days events. My own mind was still a whirl of emotions, Christain's address had released a roadblock in my head. I saw the story of Christian set in context of God the creator. Of man, and cosmic life forms, in synergy – God.

I always looked for connectivity in my writing. This is how I had attracted attention as a writer. Now I had in my mind the connectivity of the greatest story ever told. I needed to get back to Apsley, to put structure and body onto the ideas. I needed to do mammoth research into scriptures and writings of learned men. I needed help.

As Mary skipped along beside me, trying to keep up with my strides, I knew the answer lay right here. I stopped abruptly. She shot three steps ahead, and came back.

'Mary. I'm trying to get my head round all I've learned over the past months. Today has been the watershed, I know what to do! But I need help, there is a hell of a lot of research I need to do, I can't do it on my own.'

I looked earnestly into her eyes as they sparkled back at me behind her glasses. Then I knew! She had known all along, waiting patiently for me to ask. I continued somewhat lamely.

'Look, I know you do research, would you be prepared to work for me on this project, sort of personal assistant, - to do the research I mean,' I added hastily.

'Of course Matthew,' she said seriously then grinned, her face lighting up with excitement.

We were still discussing events as we reached Waterloo, Mary's mobile rang, her face paled as she listened.. 'He's here with me, I'll pass him over.'

'It's John,' she said, handing over the phone, her voice shocked.

'Hello John, what's up?' I asked.

'Matt, we've got big problems, Christian has been arrested!'

'What? You can't be serious?'

'Of course I am. He's been driven off to the Notting Hill police station.'

'Why? What's' happened?'

'It was that Superintendent Hawker. All I overheard was 'complicity in a terrorist act'. Can you get over here?'

'I'm on my way. We're at Waterloo, We'll get a taxi now,' I closed the phone and stared at Mary's shocked face.

'The police are saying that Christian is involved in the bomb scare,' I said. 'We're going to the police station now.'

John was pacing the floor when we arrived.

'They won't let me speak with him,' he said without preamble.

We asked various desk people for information without getting anywhere. Eventually Superintendent Hawker himself appeared.

'There's nothing to say tonight,' he said. 'Come back tomorrow morning and We'll see what can be said.'

'Are you saying that Mr Fellowes is being charged with something to do with the bomb?' I demanded belligerently.

'Questioned, Mr Patterson, not charged, just helping us with our enquiries.'

'You can't believe that he had anything to do with the bombs?'

'He knew they were there,' observed Hawker.

'Yes, but....'

'Yes but nothing Mr Patterson. We will speak tomorrow.'

'Does Mr Fellowes have a lawyer in there?'

'Does he need one?' Hawker smiled grimly and walked off.

John, Mary and me tried to come to terms with the turn of events. We agreed that we needed to stay in London until tomorrow. We would meet up at nine o'clock and work out what to do, get a lawyer and things.

John wanted to go off somewhere so Mary and I got a taxi to a reasonable hotel just off Bayswater. At reception I was disinterestedly informed that they had no single bedrooms available, only doubles or twin bedded. I glanced quickly at Mary and back to the desk clerk.

'Two twin bedded rooms, then,' I said. We collected the keys to adjoining rooms, then walked to the nearest drugstore still open at the time of night and bought basic toiletries.

Back at the hotel, we paused outside our doors.

'Coffee?' Mary asked, unlocking her door, avoiding my eyes.

I felt a bit uncomfortable.

'Thanks, okay. I'll just freshen up and check the room out. Give me five minutes.'

It was fifteen minutes before I called back at her door. She let me in, dressed in a towelling robe, courtesy of the room service. We sat on the edge of her bed, coffee in hand, going over the events of the day.

It was getting late as I took my leave, Mary stood to let me out, she was close. I felt her warmth, could smell her perfume, sense her vitality. She looked up at me to say goodnight. She still wore her glasses, her eyes searching mine. I was drowning, I ached, I was confused.

'Matt,' she said. 'Thank you for employing me,' and grinned.

It broke the moment, and I grinned too.

'Think nothing of it,' I said light-heartedly. 'Goodnight, and thanks for the coffee,' I gave her a hug and she snuggled into my chest.

'Good night, Matt, see you in the morning.'

The next day brought hours of futility as we tried to speak with Christian. The police were obdurate, and would not offer any opinion about the length of time that Christian would continue to 'help with enquiries'. John arranged for a solicitor and barrister from Lincolns Inn to be on hand to attend Notting Hill station if Christian needed representation.

The situation grew worse as the day wore on. Somehow the world's media had got news of

Christain's arrest and were now camped outside the police station. I could visualize the headlines with horror. *'Man of God held in terrorist plot'*.

The day's newspapers and media were already full of the Wembley car crash scenes. Fortunately, as yet, there was no mention of Christain's part in the events, or of the delay in evacuating the stadium. The event itself featured in pages of pictures, also the scene of the terrorist car on fire and police cars strewn across the road made front page viewing.

By the end of the day John agreed that Mary and I should return home and he would stay in London. He would call me back immediately if required. So Mary and I caught an early evening train back to Brockenhurst. As the train neared our destination and I watched the forest stream by I thought how far away everything seemed. The events of the past forty eight hours had pushed the peace and tranquillity of the New Forest to the back of my thoughts. Only now as we passed a small Hurd of deer grazing in the long enclosure did my mind reconnect with normal life.

We collected the car from the station car park and I ran Mary home. I got out of the car to say goodnight at her front gate.

'Well, goodnight Mary,' I said. 'Thanks for the support and everything. See you tomorrow at Aplsey?'

'Okay, Boss,' she grinned, and reached up and gave me a peck on the cheek. 'See you in the morning. 'Night Matt, and thank you too.'

With that she turned and let herself through the garden gate. I could see that her parents living room lights were on. She would probably be treated to a hot supper and bath.

It was different back at my apartment. I had left the heating off, it was cold and unwelcoming. There was precious little food in the fridge. In the end I made do with baked beans on stale bread toast, and black coffee.

I could not be bothered to wait for the water tank to heat up. I would bath in the morning. My thoughts, as I lay in bed were confused and jumped from scene to scene in an uncoordinated jumble.

I was up early the next morning and drove over to Kate and Mandy. Kate was still in her dressing gown, they were having breakfast. Mandy threw herself into my arms like a miniature missile.

'Hello Matt!' she squealed with excitement, hugging me tight. I grinned at Kate over her head.

'Pleased to see me then?' I said and bent to kiss the top of her head. I could see that Kate was pleased to see me as well and after a bleak night in the apartment it was good to be in a warm kitchen with family stuff around. I gave Mandy a cute stuffed bear I had bought in London. It had a Union Jack waistcoat on. It was the best I had time to do, but Mandy was ecstatic anyway.

Kate made me stay for coffee and we chatted for a short time while she multi tasked getting Mandy ready for school. Mandy was going by school bus today so I went down to the bus stop with her, and kissed her onto the bus. I felt good, it was a tonic waving to hordes of laughing faces staring back at me as the bus receded, my friend and miniature Jenny one of them.

I went back for the car and drove towards Apsley manor.

Mary was already in the library when I arrived. She greeted me with a smile and said she would get me a coffee. It was a comfortable atmosphere and I was relieved to quickly get to work.

I asked Mary to recount her viewpoint of the rally at Wembley. I was doing the same, it would good to collaborate our experiences.

All the while we waited for news of Christian from John. He called several times just to tell us that the authorities were non-communicative. The legal team had not been called. He also said that Christian could be held there for twenty eight days without any charge being made.

However, events were moving rapidly outside our control. The Newspapers and TV were building a graphic story of Christain's work over the last few years. They dredged up accounts of his lectures and addresses in a number of countries worldwide. Most were supportive, but one tabloid hinted of a global menace, stirring up religious fervour across cultural divides.

On the Friday afternoon a jaguar car swept into the gravel drive of Apsley Manor. As John was away there were few staff around and so I answered the door. Two men waited, both sharp suited, about mid thirties.

One was clearly the lead spokesman.

'Good afternoon,' he said, pleasantly enough. 'I'm Tom Chandler,' he indicated his colleague. 'Bob Tanner. Security Services. We have some questions,' he added - 'About Wembley.'

'I don't know what I can tell you,' I said guardedly.

'You are Mr Patterson, close confidant of Mr Fellowes and were with him at Wembley,' it was a statement.

'Well, yes. You assume I am Mr Patterson?'

'We know you are,' interjected the second man, - Tanner. 'We have your picture on file. Perhaps we could discuss this inside?'

I stood back and led them through the halls into the library. I could see the visitors taking in the grand furnishings and well appointed library. I wondered if they were doing a mental inventory.

Mary was still at the table, papers scattered, laptop open in front of her.

'This is Mary Richards, my personal assistant,' I said grandly.

'Ah! Yes, You were with Mr Fellowes also. Tom Chandler, - Bob Tanner,' Chandler said, indicating his colleague. He had the courtesy to offer his hand. I could see that Mary was guarded, she had clicked the laptop to screen saver and shuffled some papers together and turned them face down. I was impressed by her presence of mind.

'Mr Chandler and Mr Tanner are from the Secret Service,' I said to Mary.

Chandler smiled. 'We prefer to say Intelligence Service.'

'It wasn't very intelligent to lock up an innocent Christian figure of such high profile,' I said.

Chandler frowned. 'That's not very helpful, Mr Patterson. Mr Fellowes is not locked up, he is merely assisting us to get to the bottom of the situation wherein an explosive device was planted at his event, which,' he added, 'If exploded would have killed hundreds of people.'

'Including himself,' I observed drily.

Tanner spoke impatiently.

'The world is full of people prepared to blow themselves up in a cause!'

I bridled. 'Of all the suicide bombers in the last ten years, how many have been Christians?' I said, knowing the research I had already done and written about in an article three years ago.

'Let's get down to this weeks event,' Chandler said.

'None!' I said triumphantly, to make a point. Then we all sat. Tanner produced a pocket recorder and asked if we objected. Chandler took Mary and me through the event at Wembley, probing and questioning our role and experiences.

It was early evening before we drew to a close.

'What is Mr Fellowes's aim?' Asked Chandler.

'Aim? Well, to preach the word of God, so that everyone has the chance to learn of the truth.'

'The truth?' Tanner shrugged. 'I'm agnostic myself, so it's not necessarily the truth for me.'

'Mr Tanner,' I said, realising that my voice had taken on a power and presence that took our visitors aback. 'The truth is the truth. Whether you believe or not is irrelevant and is your prerogative. Nevertheless you are created by God and God will be your judge.'

Mary looked at me with a calculated expression. Tanner shrugged disdainfully, but I saw a moment of uncertainty and I pressed home the advantage.

'Look around you, Mr Tanner. The proof is there to see.'

'Rubbish. With respect, Sir, nothing is known which proves the existence of God.'

'I might refer you to Doctor Sagan: *Absence of evidence is not evidence of absence*!'

Chandler broke in.

'Alright, I understand the aim, Mr Patterson, but why should anyone want to bomb such an event?'

'Why should anyone want to bomb any event?'

There was a moments silence, then Chandler thanked Mary and me for our time and said they would 'get off now'. They were not able to tell us when Christian might be released, but it could be some time yet.

I saw them out and returned to the library. Mary was tidying up her things, she looked at me with admiration. 'You were inspirational, Matt,' she said.

CHAPTER TWELVE

We left Apsley in our separate cars. I had said I would not be in until Monday as I had a few domestic things to sort out. If we heard anything about Christian we would re-schedule. At home I mooched around the apartment, it seemed lonely and bare.

The next morning I went shopping for basic foods, then drove to St. Nicholas church. The Reverend Philip Rowlands was in the vestry, I called 'Hello', but remained in the Nave. I studied the notices, mooched around. Sat down, lost in thought. I got up and leafed through the handout pamphlets. I mooched around some more, studied the Saxon masonry wall. Pondered the font and wandered toward the chancel. Sat down again. Philip came and sat by me.

'Want to talk?' he asked gently.

'Uh?'

'You've wandered about here for over an hour, Matt. Something on your mind?'

'I don't know, Philip, life has been a

rollercoaster. I am really fired up about this work I am doing, but I am still unsure of myself. I miss Jenny so much.

'Sure you do. It's understandable.'

'No, not really. Most people would tell me to get a life and move on. Jenny has been gone for over two years now. Time is supposed to heal isn't it? I should be able to put things behind me and start again.'

Philip nodded. 'Time is a dimension both subjective and objective to us mortals. It is not a dimension of God.'

'Really?' I was suddenly alert. 'Why is it different for God?'

'Look at it simply, Matt. Time matters to us in the physical because it measures development, more importantly it separates physical things. I mean we cannot both exist in the same place at the same time. There would be an almighty crash wouldn't there? But in the astral sense time ceases to be a dimension.'

'You've lost me.'

'Alright. Take energy, - say radio waves, they can exist discretely at the same place at the same time. That's why your radio aerial can pick up any station, - it just needs to be tuned to the right frequency. Same with, say, mobile phones. Every mobile phone call in the world is present at your phone, but the tuning codes allow your phone to pick up only your call.'

'So, the physical world is serial, but non physical can be parallel?'

'Well, yes. That's one way of putting it. But even energy uses time. For example, light from the stars. It takes forever to get here, but it arrives and we can detect it. But this is no good to God. He is omnipresent throughout eternity and therefore time is not an acceptable concept. He can be equally here and squillions of light years away in a blink.'

'I hadn't really thought about it, but I see what you mean. - Spooky!'

Philip got up and disappeared into the vestry, returning a short time later with cups of coffee. We sat in silence for a while.

'Philip,' I ventured, 'You've met Mary Richards?'

'Yes, of course. A very attractive and intelligent woman.'

'She works for me now, - sort of research assistant,' I hesitated.

'I'm pleased, Matt. You need some help. Christian relies on you a lot you know and time is getting short.'

'Er, we get on very well and she seems to like what she's doing,' I stopped in some uncertainty, unsure of what I was trying to say.

Philip spoke gently.

'She's a nice girl, Matt, She knows what she is doing. You don't need to let go, but you can move on. It's not mutually exclusive.'

We sat in silence for a long time before I finally rose.

'Thank you Philip. I think its clear to me now.'

He rose too, put his arm round my shoulder.

'Carry on with your work, Matthew. It is vital to us all,' he took my cup and wandered off back to the vestry.

It puzzled me how many people seemed to be aware of my business and commitment to Christian. Even then in God's church, and charged with new energy, I shivered. In the periphery of my consciousness I had a foreboding of evil, watching, waiting. I shook off the feeling and walked down the church grounds. I spent a short time in the section devoted to the New Zealanders, taking in the neat and manicured enclosure. I wandered into the more unkempt graveyard, I stopped where Jenny lay and sat on the ground.

'I'm here, Jenny,' I said simply and sat for a long time. I sensed the soft sighs, the crowding spirits.

Eventually, as it was growing dusk, I pulled myself to my feet, muscles aching and cold. Damp from the ground had seeped through my trousers and pants, but there was an aura of peace and I was comforted.

On Sunday I stayed at home and tried to relax; caught up on reading the papers and generally mooched around.

Then things changed, suddenly events went into fast forward. I had called John in the morning; there was no news about a release date for Christian. At lunchtime the BBC World News reported that demonstrations in Westminster to protest about Christain's detention had swollen and was growing angry. There were several arrests; opposing groups of radicals had begun to assemble and were barracking the demonstrators; tempers were fraying and several fights had broken out. The TV showed crowds of people milling about in Westminster; a few close up shots of parents and children; generally noisy and laughing, but here and there more feral groups, angry faces, spoiling for a fight. One group had snatched placards from demonstrators and was smashing them up.

The news reported that other demonstrations were causing disruption in India and Africa. It was still early in the USA and so no reports of similar happenings were coming from the news wires there.

At tea time I received an email from Samuel in Lagos.

Matthew Patterson
From: 'Rev.Samuel <Samuel.JohnJohn@lagosdiocise.com
To: Matthew.Patterson@satnet.com
Subject: Urgent Meeting

Hello Matt,

I know you and John are doing all you can to get Christian released, but the news is bad; time is getting v.short. We need to discuss future security

arrangements for Christian. I have called an emergency meeting to discuss this and other matters. All disciples are arriving London tomorrow and Tuesday. I have fixed a meeting room at the Shereton Skyline Hotel, Heathrow.
I've copied John and Mary. See you there Wednesday at 11.00

Regards
Samuel.

I stared at the screen for a few minutes, then replied that I would be there. I called Mary.

'Matt! I was just going to call you,' she said. 'You've got the email from Samuel?'

'That's why I am calling. I'll be in Apsley at ten tomorrow, I can't make it any earlier, we need to discuss what's going on.'

'Of course, I'll be there,' she paused. 'Matt, what is happening? Are things bad?'

The foreboding I had felt in St. Nicholas crept up the back of my neck and I shivered.

'Yes, Mary they are bad, but not in the way you think. We'll talk in the morning, I need to sound out a few things with you.'

We spoke for a moment longer then hung up.

I drove round to Kate's. Ensconced in the kitchen I told Kate that I would be going to London on Wednesday and not sure if I would be back until later in the week. Mandy was listening, she had seemed secretly excited and now her face fell; she was close to tears. I glanced enquiringly at Kate who also looked put out.

'What? What's up Mands, what have I said?'

'Nothing. Its nothing,' she sniffed, this time a tear made its appearance and coursed down her cheek. She was making a grown up effort not to cry.

'Come on darling, you can tell me.'

I reached out to wrap her in my arms; she resisted for a moment as if to get away, then gave in and collapsed against my chest, now fully crying.

I held her close, stroking her hair; her hand was resting on my knee and I saw her thumb tucked into her palm and I hurt, I hurt so much I all but joined her in tears.

Mastering my emotions I coaxed her.

'Come on Mands, tell Matt what's wrong, eh?'

Her words were a bit muffled against my chest and came out between sobs.

'Sob, - There's a musical evening at school on Thursday, Sob, - and all the Daddies are going. I, Sob, - thought you might come with Mummy.'

I sat, pierced through the heart; I stared at Kate above Mandy's head, my look stricken.

Kate didn't look at me but I saw loneliness in her face. Suddenly I was angry and remorseful at the same time. This was not my child, not my wife, but now I could see that I had gradually become a surrogate male figure in their life.

I had used them. It was I that saw in Mandy an incarnation of my Jenny, and I had deliberately waylaid them, salving my own misery without real concern for their feelings. Anger was quickly replaced with shame, and in that shame I realised that that I did love Mandy, and did have feelings for Kate, but nothing had progressed to expression.

'Hey! Mands,' I whispered to the blonde head buried against my chest. 'I've got to be in London for a meeting on Wednesday, - what if I really try to get back on Thursday? - I mean *really* try.'

Mandy's now tear stained face looked up at me with hope.

'Really, Matt. You will try?'

'Yes, Mands, I will really try. But even if I can't get back in time You'll know I tried won't you? …'

Then I said it!

' … You know I do love you, don't you?'

Mandy's face was radiant. It was Kate that now looked tearful, biting her lower lip tremulously, her eyes met mine with an unfathomable expression.

Monday and Tuesday Mary and I worked flat out at Apsley preparing for the meeting on Wednesday. We were both using the internet to update information and using my old researcher experience we were able to produce a somewhat hurried report.

On Tuesday, just before Mary and I left for home, I answered a call, to be dumbstruck to hear Christain's voice.

'Christian!' I exclaimed. 'Where are you? Are you out of the police station?'

'Regrettably not, Matt. But John has been able to update me daily. I understand that I shall be cleared next week some time, meanwhile I will miss the meeting tomorrow; I am calling to ask you to chair it for me.'

The image of the eleven charismatic and powerful characters of the disciples ran though my mind; why would Christian choose me to organise them; why not Samuel, - affable, and liked by all. Christian sensed my hesitation.

'It has been agreed by us all Matthew. We hold you in great esteem, your service to God is not unnoticed.'

'Christian. I'm sorry, I did not mean to be rude, my hesitation was only to reflect on my worthiness to guide so exalted a team. Of course I am honoured to chair the group tomorrow.'

'Thank you, Matthew. Your record of the event will prove invaluable. Go in faith, I shall be beside you.'

I had decided to drive to London. After picking up Mary from her home we drove through Lyndhurst to join the M3, then taking the M25 and the M4 to London. The Heathrow area is easy to reach and we arrived at the hotel an hour before the meeting was scheduled to begin. We were to be in the London Room, Mary went off to check what arrangements had been made; meanwhile I was able to find the disciples in the public rooms and greet them individually. I also thanked them for their warm support and prompt responses to my many emails and calls I made since we had last all met.

At eleven o'clock we gathered in the London meeting room. I went self-consciously to the head of the table, while the others took the remaining chairs. Mary, uncertain, sat on a side chair near the door, notebook balanced on her lap. I caught her eye and indicated the space beside me.

'Mary, please sit here beside me. We will all appreciate your assistance in keeping a record,' I smiled.

As the delegates settled and their minds focussed on the business in hand I could feel the force of personality; the room became charged with tension. I was nervous and began to perspire. I wanted to stand to invoke the meeting, as I did so eleven pairs of eyes fixed on me. Their looks were friendly, some smiling encouragement, Samuel positively grinned, but behind the group bonhomie was a power not of this world; I sensed that these people together wielded more power than any government. As I started to speak, and wrought with nerves, I sensed sudden chill, then my nerves vanished and I returned the gaze of the delegates with a feeling of exultation; my voice steady and emphatic.

'Dear colleagues,' I began. 'Thank you extending your confidence in me to guide this meeting. I would first like us to review the situation concerning Christian's internment, and then I propose we each take the floor, so to speak, to report their own experiences and views, I will speak for the situation here in England, then we will have, say, an hours open discussion. I am suggesting twenty minutes each delegate, giving us a meeting length of about five and a half hours plus an hours break for lunch.' I glanced at Mary to confirm the lunch arrangements.

'I have arranged a light lunch to be ready at one o'clock,' she said.

So I started the meeting off by describing the event of Christain's arrest and the subsequent meeting between me and the officers Chandler and Tanner. I told them of the current position including the hope that Christian would be free in the next few days.

Then each disciple in turn spoke; I listened carefully, trying to make notes as the meeting progressed. The last speaker was Paul Yu; he lived in Beijing, from where his organisation preached to over 50 million Christians and over 400 million people overall.

An open debate followed Paul's contribution; it was late afternoon before a natural pause occurred, and the delegates turned to me enquiringly. Up until then I had enjoyed following the course of the presentations, now, as I looked at their expectant faces, I knew I had to call on every ounce of my skills to bind all their statements and experiences into a coherent summary. I had always excelled in taking normally disparate areas of information and connecting them into a coherent theme. Now, without preparation, I was standing before the most powerful group of people in the world to set out their collective views.

I began by noting a new hunger in man to learn the way of God; that science, far from destroying belief, was causing a re-evaluation among ordinary people. However, evil was again stalking our civilisation from all sides: The breakdown of society; the degradation showered on society by the media; Murder; rape and sodomy were every day normalities. Hurt and genocide was still common around the world.

I summarised our collective view that the churches of all faiths were failing to keep evil at bay, were failing to get the true message of God across to the populous.

I spoke of man's ignorance, which focussed entirely on mortal life; tinkering, to extend mortality by marginal amounts while missing entirely the research and development that would achieve the immortality that our creator promised.

Then I homed in on the findings of the disciples during their speech, connecting their experiences to a common thread across the globe.

I paused.

'My colleagues, with great respect to you all, I now have to admit being uneasy. Somewhere in all that we have done, all we have said, I detect uncertainty. We all agree that Armageddon is close upon us, - the last battle between good and evil before the day of judgement. But collectively, we still seek our role in these final days. I humbly set out before you my perceived views of all we have said today. This will then give us a blueprint to take away and act on.'

I then set out my understanding of the role of the disciples over the coming months. As I spoke I felt the comfort of Christain's presence at my shoulder and I concluded. 'Thank you Ladies and Gentlemen, I hope I have summarised our collective views satisfactorily.'

There was a silence. Then a quiet applause, Samuel stood up.

'Matthew, my dear friend, speaking for myself,' he paused and looked around at his colleagues, 'I am reminded again of the astonishing insight you have and ability to set out the connections between the astral and physical nature of God. Thank you,' he sat down to quiet murmurs of 'Hear. Hear'.

I stood again.

'I have omitted one topic in all this,' there was dead silence in the room, I continued.

'I have been reluctant to discuss this with anyone before. I sense that there is something unknown, but specific, waiting in the wings, a satanic presence. It worries me. I feel a malevolent gaze on us all, waiting, waiting. I cannot yet determine its place but I am sure it is responsible for the ills of the world. It seems to me that we should all be aware of it and to prepare for its manifestation.'

Heads nodded, I had touched a chord that clearly worried them also. It was a sober group that split up. While speaking, I had kept a surreptitious eye on Simon. As we broke up I caught his eye, and for a second I was chilled by his look, then he smiled and nodded pleasantly.

CHAPTER THIRTEEN

The next evening, promptly at 6p.m. I was at the school to attend the music evening. It was the first time I had entered a school for many years. I was surprised at the high security. A teacher at the door checked my identity and then ticked my name off on a list before allowing me in.

I was directed to a hall (gymnasium) which had a stage at the far end. The front part was decked out with folding chairs; in the rear half an excited hoard of children with smiling parents milled around waiting for the event to start.

Across the room I saw Mandy and Kate, Mandy stood holding her mother's hand looking pensively at other family groups; then she saw me and the joy in her face as she ran forward brought a lump to my throat.

'Matt!' she cried. 'You've come! You've come.'

'Hello, Mands,' I laughed scooping her up in my arms. 'I've made it, like I said I would.'

Kate mouthed 'Thank you'. from across the room. Mandy held onto my hand tightly as we joined her mother, but then moved away happily as I said hello to Kate. We chatted for a while.

Mandy returned accompanied by another girl about the same age.

'Matt, - this is Stephanie, she's in my class.'

'Hi, Stephanie,' I said. They giggled a bit, running off excitedly. A teacher appeared on stage, her voice amplified, asking us to take our places. The children were disappearing behind the stage curtain.

Eventually everyone found a chair and settled down. A teacher, (The Head Teacher I afterwards found out), made an appearance and introduced the evening. The curtain pulled back revealing most of the children, standing to face the audience in serried rows, were now disciplined and serious. A teacher sat at a piano at one side.

A young woman entered from the wings, bowed to the audience, held her arm out towards the gathered children.

'Ladies and Gentlemen, the Lymington Primary School choir.'

Proud parents applauded, then everyone settled down to the musical evening. I enjoyed watching the children perform; they were quite talented and sang with enthusiasm, faces shining with excitement and showing off to their parents. After the choir sang the conductor introduced Tony, about Mandy's age, who sang, his voice untrained yet confident and pure.

Then came a duet, both were girls, who gave a violin recital.

Then Mandy walked on stage! She looked excited, yet nervous. My heart went out to her, and I devoured her every move.

The teacher introduced her.

'This is Mandy, she is going to sing *'The wind beneath my wings'* for us. She says it is a special song, - for her Mum,' she stood aside as Mandy took centre stage to applause.

The notes of the piano played softly, Mandy waited carefully for the entry and then she sang, her voice immature yet melodic, inspirational, and I was spellbound.

It must have been cold there in my shadow,
to never have sunlight on your face.
You were content to let me shine, that's your way.
You always walked a step behind.

So I was the one with all the glory,
while you were the one with all the strength.
A beautiful face without a name for so long.
A beautiful smile to hide the pain.

As Mandy got into the song her voice gained in confidence, she sought out her mother's face and the words came from her heart:

Did you ever know that you're my hero,
and everything I would like to be?
I can fly higher than an eagle,
'cause you are the wind beneath my wings.

Did I ever tell you you're my hero?
You're everything, everything I wish I could be.
Oh, and I, I could fly higher than an eagle,
'cause you are the wind beneath my wings,
'cause you are the wind beneath my wings.

Oh, the wind beneath my wings.
You, you, you, you are the wind beneath my wings.
Fly, fly, fly away. You let me fly so high.

I couldn't believe it! I didn't know! Kate had never said that Mandy could sing. I sat motionless for the whole short rendition and at the end joined in the applause with tears in my eyes. I glanced at Kate and saw she, too, was moved, unashamedly weeping. I could think of nothing else for the rest of the performance and when the children all swarmed back into the hall I held Mandy tight.

'I had a lovely evening, Mands,' I said. 'And you were absolutely fantastic!'

Mandy was still excited and laughed a lot, I had not seen her so happy. We drove home; I picked up fish and chips on the way. Later in the evening, way past Mandy's bedtime, we were still chatting. She was sitting on the sofa close against me, now fighting tiredness.

'Matt,' she said, her voice drooping.

'Umm?'

'Do you believe in Angels?'

I, too, had been tired, now I came awake fast.

'I'm sure they are around,' I said cautiously.

'I believe in them,' she said. 'That lady, - when I was in hospital, - she was an angel.'

'I think you might be right, Mands.'

There was a contented silence and as Kate came in from clearing up in the kitchen I could see that Mandy was asleep.

Later, I still sat on the sofa, Kate had put Mandy to bed and she sat in the fireside arm chair opposite me. Over the past weeks I had noted the strain in her face, and loneliness, but tonight softened with pleasure over Mandy's star evening.

'Thank you Matt,' she said.

'Umm. Er, Kate, I don't want to poke my nose in things, but Mandy has a wonderful voice hasn't she?'

'Yes she has, I must admit.'

'Do you think it would be a good idea to get her some voice training?'

Kate grimaced. 'It would be wonderful for her, but I can't afford it Matt.'

'But I can,' I said earnestly. 'I would be really pleased to organise it.'

'Why, Matt?'

'Well, we're friends, aren't we!'

Kate looked uncertain, tiredness and loneliness etched on her face. I patted the sofa beside me.

'Come and sit here,' I said.

Kate came and sat beside me, I draped an arm over her shoulder and she pulled close and leant her head on my shoulder. I tickled the hair at the nape of her neck. We talked a little, growing tired.

'Kate,' I said drowsily. 'How about you helping us out at Apsley Manor. Things are moving fast and we need help.'

She stirred, coming awake a little.

'You mean help with the Christian movement that you're involved in?'

'Well, yes. There are dozens of 'congregations' meeting now just in our county areas alone. We run courses every month for teachers from across the country, some from abroad. We are really short of dedicated helpers. It would be properly paid of course.'

I paused. 'You could come along after Mandy is at school, - flexible hours and all that.'

'Okay,' she said simply, pleasure in her voice. 'I think I would like that.'

We subsided into silence; it grew late and I was bushed.

'Tired, Matt?'

'Umm. I'm trying to gather energy to drive home.'

Her voice was drowsy.

'Why don't you stay over?' She said.

It seemed a good idea, so I stayed.

CHAPTER FOURTEEN

Monday was very busy at Apsley Manor. Many of Christain's staff were back preparing for the world rally to be held early next year. I had called Jeffery Bowman over the weekend and told him that I had a full time assistant for him, - well, school hours, to help in the administration of the Hampshire and Dorset Followers meetings and could he call in on Monday morning. Mary had turned up early and was in the library, scouring the internet for something. Kate's car pulled into the gravel circuit at the front of the Manor. She had seen Mandy onto the school bus and now reported for duty. As I greeted her at the front door I could see she was both excited and apprehensive. I gave her a hug for confidence and ushered her into the library.

Mary looked up as we entered, she had met Kate on several occasions and now grinned delightedly.

'Hello, Kate,' she said. 'Welcome to Aplsey Manor.'

We were still chatting when Jeffery came in. I introduced him to Kate and noted with a smile the flash of interest in Jeffery's eyes. After a few moments of pleasantries I suggested that Jeffery take Kate off to show her around. He had an office in the far reaches of the Manor, next to the large hall that had been turned into a one hundred seat conference hall, with a stage set at the end.

I called John to find out the latest about Christian.

'Things are getting a bit tense here,' he said. 'There is a vigil At Westminster with numbers growing fast.'

'Yes, I saw it on the news this morning, looked like hundreds.'

'The police have said a thousand, with more arriving by the hour, they are trying to move everyone away, unlawful assembly and all that.'

'Rubbish! If they don't release Christian soon there will enough people there to bring London to a stand still. How is Christian anyway?'

'Quite well. In fact we are thinking that this is working in our favour. The Wembley thing has brought a lot of media attention; they are beginning to ask about our message and we are getting a lot of free publicity. I understand that Christian will be released later this week and then we have to concentrate on the big rally.'

'Okay. Oh! When you see Christian next tell him that I have just about completed my draft of the er, - gospel to date. Some of it has been scanned by Samuel, Marc and Peter. I would like to put it out to all the disciples if Christian agrees.'

There was a pause.

'Matt, when do you think it will be ready to publish?'

'Events to date?'

'Events and message.'

'Well, if I gave everyone say a month to comment, I would say about three months.'

John pressed me. 'July?'

'Well, yes, I guess so.'

'That will be an important date, Matt,' John said quietly and with that changed the subject, we discussed the forthcoming rally.

I spent the remainder of the day working at my laptop. Mary had a work ethic at which I could only marvel. She would work for hours at a time, silently, writing or deep into the internet. Sometimes she would be riffling through newspaper archives kept in the library, but would rarely open a conversation unless I invited it. She would quietly place documents for my attention in a serried rank just out of my right hand reach. When she did want to inform me about something a yellow 'post it' note would be placed discretely on my left hand side. I need never break my concentration and I found I could accomplish a satisfying amount of work.

I liked working with Mary; occasionally, when I paused, seeking inspiration, I would glance across the vast table at her three quarter profile concentrating on the work in hand; her eyes behind her bookish glasses would be taking in the information on screen, sometimes biting her bottom lip in thought, oblivious to her surroundings. I felt comfortable working near her and once or twice realised I was spending time watching her instead of getting on with my own work. I would watch her glance flick from screen to notebook, pause, write something, then pause again before returning to the screen.

Once, she glanced up and caught me staring at her. I smiled, looking away quickly, but not before I caught the quizzical tilt of her head, her eyes amused.

Later I got another call from John.

'Good news!' he said breathlessly. 'Christian has been released. They have provided a car to bring him here. He's on his way now!'

'Fantastic!' I exclaimed; suddenly the day took on renewed vitality and everyone walked with a spring in their step. I returned to my work with a sense of purpose.

Later, in the middle of the afternoon, news of the arrival of the unmarked police car quickly spread and most of the staff contrived to be at the front of the house to welcome Christian home.

Writing the account of Christain's movement, - 'The Gospel' as it had become known, - was more challenging than any work I had ever undertaken. I set myself a target date to hand over the draft to Christian for approval and although I sensed an increasing portent of a world changing event, he had never placed pressure on me to complete the work. However as the day approached I began to panic; had I interpreted Christain's requirements correctly? Was the record factual? Did it send out the right message? I had written hundreds of important reports in my journalistic career but never had it seemed so important to get the intricate story right. I constantly revised the text, something I was adverse to, believing that the original thought flowing onto paper, - or in this case, laptop, was the most powerful. I tried to maintain a taut text yet imbue the connectivity that was the hallmark of my work.

I would take the work home and spend long hours into the night going over the story, feeling the import of every word; I became tired and tetchy.

Mary had assembled separate files, one for each disciple: Andrew, America; Peter, Russia; Sybil, India; Marc, Germany; Simon, Pakistan; Paul, China; Philip, Australia; John, Israel; Yvonne, Brazil; Samuel, Nigeria. Each file bulged with supporting data acquired during over a year of effort. The gospel itself was at last in the format I wanted to achieve and told a story from Christain's early attendances at evangelical meetings to the worldwide ministry it now was.

The Christian Fellowes's movement now formed an international power house for the promulgation of the story of the creation and the glory of God.

Subjugating my own views I had to write an account that was pithy for modern day readers, but behind the great new message I needed to remain true to the views of the individual disciples while leading the reader to the pre-eminence of Christian's message.

On the Friday I laid the book on Christain's desk and was overcome with doubt about its adequacy.

On Monday I was at Apsley Manor early, the weekend had quietened my nerves, but I still felt apprehensive and as I straightened papers and looked at incoming emails I sensed an aura and I knew from experience that Christian was entering the room. I felt my throat tighten, involuntarily I swallowed and turned to greet him.

'My dear Matt, good morning,' he said. 'At last the assignment you so graciously took on is ready.'

'Good morning, Christian. Yes I believe it is complete, I have laid it on your desk.'

'Yes, I have studied it, but I regret it is *not* complete.'

My heart sank.

'But you have seen it only since Friday, there is a lot to read, - a week perhaps?'

'I am fully aware of the content, Matt,' Christian said. 'The draft is quintessentially the story and message I am charged to bring to mankind. But, - there is an omission, I do not see your own account!'

I was astounded.

'*My account?* - I wrote it as an account of the disciples and yourself Christian, ghosting the words for you all.'

'As well you have done. But you are part of us are you not?'

As Christian looked at me, I was aware of a warm friendship, almost tenderness. After a pause in which his eyes locked to mine he went on.'Matt, please add your own experience to the record. I do not need to see the final draft, you may then send it to the publishers for any proofing and printing.'

He crossed the floor to leave as Mary arrived. He paused and spoke to her for a short time and then returned to his suite of offices.

I told Mary of the exchange and with shining eyes she sat at her place waiting for instructions.

It took Mary and I a full two weeks to add a section for *'Matthew'* I made sure that the content was factual and although I kept the length to slightly less that allocated to the other disciples I did allow myself some conclusions more in the style and trade mark of my writings.

We had for months beforehand planned the publication and distribution of the gospel once it was approved. Now the plans went into fast forward drive and a number of Apsley staff were drafted in to prepare for the day of publication.

So it was, that after two more months of design work and proof reading, the first run was coming off the presses. Advance copies were sent to prearranged publicists, distributors, religious and political organisations and of course a large batch to each disciple. The book was to be made available on all outlets including online retailers.

It was not long before the reactions were flooding into Aplsey Manor. The disciples, who had been on board, and fully informed throughout the writing, were now overjoyed at the result. The book was greeted with rapture from most religious groups and strangely, there was only a muted response from the atheist and scientific recipients. Maybe their fire was to come?

Three months later, the book was a 'must read' by tens of millions throughout the world. It was to be used by many institutions as a text book for teaching purposes. Work was underway to urgently translate the text into over twenty languages.

It was October, the end of the first week brought a high state of excitement and speculation to Apsley Manor. John summoned everyone to the reception hall.

As we stood around waiting for everyone to gather I saw that staff who had been off for the day had also been called in and noted in some surprise that some thirty people were assembled. The air buzzed with questions, becoming stilled as Christian entered the room.

'My friends, I have asked you here at short notice because we shall have visitors here tomorrow, and it is very important that for the time being no word of the visitors gets out. I know you will continue to apply dedication to your work here and I thank you for that.' Christian paused, his charismatic body language holding everyone's attention.

'Tomorrow morning at eleven o'clock the Most Reverend and Right Honourable the Lord Archbishop of Canterbury, Ralph Worthing and party are attending a very private meeting here.'

There was an audible intake of breath from the assembly. Christian continued.

'We shall hold the meeting in the gallery room and take lunch in the blue room. If the weather is good we may take a stroll in the grounds,' his gaze swept every eye in the room.

'It would be a pity if word got to the media before the Archbishop wishes to announce it. Please do not relate any of this to anyone, even family or friends, not even as a secret.

Matthew I would like you to attend. – and Joan,' he added, addressing the head housekeeper, 'Would you spare me time now so that we can discuss the arrangements. Thank you everyone.'

Christian left the room and people dispersed to their work conversing in quiet astonishment.

I arrived early the next day but found I could not concentrate on my work. At last, at half past ten I walked the long corridors to the gallery room, so called because it was a very large and very light room whose walls were adorned with paintings, a number of which were masterworks of art. The furnishings were elegant and classical, the centre taken up with a conference table seating up to twenty people. There were large areas each end of the room free of furniture, except for antique chairs placed at intervals along the walls.

The scene that greeted me filled me with surprise. A number of Christain's disciples were gathered at the far end of the room. This was amazing, I had no idea that Christian had called in some of his acolytes from abroad at such short notice.

John was talking with Faith and Samuel. I had thought Samuel was back in Lagos! He was pleased to see me and greeted me with his customary wide grin.

I was also surprised to see Simon.

'I flew in from Pakistan on Wednesday,' he explained as we shook hands, 'Pleased to see you Matthew. This is going to be a defining day.'

I also greeted Yvonne the devastatingly attractive Brazilian. I greeted her with a chaste peck on both cheeks, the close encounter unsettling me. She noticed, and her eyes, as they stripped away my veneer of casualness, expressed amusement.

The big Russian, Peter, was also present.

There was activity at the door and Christian entered, escorting The Most Reverend and Right Honourable the Lord Archbishop of Canterbury, Ralph Worthing. He was accompanied by five other, clearly ecclesiastical suited gentlemen.

My head spun, - I recognised, too, The Most Reverend and Right Honourable the Lord Archbishop of York, Samson Oguntade.

Coffee and biscuits were brought in as introductions were being made.

'Matthew Patterson,' murmured Christian as he introduced Ralph Worthing to me.

The Archbishop studied me carefully as we shook hands.

'I've read your work, Matthew, which is, in part, responsible for this meeting.'

My heart lurched. Had I said something to offend?

Archbishop Samson Oguntade shook my hand enthusiastically.

'Well, Matthew. I'm pleased to meet you at last. I hope we can get to know each other more today.'

Four further members of the Archbishops party were introduced; Professor John Smith; The Right Reverend Tony Hollis; The Reverend John Foley; The Reverend Dr Ron Blakely.

Christian spoke amiably to the visitors, but it was clear that the force of his personality dominated the room, and there was some unease between the Archbishops and their acolytes. I am sure they felt the power of Christain's presence, a power that they could only dream of. I joined in the general conversation.

While John held the floor with generalities Christian drew me to one side.

'Matthew, I wonder if Mary should join us, she would be a help to you?'

I readily agreed and went to a phone in the corner of the room; Mary joined us a few moments later. We all stood around exchanging pleasantries, coffee cups in hand. Eventually we assembled at the table, there were thirteen of us. Unconsciously we took chairs on either side of the table so that the visitors were opposite us, Mary sat by my side, she was armed with notebook and pen.

Christian opened the meeting; he welcomed the visitors to Apsley Manor and noted that the meeting was assembled in response to a request from Lambeth Palace. He suggested that we take our lead in the discussion from the Archbishop and his team; he then deferred to Ralph Worthing.

The Archbishop cleared his throat, speaking carefully.

'Firstly thank you for accepting this, er, somewhat clandestine meeting. I, and my colleagues here, find ourselves in a very difficult and sensitive situation. It is my role as Primate of all England to nurture and lead the Anglican Christian faith in the 30 dioceses of England; Samson has metro political authority for another 14 dioceses in northern England.

Further, as leader of the global Anglican Communion one could say that I have responsibilities for the Anglican Christian faith of over 70 million souls worldwide.

But, - we must include, in whatever discussions follows here, the global Christian population. There are of course five other Christian ecclesiastical groupings; Over 1.1 billion people are of Catholic denomination; Protestants 376 million; Orthodox 220 million; Independent denominations make up for 427 million and a further marginal grouping account for some 35 million souls.

Ladies and Gentlemen, there are therefore over 2 billion souls in the world today who profess, in some measure, to following the Christian faith.

However, today, I am here solely as the leader

of 38 million of professing Christians in the UK,' he paused and added ruefully. 'That is not to say that anywhere near this number are church goers. I would like to hope that in due course I can present anything we achieve here today to the total of 70 million of Anglican Christians worldwide.'

The Archbishop fiddled with a notebook in front of him.

'What is taxing us, - the leadership that is, is the dwindling church population in this country, coupled with the rise of alternative strands of Christianity; and the emergence of other religions onto the global stage. For example, the Islamic religion with some 1.5 billion followers worldwide and is growing.

Of greater concern of course is the rise of the non believer.'

Ralph Worthing paused to allow his introduction to sink in. He seemed to hesitate, almost as if what he was about to say would seal his fate as a heretic.

'Mr Fellowes, What we have witnessed during the past two years is deeply troubling us. We have read the reports of your well publicised, er, lecture tours, indeed, some of our officers have attended such meetings to report back to us.

We noted, - with sadness I hasten to add, your incarceration, and the astonishing upsurge of worldwide support following that; finally the publication of the, er, ah, 'gospel' by Matthew Patterson here and the quite incredible response to it. In a nutshell this is the background to our dilemma.'

Ralph Worthing paused again. He poured a glass of water from a carafe close to him, and fiddled with his notebook again.

There was total silence in the room.

'My colleague, Archbishop Samson Oguntade,' he nodded to the Archbishop in recognition. 'Is continually urging me to be more receptive to the Christian philosophy of the return of Christ.

'What I am trying to say, Mr Fellowes, is that your activities and the publication of Matthew's work has opened our eyes. Perhaps we have been blind, perhaps we have been delinquent in our teachings, and, well, - I'll say it here and now; we wish to place a select team, in confidence, from the Anglican Communion with your organisation to explore any common ground that would benefit the members of Christendom.'

There were murmurs from the Apsley Manor party. Christian was impassive. Ralph Worthing drank more water, Samson and his colleagues, seeking reaction, glanced cautiously round the table. All looked to Christian, whose eyes glittered with unfathomable light; his voice, when he spoke, was commanding yet gentle.

'Archbishop Worthing, you are a courageous man, I salute you. Your decision today will prove to be a defining day in the kingdom of God. You have referred to Matthew's work. It is fitting that he take the floor next and set out the facts for us to build an agenda around.'

Christian looked across at my startled face, he smiled, and in an expression which perhaps only

I could see, conveyed warmth, appreciation, and yes, love. It was a fast ball; I was totally unprepared to field it. Looking down at my notebook I saw the two or three single words I had scribbled. I just didn't know where to start, or what I was expected to say.

I felt Christain's power emanating across the room, and discreetly, under the table, Mary squeezed my knee; it was a gesture of support; as I stood an eerie feeling washed over me and I had an uncanny sense of well being, of a power welling from within, and something else! Something that nearly turned my mind, but I clung on and stood as if clearing my mind; it was the perfume! I knew then. - I don't care how stupid it sounded, - *Jenny was in the room!*

'Thank you Christian,' I said, my voice clear; calm.

'Archbishop Worthing. With regard to my literary efforts, thank you for your kind words. I must say I am galvanised by the potential your own words have invoked in me. It is from Christian that I have learned; it is his strength that has sustained me; his wisdom counselled me; I see clearly now.'

I drew a breath, rubbed my finger tips on my chin and addressed the visitors. I spoke for over an hour. I took as a starting point the huge following for Christian and his doctrine; add in the vast worldwide established Christian church and organisation, and we have an awesome hunger for God's Grace.

I assured the visitors that we all worshipped the same God; indeed all the major religions worshipped the same God. They may not accept the statement, but as there is only one creator, ergo, in their own way the major religions took a different view of the same God.

There could be said to be a failing of the Christian church in that it promulgated its message using an archaic, biblical setting of a very small known world at the time of Christ, and carrying it, without modification, into the twenty first century. Ordinary people struggled to identify their life, their everyday problems, their aspirations, with a message that was prescribed in a geographically limited area of the biblical lands at the time of Jesus; the eastern Mediterranean lands

That said, nothing has changed in the message itself.

The first need was to acknowledge the one creator of all heaven and earth; to accept the fact that man was created by God, in his image. That is, the astral image, not the physical image.

The second need was to acknowledge that man was on a journey, not just a physical birth to mortal death, but that his soul was destined for immortality to exist for eternity; this immortality would be gained through the Grace of God

The third need was to acknowledge that man, in turning away from God had taken his eye off the ball; now without compass, he was on a path of moral and social destruction. In devoting science and physics to material gratification he had all but ignored the 'raison detre' of mankind, - which is, to develop the psyche until it was ready to exist outside the physical.

The fourth and last need was to acknowledge that, in return for free will, God demanded a reckoning; that day was fast approaching.

I turned to Ralph Worthing.

'Archbishop, you spoke of the need for vigilance, and you are correct. The return of Christ is prophesied in hundreds of passages throughout the Scriptures, in various faiths, taught and explained in the most vivid and varied of ways around the world; the return of Jesus Christ to this earth will be one of the most breathtaking and glorious events ever to be experienced by man. Its awesome significance to believer and unbeliever alike completely dwarfs all other considerations put together. - Why? Because, at long last, after millennia, God will show his hand. We do not know what will happen or when, only God will decide, but the forces of evil will make one last catastrophic bid for the planet.'

I paused. My next words were dramatic, I stunned myself, - they were uttered without plan and which brought gasps from the assembled delegates.

'Gentlemen, in my deepest thoughts, I believe that Jesus Christ has already arrived on our earth! The era of the second coming has started.'

From the corner of my eye I glanced fleetingly at Christian, his face was inscrutable.

I went on.

'Finally, Sir, I would suggest that if the church preached the unchanged message with today's science and language the churches would be packed with people seeking God's Grace.'

I stopped, aware that I had spoken for well over an hour, I had exerted every ounce of skill and understanding I had to tell a coherent account.

I sat; there was silence which went for a long time; I could sense those present turning over my address in their minds, conjuring up the vision.

Eventually, as Christian waited, calm, silent, Ralph Worthing coughed slightly.

'Matthew. I am humble before you. Your insight to the theological structure of God's purpose has left us confounded. We see now that our visit here has been divinely guided.'

I felt sure I reddened, I looked to Christian for help. He smiled and with some observations suggested that the meeting be reconvened after lunch.

The afternoon progressed with an open debate, in which all the visitors engaged. I could see that they were enthusiastic about further collaboration. In a summing up, Christian and the Archbishop agreed to arrange a cadre session at Apsley for a selected group of clergy. The Archbishop would assess the outcome as an input to the long committee processes he would have to endure to get any change to traditional doctrine.

The Archbishop made a final statement. (By now we were on Christian and Ralph terms).

'Christian. It will take a long time to bring into

the Anglican Church a formal collaboration, if indeed the synod would even discuss it, or even use any aspects of Matt's work, but, if I may, I have a proposal: We do sanction, from time to time, er, invitations from clergy to other faiths to visit our services in order to engender understanding and tolerance between faiths. Would you accept such invitations under the guise of 'inter faith' invitations, - to seize the moment, so to speak?'

'My dear Ralph,' Christian said with quiet warmth. 'It would be an honour for me or any of my followers to attend God's gatherings under any circumstances. Please send as many invitations as you are able to arrange, we will respond positively.'

The meeting broke up in friendly chatter, the air charged with energy and excitement.

CHAPTER FIFTEEN

Over the weekend Paul Kneale called. While writing for Christian, my professional articles had taken a back seat. Now the 'gospel' was finished I had told Paul I would be producing more papers for publication. 'You write 'em, I'll sell 'em,' he had said. He rang to tell me that a couple of quack scientists were 'Banging on' about creating artificial life. What did I know about the subject?

'Only that it's impossible,' I said drily.

'Come on, Matt. These guys are serious beards.'

I knew Paul was winding me up.

'They may be able to produce something, but it will be more mutated than artificial,' I said.

'So you *do* know something about it?'

'More a view on the morality than the science I 'Spose. I never could understand the need to create monsters when there is no shortage of the genuine article.'

'Good. I'll hear from you then?' I could almost hear him chuckling as he said goodbye and rang off.'

I thought about the subject as I drove into Apsley on Monday morning. The Manor was alive with activity. Christian and John, I know, were preparing for the world rally.

An acolyte of Christain's, Roderick Pearce, 'Roddy' was in charge of the lecture programme in the Manor lecture hall. Every month about fifty practicing Christians from different nationalities, denominations and independents arrived for two days of presentations and discussion. They would then return to their own diocese around the world to further the message of God's salvation as taught by Christain's followers.

The library was, however, kept off limits to most, so that I could work, in the main, uninterrupted. Mary, working at her laptop, looked up as I entered. We chatted for a short time about the weekend. I told her about Paul's call and asked her to research the current thinking on the subject.

We worked the whole day; I put together my view of the subject of artificial life and wanted to test it against any 'evidence' that Mary was able to uncover.

The week was going by too quickly. On Thursday I had completed a satisfactory draft and got Mary to read it.

The basic premise was that truly artificial life was not possible; Scientists were close to being able to take already living elements, even down to genome level, and mutate them to achieve a quasi form of life. In any case what did we mean by

'Life'? Did we mean something that merely existed, or could perhaps move of its own volition; divide perhaps, or did we mean something that could evolve into a 'thinking' organism; man even?

In all cases scientist were playing the devil's game for him; it is one thing to research in order to heal or maintain health; quite another to tinker with the mechanism of life itself. The spectre of unleashing an uncontrollable outcome was the stuff of films.

I linked the so called artificial life creation to the research into producing artificial life in a woman without a biological father. Technically feasible to produce foetuses from cells other than eggs and sperm, it was nevertheless abhorrent and totally unnecessary. Little thought is given to the poor creature, who would grow up in the knowledge that it not only had an unknown father, but no father at all! What sort of world would it be when a critical number of such monsters existed?

I set out the reasoning behind my contention that creating life other than by mutation was impossible. Man cannot take a non living (mineral) material and create life; He may be able to take components from living organisms, (animal or vegetable) and create quasi life. A bit like building a working car from other scrap vehicles.

Mary took her time to read and ponder the article. In the end she looked up, her eyes slightly haunted.

'Matt,' she said quietly, 'I begin to see the point when God will call 'time'.'

I lightened the subject, and we talked about going with Christian to the world rally. Sitting there, in the warmth of the library, I realised how much I enjoyed Mary's company. I enjoyed watching the changing moods in her eyes, expressive behind the heavy rimmed glasses.

'Mary,' I said on impulse, 'What are you doing on Sunday?'

'Er, nothing special,' she said.

'How about coming to church with me in the morning and then We'll go on for lunch?'

She looked surprised, then smiled in pleasure.

'Yes, I'd love to,' she said.

Apart from business trips to London and my fascination with Mandy and her mother I had let no one into my life for over three years, since, well, - since Jenny. I was as surprised as Mary and suddenly worried how it would work out, I had forgotten how to relax and socialise.

Mary and I worked at Apsley all day Friday; we collaborated on a couple of reports as if everything was normal, but I hid an amount of suppressed anticipation and worry.

I sent the paper on artificial life to Paul; did some parallel work on the search for consciousness, controlling the mental and physical man.

By five o'clock Mary and I were ready to leave. I suggested that I pick her up at her house at ten thirty on Sunday. She happily agreed.

On Saturday I tried to get interested in cleaning the apartment. I must say it did look better after an hour or so of work. I went to the superstore, without a list and only a general idea of what I needed. Most times I shopped by impulse. I didn't see Kate or Mandy.

On Sunday morning I picked Mary up at her house on time. She looked, well, different, - even in a simple two piece she looked more glamorous. Her hair was groomed into a high pony tail; She still wore the bookish glasses of course, which seemed to accentuate her appeal. I realised that she had ditched the long coat and university scarf.

I, too, had made an effort; I wore fairly good mustard cord trousers and a navy blue sports jacket. I agonised for a long time about tie or no tie, in the end I decided I looked better with a tie. So I wore one.

We drove to Brockenhurst and St Nicholas church. I had difficulty in trying to park the car in the small, already crowded, parking area. It was nearly a capacity congregation, - most of whom I knew quite well. Philip welcomed us at the door, his face smiling, un-remarking.

'Good morning Philip,' I said, 'Can I introduce you, - Mary, - Philip. Mary works with me,' I added, defensively.

Hello, Mary, you are most welcome.'

Philip took Mary's hand in his hands. 'We've met before. I hope you enjoy our service.'

As we found seats in the nave I was greeted with smiles and some salutations. For three years I had attended this church alone, and today I had company.

After the service and the short chats at the

doorway I suggested to Mary that we stroll through the church yard. We walked gently in the sunshine, through the narrow gate into the graveyard that stretched through the trees and down the hill towards the village. I pointed out the war cemetery of New Zealanders, and the tombstone of the local snake catcher. We meandered slowly on, until I stopped by Jenny's grave.

'Here is Jenny,' I said softly, matter of factly.

Mary was silent, head slightly bowed, looking at the mound and the headstone which read:

'Here lies Jenny Patterson. Much loved wife of Matthew'

The dates were inscribed underneath. We moved on, and further down sat on Jenny's and my bench, looking at the view. After a while Mary got up and walked slowly to and fro looking at the tombstones, she wandered back up the hill into the immaculate war cemetery enclosure. She studied inscriptions and then slowly returned. I glanced round and saw that she had stopped by Jenny's grave, and sitting on her haunches had placed her hand on the mound as I so often did.

I turned back, not wanting to intrude. There was no wind, the sun shone weakly; the aura enveloped us peacefully.

After some time Mary appeared back at my side, I smiled and stood up,

'Lunch?' I asked.

CHAPTER SIXTEEN

A fax, on formal Lambeth Palace letter heading, was received at Apsley Manor. On six pages, it referred to the ecumenical meeting between the Archbishop and Christian, and listed an initial twenty churches spread across the country that would welcome a visit from Christain's followers as 'other faith guest speakers'.

Christian called John and me into his study to discuss the invitation. We examined copies of the fax. It named the clergy, giving their contact details and suggesting a specific Sunday three weeks hence. A reply was appreciated.

It would be easy to produce twenty experienced speakers from various locations around the country.

John agreed to reply to the Archbishop in the affirmative. He would match up geographically placed speakers and ask them to contact the relevant clergy and to make arrangements directly.

'We three must be a part of this initiative,' Christian said thoughtfully, he seemed distant, his face heavy and brooding. Suddenly I was uneasy, Christain's mood had a habit of transmitting itself to me and I had a sense of foreboding. The atmosphere in the room had changed, I had an eerie feeling of a malevolence in the corners of the room and I shivered.

I rose from the table and walked around, rubbing my arms, feigning thoughtfulness about the invitation. John ignored me, busy writing possible names on the fax, but Christian noticed my behaviour, his eyes thoughtful as he regarded me.

John suggested that Christian would be most effective going to London. He would go to Birmingham and would I go to Norwich. We all agreed; the remaining seventeen locations John would allocate to experienced followers.

John tapped his teeth with his pen.

'Would it be a good idea if we all gave the same sermon?'

Christian nodded.

'Yes, it would. - Matt you are our narrator, would you produce some notes on a topic, tomorrow, and get them to John to send to all of us?'

I was taken aback. *Me?* - To give Christian and other major lights in the movement a subject to sermonise on? I looked at Christian as if to divine what subject he would have in mind, but he returned my enquiry with a steady gaze.

'Er, of course I will,' I said. I didn't ask about the subject, I knew Christian didn't expect me to.

As we were about to break off I held up my hand.

'Uh, John. I suppose the clergy will put out advance notices about the guest speakers?' I asked rhetorically and went on. 'I think you should ask the clergy to be sure to lay on a public address system at each venue, er, - in case there is an overflow.'

John nodded and noted it, Christian smiled.

The sermon was to be called *'Man in God's image'*.

Mary and I had spent the next day drawing up a page of headings for the speakers and in the following two weeks I thought long and hard about my task.

Mary was to come with me; I suggested we drive up to Norwich; she arranged an hotel for the night. The days passed in a whirl of activity at Apsley until the day of the visit came. We left Brockenhurst very early in the morning and arrived at our venue an hour before the service was due to start.

Finally the service began, and at the appropriate point I stood in the pulpit looking at the massed congregation stretching away from me; my initial nerves fell away as a power and lucidity coursed through my mind.

As I had anticipated, the notices had gone out publicising the sermon and had resulted in a packed church with hundreds more gathered outside to hear the service over the public address system.

The Reverend Thomas addressed his congregation.

'Today we are pleased to welcome Matthew Patterson. I'm sure most of you will know him for his work *'The Gospel of Revelation'* and much more. Today Matthew is going to tell us about the Christian Fellowes's view of God and creation. God has room for all those who believe and I am sure that we shall benefit from other views.'

Mary was in the front row; she seemed a long way down, but I felt encouragement radiating from her face as she looked up at me.

I resisted the urge to tap the microphone, instead I spoke directly to the assembly and was reassured by the amplified words filling the vaulted church.

'Thank you,' I said. 'I am heartened that so many have turned out to attend this wonderful church today. To those of you outside, - please know that I am aware of you; you are part of my audience as if you were here in front of me.

The Reverend Thomas has introduced my talk to you as *'Man in God's image'*.'

I paused.

'Yes, God made man in his own image. In Genesis 1:27 the Bible says: '*So God created man in his own image, in the image of God he created him; male and female he created them.*'

So, if we are in God's image, what does it mean to us? And why? These are questions older than the hills, - its all quite confusing really and is made difficult because the explanations are not really forthcoming from the teachers, or perhaps because the words are archaic, told to us here in biblical language, designed for a biblical era and a geographically limited biblical land.

But bringing the language up to date is not enough, indeed could make the word of God more incomprehensible, not less.

The result is that we have left the field open to scientists to denounce the word of God and replace it with a view based solely on the observation of physical phenomenon.

As for atheists, they do not seek the essence of the human spirit at all.

If you listen to lectures by Christian Fellowes you would understand how creation and evolution are not mutually exclusive. So what can we believe in? What is true and what is fiction?

In the short time I have been given today let me set out some pegs in the ground; this is what you should be learning about in a scientific way; be aware of our modern knowledge, yet not misdirected by the conclusions of the atheists in our midst.

There is only one God, - the creator of all heaven and earth, ergo, in our own way we all worship *THE* God. Each faith is looking from a different vantage point. We must take the premise that our earth is not a happy accident, appearing as it does, an insignificant planet in the firmament of stars and galaxies.

Our vantage point is through Jesus Christ, others through different perspectives.

God created man, Yes he did! - and woman, of course,' I added. There was a murmur of amusement from the attentive crowd.

'Man did not accidentally evolve out of the primeval mud as atheists would have us believe.

But, yes of course life has evolved, and is evolving even today; Christian Fellowes tells us that life was well evolved hundreds of millions of years before the spirit of God was conceived into man, by God himself into a prepared environment! God had prepared the ground, so to speak, so that mankind could receive the precious eternal life, and would there incubate until capable of astral existence.'

I paused, as if daring any voice of dissent; there was only attentive silence.

I moved on, to put other pegs in the ground of faith in God. Man was in the image of God referring to the spiritual image not the physical image; that God was not a photo fit picture of any specific race on earth, but that each of all races were spiritually an infinitesimal component of God himself.

I touched on Good and evil; I told of God's hurt and anger when his munificence was mired in crass behaviour, in evil acts that defiled life and obscured the grace of God.

I touched on the 'Why' and purpose of life; that God was a cosmic energy and power that needed the human soul to mature in order to recharge the God force. God was the synergetic sum of all life, not just here on earth, but throughout the infinite universes of heaven.

I spoke with passion of the coming salvation when God would call his children home to immortal life; the atheists condemned to mortal oblivion; the evildoers vanquished to purgatory.

In the closing moments I said that what I had touched on throughout my talk were the facts, and I beseeched all to take time to learn more about the proof of what I said.

'The clues are all around you. There is sound evidence of God and his work, even if obscured by misdirection of the unGodly. I wish you the strength of God in your endeavours.'

I stepped down from the pulpit to quiet murmurings. I glanced at Mary and was sure her eyes glistened. I had prearranged that the closing hymn would be '*Bring me Home*', the new hymn now on charts around the world. I was not surprised that the congregation knew it well, its aching refrain still stirred my soul. At the end of the service I stood at the Church door with the Vicar, besieged by those outside and hassled by the people trying to exit; all thanking me for my contribution.

CHAPTER SEVENTEEN

Mary had taken a call on her mobile phone. I was still shaking hands with whole families who had come to the service, some from far afield. I saw Mary's stricken face over the heads of the nearest well wishers. She beckoned me urgently; I uttered 'thank you' and 'excuse me' to the couple I was talking to and disengaged as politely as possible, hurrying over to her.

'Christain's been attacked!' she cried, distraught.

An iron band wrapped itself around my heart.

'Oh my God!' I whispered. 'What's happened? How is he?'

'He's been rushed to hospital. He was outside the church talking, - like us, when he was attacked by two men. That's all I know. John is at the hospital now.'

'We'll have to get there, now!' I said urgently. 'Come on.'

I quickly returned to our host vicar, still talking to people thronging the churchyard.

'Reverend Thomas, I'm sorry to break in.

Christian Fellowes has been in an accident, he's been taken to hospital. We have to leave you immediately and get to London.'

Goodbyes were quickly said, Mary and me making our way with difficulty through the crowd to the car park. The word of Christain's attack had been overheard, a swell of shock and anger and spreading like wild fire through the crowd. By the time we got to the car word was already there and paths were cleared for us to make a hurried departure; as we cleared the crowd we waved in thanks and I settled down for a fast drive to London.

It took a long time to get onto the southbound carriageway of the M1, then I stayed on the outside lane all the way into London, half expecting a police car to appear behind us at any time.

As we pulled into the hospital car park I was astonished to see large crowds gathered at the hospital entrance and spilling onto the car park. I found somewhere to leave the car on the edge of the crowd and we struggled through the throng to the hospital entrance. By now I had been on the go for twelve hours, adrenaline fuelled my body and overwhelmed tiredness.

Four policemen were at the entrance preventing admission to any not on legitimate business, the waiting crowd was held back behind an imaginary line. The mood was calm, sombre. Such was my growing celebrity status that several in the crowd recognised me and shouted messages of encouragement. Fortunately one of the policemen recognised me too; Mary and I were allowed into reception.

We had had called John on Mary's mobile, he was in reception waiting.

'Thank God you are here,' he said, his haggard grey face revealing the desperate situation. His right arm was bandaged. 'He is in surgery now. We have to wait. There's nothing we can do.'

I could see he was in shock and I placed my arm round his shoulder, drawing him to a quiet corner.

'It's alright, John,' I said gently, 'I know you have done all you can,' I indicated his arm. How did that happen? Now, have you eaten, or even had a drink?'

He shook his head, near to tears, overcome with relief that I was now there to share the worry.

'It's nothing. I put up my arm to shield Christian, but they stabbed it with a knife and one of them jumped me and hit me in the stomach.'

I took charge.

'Mary, would you find if there is coffee and food please.'

She nodded and hurried off.

'What happened, John?' I asked.

'We were outside the church, Christian had given a very powerful sermon and there were masses of people milling around. There was even a TV crew filming. Christian stood on the steps for a while holding court, then we started through the crowds towards the car. Everyone seemed so, - well, friendly, and desperate to speak to Christian and touch him. There was some heckling at the back, but there always is! Then a group of men barged through everyone and two of them attacked Christian.'

'How?' I prompted. 'What did they do?'

'Well, two had knives and seemed to stab at him in a frenzy, Then Christian collapsed to the floor, a couple of the men kicked him and they tried to run off.'

'Tried?'

'Yes. It was pandemonium, women were screaming. Men close by started shouting and trying to stop the attackers. Then fights broke out with more people at the back and as they pushed forwards there was a huge crush, people were being pushed onto Christian and me. - But they got the attackers and held them down. About six people were stabbed,' he looked around dazedly. 'They're here somewhere.'

Mary returned.

'There's a sort of canteen, we can sit down and get something to eat and drink.'

'Good. Mary, take John and order up something; get me a coffee and a sandwich. I'll join you in a minute.'

Mary took John's good arm and they moved off. I went to the reception to get information on Christain's situation. The receptionist was extremely helpful and after making a phone call told me that the surgical team were still working. Christian was in a critical state and would be in surgery for a while yet. A nurse would come and tell me when they had more information.

I went to the entrance to speak with the police and was surprised to see Superintendant Tom Chandler talking to one of the uniformed officers. The crowd surrounding the hospital front had increased, quiet, patient.

I saw a TV camera crew off to the right looking towards us, recording the crowd scenes and presence of the police.

I approached the Superintendent.

'Superintendent Chandler, I didn't expect to see you here,' I said, adding anxiously. 'There is not a bomb element to all this, is there? It's just some anti religious thugs?'

Chandler smiled grimly.

'Ah, hello Mr Patterson. We meet again. No, there is no bomb threat that we know of. But these boys aren't just fundamentalist thugs. We picked up five of them, held down by the public, at your church meeting - I might say. They have known links to extremist organisations!'

He nodded towards the TV crew. 'You've seen the news?'

'No. I've been travelling. I've been driving down from Norwich, just got here about thirty minutes ago.'

'Well it seems that your lot are brewing up a storm. The word is spreading like wildfire; there are demos every where.'

'Not 'my lot' Superintendent. Most are ordinary people who are exercising their right to freedom of religious belief. It's the oddballs, extremists and the like who stir up trouble. In any case,' I added, 'Why are you here anyway?'

Chandler waved an arm in the general direction of the world.

'Trouble, Mr Patterson, - trouble. We are watching very closely…' We were interrupted by a man in sweater and jeans.

'Hello. - Mr Patterson isn't it? Any chance of a comment for the TV?' We all glanced across at the TV eyes watching us.

'Well, apart from being appalled at what has happened, and worried sick for the health of Mr Fellowes, there is not a lot to say until he recovers.'

'He is going to recover okay then?'

I glared at the man. 'I don't know yet, he is still in surgery.'

'What do you say to the people who did this?'

My irritation and tiredness was about to erupt into a tirade against the fatuous question, but Chandler stepped in and saved me.

'The matter will be dealt with by the authorities sir, there is nothing to say until then.'

I looked at Tom Chandler with gratitude, receiving a glimmer of sympathy in return.

I went back into the hospital and the canteen. My coffee was cold.

Mary and John sat near the door looking up anxiously every time someone entered. John, haggard, was pulling himself together and sat with a paper and pen talking earnestly on his mobile phone.

Mary looked tired but brightened up when she saw me.

'John has been phoning the Disciples,' she said. 'They all know what has happened. They are saying that people are using churches as focal points and huge crowds are gathering all round the world, even though it's the middle of the night in Asia.'

I grimaced at the coffee, and picked up a sandwich.

Mary immediately said.

'I'll get you a fresh coffee.'

'Has anyone come in?' I asked.

'No,' she suddenly looked defeated. 'Matt, I'm frightened.'

I put out my hand and held hers.

'He's going to be alright,' I said with more conviction than I felt.

Another two hours passed before, at last, a uniformed nurse and a man in a green short sleeved jacket looked round the door and, seeing us, came in.

The man spoke.

'Hello. I'm Doctor Johnson,' he inclined his head towards the nurse. '- Sister Freeman.' They both looked tired; serious.

'Well, Mr Fellowes is now in intensive care,' Dr Johnson paused. 'Its not too good I'm afraid. Mr Fellowes suffered four significant knife wounds to the body and two superficial gashes, one to his head. The surgeons have stitched everything back together but there is severe trauma to several organs and we are concerned about organ failure. He is, if course, extremely weak. He's been given blood and all we can do now is to wait.'

John and I spoke together. Mary just looked miserable.

'Is he conscious?'

'Can we see him?'

The doctor looked from John to me. 'Sister Freeman here is now in charge. She will take you to the care unit. You can stay there, but I warn you there is nothing happening. Mr Fellowes is in a coma and you must not attempt to arouse him with questions, but gentle background talking can do no harm.'

Sister Freeman escorted us back into reception. There were still police at the entrance. We walked along a corridor for a short distance then into a lift to the first floor. Along another corridor, left turn, more corridor. The doors were labelled 'Dependency unit 1' and so on. We stopped at unit 4. I noted there were two more doors, - 6 units in all.

The nurse ushered us in.

The sight of Christian brought a sudden welling of tears to my eyes, Mary openly wept. Christian lay in a pristine white bed, his head and shoulders half raised by masses of pillows. At first glance seemingly dozens of wires and pipes snaked from various parts of him to a tall rack of medical equipment beside the bed. Later I noted that there were in fact only five lines. He lay still, eyes closed, patriarchal features composed; beside him, the equipment rack hummed with activity; a visual monitor showed coloured graphs dancing along a screen; the bottom line blipped every centimetre. Bellows moved very gently up and down, while an audio monitor beeped softly, regularly, in time with the blips on the screen. Other lamps on the equipment glowed in multi colours.

There were two chairs in the room. Sister Freeman said she would get another chair for us and would ask nurse Daisy to come in.

'Nurse Daisy is the one to one nurse for this unit,' the sister explained.

We stood numbly beside the bed. Christain's hand lay on top of the covers, I gently placed my hand over his, and stayed thus for the next hour, willing him to come round and look at us with his piercing gaze that so awed me.

Nurse Daisy came in with another chair. She was a cheerful, competent lady of Asian origin. She fussed around the bed, checking the cover and the lines to the machine, then looked at the equipment rack, the monitors and lights. Apparently all was as it should be. John introduced us all to her, while I remained gently clasping Christain's hand. She smiled quietly at us, said she was always on call, just 'push that call button', indicating a large red domed button on the wall.

'Would you all like a coffee,' she asked and quietly disappeared out of the room.

Reaction began to set in, we were all tired; defeated. There was nothing we could do. As I listened to the steady beeping of the monitor I suddenly thought of the dire consequences if Christian didn't make it, he was the lynch pin embracing and unifying hundreds of faiths and denominations comprising over two billion people. He fired them with hope and reconciliation in a faith far greater than ever witnessed before.

Christian had preached the mystery of the cosmos, the creation of man, the divine power of the true God; who demanded loyalty as the price for passing into immortality and joining him in eternity.

I panicked as I thought of two billion people rudderless, blaming extremists for the loss of a unifying preacher.

I thought of the loss to me personally; he had inculcated into me a new life from despair; he had reunited me with Jenny.

I thought of the brooding malevolence that dogged the world, manifesting itself in fear, arrogance, evil; materialism and even now sawing away at the fabric of society.

We needed Christian as never before; he had preached the coming salvation, we needed his guiding hand; his mental power to inspire and help us through the coming storm. We needed Christian alive and well when Armageddon arrived, the final battle between good and evil on the day of judgement.

All these thoughts coursed through my mind as I held Christain's hand and I prayed for his recovery.

The night wore on, we had yet more coffee, and sat exhausted, half asleep. Nurse Daisy came and went. She came in during the early hours, and, looking at the monitors left quickly, returning with the doctor. They checked the monitors yet again.

The doctor said quietly.

'He's getting weaker, Mr Patterson. The next hour or so is going to be critical,' he and the nurse stayed on. The doctor telling us quietly about the growing crowds in every country, mainly silent, praying; but in several countries trouble had erupted, and around the world police forces were on the streets and around institutional buildings.

The doctor was in the middle of a sentence, - *SUDDENLY THE BEEPING STOPPED!* The silence was like a thunderclap! Then a continuously urgent 'B*e-ee—eee*' sound. For a second we froze, then the nurse leapt forward and hit the red button.

'Stand away,' she ordered sharply; we backed away hurriedly while she and the doctor busied themselves around Christian and the machines. The door opened and three more hospital staff quickly joined the bedside activity. Nurse Daisy had changed from an amiable Asian lady in uniform into an efficient expert in her field.

From the corner of the room I could see them preparing what looked like defibrillation equipment. The audio monitor continued its single long beep; the visual monitor green blips were now a flat line, but the coloured graphs above still danced across the screen. I could see that the bellows had stopped their quiet sighing.

Fear and horror gripped me. I found Mary was hanging onto my arm her face ashen. John seemed collected, but stared unseeingly at the activity.

People came and left the room. Two more came and stayed working with the team. I noted that even Superintendent Chandler poked his head round the door. He stared across at the bed to the calm but urgent activity, then across at us. After a moment he withdrew.

The doctor in charge directed the activity, he continually glanced at the coloured waveforms dancing across the screen of the visual monitor, they seemed to get more erratic.

I heard the whack of defibrillation shocks. I heard the doctor call for something, I know not what; after thirty minutes the activity slowed and the team began to stand back.

The doctor consulted the screen, the waveforms had ceased.

There was silence, a sort of stunned unbelieving silence. One of the team left the room; five others and us three just stood, we didn't know what to do, we were lost.

'NOooh!' Mary's anguished cry brought everyone back to reality.

I stepped towards the doctor.

'*DO* something,' I implored him, 'What can you do?'

He knew who his patient was and he was devastated. He looked again at the monitors, the insistent 'B*e-ee—eee*' continued, the green line was flat and the coloured waveforms gone. The digital clock now registered 40 minutes since flatlining. He turned to me, his grey face empty.

'He's gone, Mr Patterson. He's gone. I'm so sorry.'

Suddenly everyone was talking. Chandler

reappeared, his face grim. A senior executive of the hospital came in and was in urgent discussion with the doctor, - I thought probably worried about possible litigation charges.

The room was full of people talking; moving around. I stared at the scene. Then I saw her! My heart skipped a beat; I could not take much more of this.

Across the room, close to Christain's bed head, stood Faith!

I had not seen her come in. Tall, blonde and beautiful she gazed impassively at the commotion.

Chandler came quietly to my side speaking above the din of voices.

'We've got a problem Mr Patterson.'

A problem! I could think of no greater problem that here, the death of a great preacher, a man whose power and psychic abilities was leading mankind, unified, to the true God.

'We've got a problem,' repeated Chandler, trying to break into my thoughts.

The digital clock now registered 50 minutes, and already people were planning how to cope with the aftermath.

I looked at Chandler blearily through red rimmed eyes.

'Go on,' I said

'Someone has told the press about Mr Fellowes. The media have sent it around the world. There is pandemonium in some parts, looting, fires and reports of killings already.'

I retorted angrily.

'Why? Why do people react like this? What good does it do?' I felt empty, dispirited.

'Er, some have it that Mr Fellowes was attacked by Muslim fundamentalists, Now Muslims around the world are fearing for their lives. Mosques and Muslim enclaves are being sacked'

'Hopeless!' I shouted, suddenly galvanised; the room fell silent at my outburst. 'Absolutely bloody hopeless! Don't these people understand? Have they not been listening? Muslims believe in God too. What's the point in killing? Christian was bringing the faiths together! These people that attacked Christian, - they were not Muslims! They are Godless extremists, doing the work of the antichrist!'

Chandler looked shocked at my outburst.

'Mr Patterson, - er, Matt, would you be prepared to go on television and calm things down? It would help to get some proportion back into the situation.'

'What? - What can I say, Superintendent Chandler?' I practically shouted at him. 'That they have killed the one person who could have saved the world, - and now would you please all settle down and all go home! Eh, - Eh!'

I buried my face in my hands.

The digital clock registered 65 minutes.

Everyone in the room shuffled uncomfortably, unsure what to do next.

What did happen next caused uproar, one nurse fainted. The blood drained from my face, there was a collective intake of breath.

The continuous 'B*e-ee—eee*' sound suddenly stopped.

There was utter silence in the room. The staff had not turned off the monitors and the continuous sound had impinged itself onto our subconscious until we ignored it, now the sudden silence was as if the whole world had shuddered to a halt. . No one spoke; No one moved.

The monitor gave a single beep. We collectively jumped as if electrocuted.

My eye caught the green blip on the visual monitor. Another beep, another blip; then the beeping faltered into existence and the unsteady blips sorted themselves into a regular sequence.

We all stood transfixed, absolutely transfixed. The visual monitor now blazed with colour graphs racing across the screen.

Still we stood.

I could feel the blood pounding in my head, I dashed across the room and threw myself on my knees beside the bed. I held Christain's hand in mine. As I did so the bellows gave a deep sigh, and began a slow imperceptible rising and falling.

'Christian!' I cried, holding his hand to my lips.

Then pandemonium broke out, people were laughing and crying at the same time. The doctors tried to take control, but I refused to move, and they fussed around me.

Chandler stood open mouthed, uncomprehending. Then he pulled himself together. He addressed the doctor.

'Doctor!' his voice stern above the noise. 'Is Mr Fellowes stable? Are you saying that he is really alive?'

The doctor looked shocked, he glanced at the monitors, then back to Christian.

'Yes. - Mr Fellowes has a higher stability than before he , er, lapsed. I don't know, I just don't know. I would expect a recovery progress from here on.'

Chandler looked at me.

'I'll come back shortly Mr Patterson. Then I want you to announce this extraordinary situation to the media.'

It wasn't a request.

He shouldered his way to the door. People began to leave. Nurse Daisy tried to bring order and take control. John left to impart the news to the disciples by mobile phone.

In the end there was just me, Mary and Faith. We stood quietly around Christian. He seemed to sigh, his eyes half opened and he looked weakly at me. He was saying something, I had to place my ear close to his mouth to hear his words.

'Matthew, my friend, you have been here when I needed you. God bless you,' he paused, his eyes taking in his surroundings. 'Matthew, you must go and tell the people I shall be attending the rally, and I will have a message for the world.'

His eyes drooped and he lapsed into sleep, but not before he had weakly raised his free hand; Faith took it into hers.

'He is well now,' she said quietly. There was an

ethereal air about her that I never seemed to fully understand.

'I didn't see you before,' I said, 'I'm sorry, I should have called you earlier.'

'I was here,' she said simply.

We sat with Christian for another hour. I arranged with Faith that Mary and I would find the nearest hotel and crash out for a while. Chandler came back and asked me to go with him and address the media. I was so tired I weaved slightly as I walked.

Outside the entrance to the hospital the world's media had set up an untidy forest of cameras and microphones. Behind the paparazzi, crowds stretched into the car parks as far as my eyes could see.

As we came out of the entrance, a collective hush descended on the assembled media.

I stood on the designated spot, Chandler introduced himself and then me. He told the massed media that Mr Fellowes had been attacked while a guest of the church; that he had received a number of vicious stab wounds and was rushed into hospital at three twenty last afternoon. The perpetrators had been apprehended and were now in custody; that events over the past hours had created turmoil across the world and caused harm to many people, mostly based on incorrect information. He then turned to me and asked me to tell the waiting world what had happened and what was the current state.

I was tired to distraction. I didn't want to spend a long time discussing events, so I was brief. I told of Christain's fight for life; that the hospital had responded to all calls made on them with impeccable professionalism; that Christian had been in a coma, and teetered on the brink of death, but that he had pulled through during the night and was now recovering. I assured everyone that Christian would be at the world rally. I thanked all who cared for Christian around the world and said how their prayers had saved his life. I asked them now to thank God for Christain's deliverance and would they now return home, continue their prayers and be sure to attend the rally either in person or by TV.

I said I was very tired; too tired to answer questions, but I would arrange a press release later in the day.

Even so, the reporters would not accept 'no questions' and hurled them at me anyway.

'Can you comment about the statement that Mr Fellowes had died?' shouted the loudest.

'There was a hard struggle to save his life,' I said. 'He is alive and recovering well. I am sure you will see him yourself soon.'

I ducked any further questions, Chandler called a police car forward. Mary joined me, bringing our overnight bags and we were driven off to an hotel.

Mary sat in an arm chair in reception while I booked us in. It was the wrong time to check in, but the hotel seemed aware of the exceptional circumstances and fixed me up with two rooms ready for occupancy.

I returned to Mary, keys in hand. Her head was resting on the back of the chair, tilted slightly to the side, she was sound asleep. I stood quietly observing her. Dear Mary! - From the start she had supported me without complaint; setting off with me on our journey to Norwich and by my side throughout the traumas that followed. As a Personal Assistant she had excelled, providing material, bookings, phone calls, - whatever I had asked for she had produced, efficiently and with good humour. The events that occurred were as hard for her as for me.

Her attractive face in repose looked alluring, generous lips slightly parted, the light catching a dusting of freckles on her cheeks that I had not noticed before. Her eyes normally bright, intelligent, were closed behind her heavy framed glasses. Her coat had fallen open revealing a revered blouse and glimpse of a lacy bra; I leaned over and kissed her gently on her forehead.

'Come on,' I said gently, 'I've got you a room.'

We took the lift to the first floor; I found our rooms and unlocking the first door entered with Mary, putting her overnight bag on the bed.

'I want you to get properly undressed and into bed, - no dozing on a chair!'

Mary nodded.

'Will you be okay? Can you manage?' I asked.

Again a nod.

'Right,' I said looking at my watch, 'I'll call at about six o'clock, then We'll get something to eat.'

Another nod. I looked at her carefully, she was just about dead on her feet. I wanted to gather her into my arms, instead I pointed to the bed.

'Undressed and into bed,' I said firmly, and closed the door gently. My room was next door.

I followed my own instruction and fell into bed, exhausted. I slept all day, and was still asleep at half past six when Mary knocked on the door. I quickly put on my pants and trousers to let her in. She looked sparkling bright, the sleep had done the world of good. I could see that she had just bathed or showered, she smelt soft and fresh. I left her tinkering with the TV while I showered and dressed.

As I came out of the bathroom she was watching BBC news 24. The presenter was describing the attack and return from death of Christian. Crowd scenes followed. We watched for a while. I called John and told him that we would eat and then visit Christian at the hospital, then we went downstairs to find the restaurant.

When we later arrived at the hospital I found that my car had been clamped. After remonstrating with the hospital management and receiving an agreement to release the car we walked to Christain's room, he was sitting up looking remarkably normal. John was by his side and I could sense that he had been remonstrating with Christian. They both looked up as we entered. Christain's eyes gazed at me intensely, I felt again the unearthly power, - a strength I would not have believed from someone who had been at death's door only twelve hours ago.

John was agitated.

'Ah! Matthew, Christian intends to leave in the morning! I have been telling him that he must stay here for a while, a few days at least. Don't you agree?'

I looked at Christian and smiled.

'We worry for you, Christian. I watched the TV news earlier this evening; the people of the world, they call for you. Only you truly know the power that sustains you, if you decide you can leave soon we must accept your decision.'

John looked sceptical. We all talked about the sermons we had given, little was said of the night's horrific events.

Christian beckoned Mary closer, he took her hand.

'Dear Mary,' he said. 'You, too, were here when I needed you. I took your strength, I am here, in part, through your devotion. You are truly one of us. The Grace of God be with you always.'

Mary looked startled to be singled out, then leaning towards him demurely kissed his cheek.

He went on,

'Matthew, you must return to Apsley Manor, there is much to be done John and I have other business and we will join you in three days time.'

CHAPTER EIGHTEEN

We stayed that night at the hotel. I called Kate for a chat; Mandy insisted in talking to me too. We were not late to bed; the recent events still extracting their toll, but the next morning we were up early travelling on the M3 towards the New Forest. I dropped Mary off at her house then went on to my apartment. It was cold and uninviting but I was so tired that I fell into bed and slept until tea time.

The next day I was at Apsley Manor early. There were piles of letters and a long list of emails waiting attention. Most of the disciples had emailed me with reports of activities in their country; I was left with the task of piecing together the implications of what was happening on the global scale.

On Wednesday evening I went to see Kate and Mandy. Mandy was first to the door and greeted me with her usual exuberant hug around my middle.

We chatted, Kate and I, about her work with Jeffery. I couldn't help noticing a more poised look about her, she looked attractive; happy. I put it down to her getting out and about in the community; working for the Followers.

While Kate was in the kitchen preparing a snack supper, Mandy showed me her paintings, she was an accomplished little painter, as well as a singer. She talked with excited interest, her words slightly lisped. She sounded, and looked, just like my Jenny, and I hurt.

Later, after supper and Mandy had been encouraged to bed, - (not before I had been inveigled into reading a story), Kate and I sat on the settee in comfortable peace, coffee freshly brewed in the percolator on the table.

'Matt?' she said.

'Umm.'

'Come to a proper supper on Friday?'

'Sounds good.'

'Would you mind if I invited Jeffery as well?'

Ah! I thought, is this why Kate is blossoming? I was pleased for her if so, but could not escape a pang of jealousy. Unreasonable!

'Of course not Kate. It's a good idea.'

We said little for a while, then.

'Matt?'

'Umm.' Again.

'You know that night when you thought I had, er, - well, I was in the bath and you came in?'

'Well, yes, it's not something I'm likely to forget is it?' I placed my hand behind her neck and gently massaged.

'You saw me didn't you?'

'Well I, well I tried not to, but it was difficult.'
'You saw me then?'
'Yes, I did a bit.'
'Did you think about me?'
'Hey, Kate come on! I'm only human, of course I thought about you. - Still do!' I added mischievously.
'Matt!'
'Look Kate. You are a very attractive woman. I know you had a tough time with your husband, but it wasn't down to you. You've got to get on with your life, pick yourself up, start again.'
'And you, Matt?' she asked softly.
I sat sort of pole axed. I had walked right into that!
'It's different,' I said defensively.
'Yes, of course it is,' Kate said quickly, contritely. 'I'm sorry Matt, I had no right.'
I pulled her towards me and kissed the top of her head.
'Of course you do. We're friends aren't we? Now look, about this coffee.'
About half an hour later I took my leave.
'Jeffery's a good man,' I said as we parted.

On Friday I was back at Kate's house for supper. I arrived before Jeffery. I could see that Kate was on edge, putting on a show, busy in the kitchen. I stayed out of the way in the living room talking to Mandy. She was busy drawing something.
'Is Jeffery a nice man?' She asked, concentrating on her drawing.

'Yes he is, Mands, a very nice man. I see him a lot and everyone likes him.'

'Do *you* like him, Matt?'

'Yes, Mands, I do.'

'That's all right then,' she said and we talked about other things.

On Saturday early evening, I went to St Nicholas church. Philip was in the nave, tidying up pamphlets; I stopped to say hello, then I strolled into the cemetery and down the hill towards Jenny's and my bench.

I stopped in surprise! Close to where Jenny lay, was a new bench, firmly installed in a concrete plinth and facing downhill towards the village. I halted, non-plussed, at the foot of the grave. I stood for a while, then quietly moved to the bench and sat down, reaching forward I lay my hand on the mound of her grave.

'I'm here,' I said simply.

I said no more and we sat in comfortable silence, Jenny and me.

I could sense the sighing of a thousand souls, the flitting shadows of early evening. There was nothing to disturb us.

On Monday, John was at the Manor when I arrived; he was rejuvenated Having spent a long time with Christian he had been given a lot of work to do to prepare for the final world rally.

'Final?' I asked.

'Well, yes,' he said. 'Christian has called for a

meeting of all disciples at the end of the month, - perhaps you would help me set it up Matt? The world rally will take place at Easter. Christian told me it is the last global style meeting he is planning. After that it will be down to local groups to build and develop their own spirit based on his scientific teachings. He wants the emphasis to be on micro affairs in the communities.

The keyword is to be, - Keep watch, for we none of us knows when God's salvation will be among us, but it will be told and it will be soon.'

Mary arrived and we began the week responding to thousands of emails from all faith groups wanting information about co-operation and lesson ideas.

A few weeks ago I had asked Jeffery if he could find helpers to staff an office as the work now overwhelmed us. We had turned a large room at the back of the Manor into an office and fitted it out with ten workstations connected by a LAN network to the internet; Mary and I were able to forward incoming emails to the appropriate desk for follow up action. Richard had his own team producing teaching pamphlets and also ran the monthly session in the training room.

I continued my work of getting information from the disciples around the world and kept my chronicles up to date. My original 'gospel' was expanding at a rapid rate and I knew that I would soon have to publish book two.

On Thursday Mary and I were in the library,

we were working late and the evening was already dark; she busy at her laptop, eyes studying the screen, I was taking information that had come by email from Peter, and adding it to his file.

Someone entered the room, usually it was John or Jeffery; or perhaps staff, who also quietly came and went, maintaining a coffee station I had installed.

But this time it was different; the atmosphere was charged and I sensed a static energy – *I KNEW!* I looked up quickly, - it was Christian!

I stood and went forward to greet him.

'Christian! Thank God you are here safely. We have prayed for you,' I held his grip for some moments in a high five handclasp.

'Thank God indeed,' Christian said dryly. He eyed my working space at the great library table; seemingly more and more papers covered the surface. Reports generated by Mary were placed by her, neatly, in a long serrated line of the right of my laptop. A number of 'post it' notes were dotted on the table surface and on the left several piles of letters that were received.

'I have asked a lot of you, my friend,' he said. He stood upright, no sign at all of the horrific attack of only a week ago; his patrician features calm, piercing eyes, deep-set, appraised me intently.

'I am happy,' I said. He nodded then looked to Mary, who had stood up but seemed unsure whether to approach, or simply smile from where she was.

Christian held out his hand, Mary came readily into his grasp.

'My dear girl, I, - we, - are all sustained by your devotion. I have needed your strength and you have given it unflinchingly.'

Mary lowered her eyes, she seemed embarrassed by the praise.

Christian was standing between us, he held our elbows and guided us to the large bay and opened the French windows. We stood there, Christian, Mary and me.

The air seemed charged with electricity and as we gazed out at the manor grounds, the trees in the distance, I could feel a ringing in my ears; everything seemed still and far away, almost as if time was standing still. Our eyes travelled up to the clear sky and at the stars suspended in a hypnotically wondrous sight against a blackness of infinity.

Christian spoke of the forthcoming meeting of disciples and asked me if my chronicles were in order.

'We shall have supper,' he said, his voice seemingly from a distance, 'And then my friends you shall experience a most awesome event. You shall receive the Grace of God to strengthen you for the horrors to come.'

I felt the blood throbbing in my heart, what was Christian saying; that the end was close? He read my thoughts.

'No, Matthew, it is not the end yet, you will be exalted for a short time; you will experience the glory of heaven and be one with God, free to travel throughout the cosmos; you will see the wondrous life without end; time will not exist. But you must return to live through the judgement, to assist the believers aspire to heaven. You will need all the strength imbued by God, - for the world will become a charnel house; there will be flood, destruction and disease. God's retribution will be the most awesome event since creation.

As God created, so God disposes.'

Mary and I were silent, stunned and alarmed. Christian turned to go, I saw just outside the doorway, in the hall, the figure of Faith! Waiting; it was unnerving. She turned with Christian and they left together, along the corridor, towards his office and suite.

The next few days were unsettling, I could not concentrate, then slowly my world returned to normality and the work at Apsley Manor continued apace.

The next week, on Friday afternoon I called in at St. Nicholas church, (It was usually locked up in the mornings), I was hoping to speak to Philip. He was not there and so I wandered through the churchyard and down the steps to the cemetery. As I came in sight of 'our' new bench I stopped in surprise. Mary was sitting there! She was resting her elbows on her knees, chin cupped in her hands, seemingly absorbed, as if in discussion.

She looked up as I approached.

'Matt,' she said, a little defensively.

'Hi Mary, I had come to see Philip, but he is not in.'

I sat down on the bench, placing my hand on the mound where Jenny lay. Then I sat back and my gaze wandered over the serene field and trees.

Mary said nothing and we sat in quiet communion, Mary, Jenny and me.

CHAPTER NINETEEN

A week later, on Saturday, Mary invited me home for supper.

She met me at the door wearing a soft pink jumper and black trousers. Lustrous hair denoted recent washing; her eyes, as she considered me through her glasses, were unfathomable.

'Hi, Matt. Supper in about an hour?'

'Hello, Mary. You look, well, - wonderful.'

'Thank you,' she looked slightly embarrassed, but I could see that she was pleased. 'It's a lovely evening, how about a drink on the patio before supper?'

'Good for me,' I said and went in with her to choose some wine, then we sat outside in a swing seat. It was growing dark and with little light pollution in the forest the stars were beginning to show.

I thought of other star systems out there harbouring life force and of God, King of infinity, uninhibited by time.

Mary sipped her wine. 'A lot has happened in the last year Matt, since we met.'

The evening air felt infused with anticipation, a sort of static electricity hovering over everything.

'Umm, its been life changing for me,' I said, 'And we have accomplished a lot, but so much more to do. The rally next spring will be a catalyst event for the world.

'Christian said it's the last rally, what do you think he means by that? Are we really close to retribution?'

'I don't know, Mary. No one knows when God will reveal himself. I've got two thoughts running round in my head. One, the date of judgement may be driven by another force, a force equal and opposite to God, an evil force. It could be this, and when it comes, God will also appear to collect his children and take them to safety, leaving the ungodly to stew in their own hell.'

'Matt! That's awful!' Mary exclaimed. 'Where did that come from?'

'I don't know, it's just that there always seems to some dark, brooding presence in the background. I often feel it, Mary, I feel there is a powerful force for evil, just waiting, biding its time, watching our civilisation destroy itself,' I paused.

Mary waited. 'You said two things?'

'Oh yes. The final days will be the search for consciousness. The spirit or soul that is *us*. The scientists have learned a lot about the brain, and how it might work, but they are no further forward in discovering the soul, nor will they ever be. Sure, we know the brain is made up of neurons, with nerve tendrils of dendrites and axons, but these are just the mechanics. We might see how it could work, for example in tasks like making muscles work, or recognition, even calculations. This is not yet really understood, so what hope that our soul can be 'measured'?'

'Do we want it measured?'

'Well, no. The point I'm making is that scientists may one day work out how the brain can, for example, add two and two and come up with four. Or how the brain cells store the concept of 'two' and the result 'four' in the neuron structure, - I mean, is 'two' a dab of chemical, or an electrical value, and how does it stay stable over years.

What about recognition? What happens in the neurons to store a mosaic picture of, say, a face and compare it forever with faces it sees and recognise the pattern when it meets the 'face' years later. Or connects the mosaic to a name, or the sound of the voice, and can cause the person to say 'Oh, yes that's Tom or whatever.

All these are complicated enough, and maybe the scientists will one day unravel the way it works, - but here's the clincher!

The brain can be busy adding up, or recognising things, or moving muscles, - but what *causes* it to do any one of these things at a particular time? What decides that I *'fancy'* adding up, or I *'plan'* to read a book and so on. There we have the soul! This is the immaculate guiding energy that is an infinitesimal fragment of God. It is this element we should be developing to maturity to sustain God and pass into immortality. Then we will have control over the final dimension - Time!'

Mary was silent.

'Sorry,' I said, 'I didn't mean to get into deep discussions about this.'

'It's okay, its just, well, too big to get my head around, I guess.'

I got us another glass of wine and we sat gazing into the darkening sky.

Mary sat close to me. 'What's out there, Matt, - really out there?' She spoke wistfully, as if there was something there she should know about, but was denied her.

'It's beautiful, isn't it?' I said. 'Try to look beyond what you see, look through the haze of the milky way, beyond the stars and galaxies. Look deep into the sky and see God's world, trillions of civilisations, stretching into eternity.'

I put my arm round her shoulder.

'Do you think we will be part of it, Matt.?'

'I know we will.'

I glanced at her face upturned, looking with shining eyes into the heavens. Her lips, lightly polished, were parted. I was drowning and I knew it.

I bent my head and kissed her lips gently, so gently. For long precious moments, as her softness and perfume enthralled my brain, the exuberance of existence finally flowed again in me.

We long sat in silence, reliving that ecstatic moment. Then I said softly.

'Isn't it time you left home, Mary?'

'Why?' she murmured. 'Do you love me?'

'Yes, I love you.'

'Umm. Then I could think about it, I 'Spose.'
'Would you marry me?'
There was an even longer silence,
'I'm not Jenny,' she whispered hesitantly
'I know,' I said softly. 'it's alright, Mary, I know.'

<u>THE END</u>

About the Author

Dudley Price and his wife Marion live in the New Forest area of Hampshire, England.

Dudley completed a career in the British Army, leaving to take up positions in the Aerospace industry.

Dudley and Marion have two daughters, four grandchildren and a great granddaughter, Kathryn.

Ever since a young age Dudley has been intrigued by 'deep space' and the certainty of life 'out there'. His interest in the universes has rubbed off on grandson Mark, who is a regular 'stargazer' and member of a local astronomy club.

Dudley, now retired, and Marion spend their time between their home in UK and visiting Cyprus.